THE COMPASS

THE COMPASS

A NOVEL

THE CATCH & HOLD SERIES
BOOK THREE

JENNA MALABY*

*FORMERLY WRITING AS JENNA MILES

Copyright © 2024 by Jenna Malaby, formerly writing as Jenna Miles.

All rights reserved.

No part of this book may be reproduced in any form or by any electronic or mechanical means, including information storage and retrieval systems, without written permission from the author, except for the use of brief quotations in a book review.

Cover art copyright 2025 by Jenna Miles. Created with Canva.

For C, A, and L
Thank you for sharing me with this strange obsession of mine. Never let anyone convince you your dreams are dumb, impractical, or far-fetched.

And for R
Thank you for encouraging me to fetch my far-flung dreams.

CONTENTS

CONTENT ADVISORIES

The Compass is hilarious, joyful, and tender; however, it also contains some heavy, dark themes. Please use your judgment in determining whether *The Compass* is a good fit for you.

Shown on page:

- Addiction / substance abuse
- Mental health challenges (depression, PTSD, anxiety)
- Physical abuse of a 14-year-old by an older sibling
- Attempted sexual assault of an 18-year-old and a 14-year-old in a brief scene at the beginning
- Romantic relationship difficulties
- Failure to disclose, to a casual sex partner, the existence of additional casual sex partners (all within the context of a non-committed sexual relationship)
- Death of a close family member, witnessed by a minor
- Grief
- Homophobia / homophobic slurs
- Sexism
- Racism
- Strong swearing
- HIV/AIDS
- Consensual sexual activity between adults: open door / on-page sex scenes. Sex acts and body parts are described relatively explicitly and/or using swear words. Bodily fluids and their movement are referenced, but relatively less explicitly.

Discussed as having happened in the past, but *not* shown on page:

- Sexual assault of a minor by an adult
- Parental suicide

An albatross bent upon the wind
cannot flesh out the many feathers of life
without making horror of its deeds
Carry me to the shore you shun
and deposit me on its rocks
cracking the shell
to feast on the liquor

THE COMPASS

A NOVEL

OCTOBER 1989

"YOU CAN CALL ME HAZE."

*W*illiam ripped his headphones off when an outside sound penetrated the seal around his ears. The hairs on his body bristled instinctively, even before his brain interpreted the sound.

A woman was screaming. Not outside – downstairs.

Aftershock. That was the next thought his brain seizes upon.

The last time a woman screamed like this in his house was exactly one week ago. In fact, it had been *three* women – his grandmother, mother, and sister – all screaming their heads off in the living room, where they watched the World Series. For a split second, he had been so pissed, assuming he missed a huge play – and there he was with his head stuck in the fridge, fishing around for another Coke.

But then the cabinet doors burst open and the dishes flew out, smashing into shards inches from his feet. The cereal boxes leaped from the top of the fridge and ricocheted off his head. Only when the shaking knocked him flat on his ass did his brain catch up to what was happening. It all transpired within milliseconds.

But now – today – there was no shaking, and Nonna had already taken Kelly to soccer practice. His parents were still at the processing plant, and Mike was at Uncle Bill's auto body shop.

That's when William heard the familiar raspy bark – the grating sound of Jimmy's voice when he was tweaking. And then he heard it again – a female voice, screaming.

Unmistakable peril.

His journal tumbled to the floor as he sprang out of bed. *Meddle* still spun on his turntable, but adrenaline propelled him downstairs.

He had no plan.

The screaming came from the in-law unit. He twisted the doorknob – Jimmy had forgotten to lock it. Which meant that Jimmy was going to be in bad shape.

William pushed the door open. The all-too-familiar acrid-sweet smell assailed his nostrils. Clearly Jimmy had been at it for a few days. Pipes, needles, cigarette butts, liquor bottles, vinegar, foil, spoons–

A teenage girl on the couch.

Her tank top was torn, her bra wrenched up, her blue-streaked hair matted with blood from a gash on her left temple. She looked only a few years older than William. She was giving Jimmy the fight of her life, but after all, Jimmy was six-foot-two of solid muscle, and she – well, she wasn't.

Jimmy wasn't making much sense; he never did when he got to this point. His speech had devolved into a chain of profanities strung together without other parts of speech to give them meaning. He enunciated poorly, except when he landed on the words that his unhinged mind thought were most venomous.

William had the presence of mind, finally, to realize he needed a weapon. He ran out to the patio and retrieved a baseball bat, then sprinted back to the in-law unit, where Jimmy had wrenched up the girl's skirt.

He was screaming at her to give it to him, and something about a cavity search. Some bunch of nonsense about shoving something up her cunt, or something being shoved up there.

William wouldn't kill him. He'd just knock him out of commission, just long enough for the girl to escape.

He sneaked up behind Jimmy and swung the baseball bat across his back. It landed with a feeble thud, but Jimmy flinched back just enough for the girl to punch his Adam's apple and get out from underneath him.

Wearing only one shoe and holding the shreds of her tank top together, she fled the in-law unit and burst out the front door, into the street.

That's when William knew, from the look on Jimmy's face, that he was going to die.

He dropped the baseball bat – later, he'd wonder why; maybe to run faster – and fled the same direction as the girl. Unfortunately, his legs were only half as long as Jimmy's, and he hadn't enjoyed the same head-start as the girl. On the sidewalk, Jimmy's arms banded around his torso.

William screamed for help. He saw the girl then; she had made it all the way to the stop sign at Taraval. At his plea, she turned to watch in horror as Jimmy dragged him back to the house.

William had a moment of detachment, just long enough to lock eyes with her. He had never seen her before, and for all he knew, she was just some random girl Jimmy had abducted off the street. But he realized, as if by Morse code signal to some receiver lodged in his brain – she would go get Mike. He was just five blocks down Taraval.

"Get inside, faggot!" Jimmy's spittle sprayed William's cheek. William screamed and flailed, but of course he stood no chance against his meth-addled older brother. Jimmy dragged him back inside, up the stairs, into William's bedroom.

He flung William to the floor and kicked-slammed the door behind them. William scuttled backwards into the corner like a crab.

Jimmy just stood there a minute, his chest heaving, his snarl framing his mottled teeth. His rage imparting a garish hue to the weeping sores on his sallow face.

Then he spied William's journal on the floor. It had fallen open to a page right in the middle.

"Ho-ly crap," Jimmy said ominously. "Is that really what I think it is?"

Panicked, William crawled toward it, but flinched back when Jimmy's arm swooped to snatch it from the floor. William watched with growing dread as his brother flipped through the pages.

"I thought I told you never to let me catch you doing this fairy-ass shit again," he said in a low tone, shaking the journal at William so he could hear its pages rattling.

Jimmy flipped through some more pages, sniggering at each one. Finally, in a mocking high-pitched voice, he began to read aloud William's poems. When he was done with each page, he ripped it from the notebook, sneering as he tore it to shreds.

William felt his intestines, his very soul, being gouged out with a spoon, but he dared not twitch a muscle. Jimmy had done it before, two years earlier – laid waste to all the poems and songs William had composed since he was eight years old. This time, the entire process took less than fifteen minutes.

When the entire past two years of William's life lay in a snowy heap in front of him, Jimmy lingered a moment longer, still sneering. William felt a strange sense of calm then – of acceptance. This was it. Even if his body survived the day intact, he was still dead.

Jimmy swooped again and snatched William by the hair. But that small patch of hair came right out of William's scalp, so Jimmy gripped another, larger chunk and used it to hurl William onto the bed. In one swift movement, Jimmy pinned William to the mattress with a knee to the chest.

"I bet you'd love to suck a *real* man's cock, wouldn't you?" Jimmy rasped out. William watched in horror as Jimmy notched the tab of his zipper down, one tooth at a time. "Not one of those pencil dicks you're used to sucking off in the school bathroom. Something long, thick, and hard to choke on. You'd love that, wouldn't you, faggot?"

Fully unzipped now, Jimmy's fly tumbled open, and he reached into his boxers.

"What the fuck are you doing?!" screamed William.

With that, a switch flipped, and Jimmy woke from his fever dream. For a moment, he blinked down at William, as if confused.

And then he was furious again, re-zipping his pants with a vengeance. "I'm gonna curb-stomp your fairy ass."

He again seized William by the hair and used it to haul him from the bedroom to the living room.

Where they met Mike.

"Jimmy," said Mike, with forced calmness. "What are you doing?"

"I'm curb-stomping this little faggot! It's about time one of us did it."

Jimmy knocked Mike aside and dragged William down the stairs, out the front door, to the sidewalk.

Where they met the girl Jimmy tried to rape.

"Jimmy," she pleaded. She had zipped Mike's jacket over her torn tank top, and some man – maybe Uncle Bill – had lent her one of his ill-fitting shoes.

It was as if she were invisible now. As if Jimmy couldn't even hear her. He flung William to the ground, by the curb.

"Jimmy!" she shrieked as Jimmy positioned William's head against the curb. William fought back with everything he had, but he was a Lilliputian battling a Titan. The girl launched herself onto Jimmy's back, the ill-fitting shoe tumbling from her foot.

"Stop it!" she screamed.

"Back off, Jimmy."

William didn't recognize the stern voice. Neither did Jimmy, and it stopped him in his tracks. Still holding William's head against the curb, Jimmy turned his head to look, giving William a clear view of Mike. With a gun.

Jimmy actually laughed at him. "What are you gonna do with that thing?"

Mike aimed the gun squarely at Jimmy's head. "Well, I'm certainly not going to let you kill our brother."

He was so calm, and deadly serious. Almost formal. William had never once seen him like that. Maybe that's why it silenced Jimmy for a moment – just long enough for a wary look to appear in Jimmy's eyes.

"Stop playing," he scoffed. "You don't even know how to use that thing."

"I do. As you know all too well."

William had no idea what Mike was talking about, but Jimmy looked like he did. Then another sneer crept over his face, and with a final, spiteful shove that did no real damage, he released William's head.

Slowly, Jimmy clambered to his feet. Mike kept the gun pointed at him, and Jimmy, not daring to say anything more to Mike or William, turned instead to the girl.

"I wouldn't take anything from your skanky-ass dyke-hole even if your dad paid me to."

"When my dad is done with you, you'll wish Mike had shot you," she spat back.

And that was the first time Jimmy looked truly worried. Mike said, "Get your shit, Jimmy."

"Yes. Get your shit, Jimmy," she echoed derisively.

She stood ramrod straight the whole time they waited outside. But after Jimmy gathered his wallet and his paraphernalia and peeled away in his beat-up '68 Camaro, her knees began to wobble. Mike set the gun down and caught her around the elbows.

"Shit," he said, gesturing to the blood in her hair and the gash on her forehead. Too shell-shocked to stand, William didn't even try to – he remained seated on the curb.

The girl shrugged off Mike's assistance and held her hand out to William. "Let's take care of you."

"What?"

She gestured, and only then did he feel it – the enormous abrasion on the left side of his face, where it had scraped along the curb. The stinging roared to life with a vengeance as the adrenaline simultaneously wore off.

William accepted the hand she offered, and they returned inside. While Mike scrambled to put the in-law unit in order, she tried to restore order to William's face in the bathroom upstairs. He sat on the toilet lid as she dabbed his wounds with a washcloth and soap.

He watched her face while she worked. "Is your dad going to do something to him?"

She laughed a bit. "No, but Jimmy thinks he is. And that's all that matters. Trust me, Jimmy will not come back here, ever again."

Only then did William detect the foreign inflection in her voice. It reminded him of the Russians in the Richmond District. While she continued to doctor his wounds, he said, "Why didn't you just call the cops?"

She soaked a cotton ball in hydrogen peroxide and dabbed his skinned cheek. He winced, but swallowed the hiss of pain. "You know your parents could get in a lot of trouble if the cops thought they were tolerating a meth den in their house," she replied. Pausing a moment, she lifted her eyes to his. "You don't believe me, that Jimmy won't bother you again."

William shook his head to clear it. "It's not just that. He tried to rape you, and..." He couldn't tell her what he thought Jimmy was about to do to him, in the bedroom. So he just said, "I'm afraid he's going to hurt someone else."

Her dark, heavy brows came together. She found a clean towel and blotted his wounds. Finally, she said simply, "Jimmy is not going to hurt anyone else."

"How do you know?" he demanded.

"Because he'll go to prison first."

It seemed like a feeble argument, but she looked weary, so he decided to drop the subject for now. She put a few dots of antibacterial ointment on some gauze. It finally occurred to him to ask, "What's your name?"

She taped the gauze over the skinned area on his cheek. "Serafima."

He rolled the name over and over in his mind. *Serafima.* "That's a cool name."

"Thanks." She brought the first aid supplies to the vanity and began doctoring her own wounds. "But you can call me Haze. That's what my friends call me."

SEPTEMBER 1995, PART I

"ARE YOU EVER GOING TO LET IT OUT OF ITS CAGE?"

*W*illiam had long ago programmed the alarm clock to play *I Got You Babe* at 6 A.M. so he could have the fun of smashing the snooze button every morning. Just like in *Groundhog Day*. But that morning, he smashed the off button instead. His eyes never actually opened until long after the sun penetrated the blinds.

He glanced at the clock - half an hour until his first class.

He sat up and looked toward the bathroom, considering. He could definitely use a shower. And he had never bothered to change out of the clothes he wore yesterday. He turned toward the closet, in case that presented a less-daunting prospect than the shower.

Instead, he dropped *The Dark Side of the Moon* onto his turntable and lay down again.

It didn't occur to him to eat until that evening, when his mother descended to the in-law unit and knocked on his bedroom door. "Will, are you in here?"

"Yeah," he called back, and wondered why his voice frayed. Then he remembered – he hadn't spoken all day.

"You okay in there?"

"Yeah," he mumbled.

A pause. Then his mother said, "Dinner in thirty."

"Okay."

When he still didn't emerge thirty minutes later, she knocked again. "Will?"

"Uh?"

"Are you sick?"

"No."

"Okay... well, dinner's ready. Are you coming?"

He sighed in resignation. "Yeah, okay."

He got up, finally. Opened the door, and didn't miss the way she caught her jaw before it dropped.

"Are you sure you're not sick?" she ventured.

"I guess I'm just fighting something off."

"Well then, let me bring a plate down to you. No sense giving it to the rest of us."

"Yeah... all right."

He closed the door again, and climbed back into bed. A while later, he heard another tap on his door. Got up, and accepted the tray his mother held out.

"Pastina," she explained. "I had some in the freezer."

"Thanks, Mom."

"Leave the dirty dishes outside the door," his mom called as he closed the door again.

He stared at the bowl for a while. Lifted a spoonful; watched the golden broth and the stelline dribble back into the bowl. Set it outside his door again, untouched. Climbed back into bed.

He still wore the same sweats, and his teeth were fuzzy. He dozed fitfully, disturbed by vivid dreams that he couldn't quite remember. Copper strands of hair, whipping about wind-chapped cheeks. A silver mermaid pendant against freckled skin.

Nearly twenty-four hours later, he finally emerged from bed. His head spun; he knew he should probably eat. So he went upstairs and found his sister at the dining table in her soccer uniform.

Kelly took one look at him and bellowed, *"It's aliiive!"*

He stared listlessly at the textbooks and notebook paper strewn on the table. "Stop the presses."

Kelly quirked an eyebrow. "Huh?"

"You're studying."

"I have to, or they'll kick me off the team." Giving him a quizzical once-over, she clicked her pen rapidly a few times in succession, then threw it on the table. "So what finally dragged *your* ass out of bed?"

"I'm on the schedule at work." Only then did it hit him - he hadn't been to class in two days.

His head spun again.

"Jesus, you look like shit," Kelly remarked. "Are you sick or something?"

"Yeah," he said flatly.

"Dude, fuck off. I have a game against Washington in two days."

"I mean, no. I just remembered that I missed an exam yesterday. And I need to eat."

"Fuck off anyway," she said mildly.

He went to the kitchen and made a salami and cheese sandwich. Somehow, even though he hadn't eaten in forty-eight hours, he still couldn't choke it down.

He stood in the shower, letting the water run over him until it turned cold. Brushed his teeth and put on some clean clothes; never mind whether they matched or needed ironing. No need to shave his face or tame his hair.

At work, Paul took one look at him and said, "You're not contagious, are you?"

William shook his head, and Paul said, "Good. You're on grill."

William watched him stride away. He couldn't help seizing onto that little flicker of hope – she hadn't told him yet. For his part, William wouldn't give Paul any ammunition against him. From now on, he'd attend to his grooming before work. She would hear only good things about him from her father.

It did make him feel better to get out of the house and cook for a few hours. He slept better that night, and the next morning, he felt well enough to go to class and plead his case for the make-up exam. But as he sat in the lecture hall, his mind drifted back to that day a little over a week ago. Her forgiveness, sweeping them up in successive spasms of what amounted, in the end, to little more than lust. The dying gasps of something he had assumed would last forever.

His pen idled over his notebook, and at the end of the class, he had nothing to show for his attendance.

The days when he had to work were better. But when he had a string of days off, he found himself sinking back into that sort of flu. And after he failed to emerge for dinner for the third day in a row, his mother knocked on his bedroom door.

"Can I come in a minute?"

He glanced back apprehensively into his room, but held the door open for her. Her eyes surveyed the rumpled bed sheets and appraised the empty soda cans and beer bottles on his bedside table. She wrinkled her nose at the stench, and found its source in the fetid clothes he wore and the rotting food atop his dresser.

She said, "Will, you might be fooling some people, but you're not fooling me."

He shoved his hands into the pockets of his sweatpants and avoided her gaze.

"The last time this happened was about three years ago," she persisted. "You know what happened three years ago?"

He sniffed, and took a sudden keen interest in the wobble of the ceiling fan.

"Three years ago," she prompted again. But he still refused to fill in the blank for her.

He lowered himself onto the edge of his bed. Stared listlessly at his fingernails. They could use a trim and a good scrubbing.

She folded her arms across her chest. "What happened this time, Will?"

"Mom, I know you want to help, but there's really nothing you can do."

"Maybe not. But if you think you can fight this one out in your head, I would just invite you to look around yourself right now."

When he still remained silent, she ventured, "If you're missing Julia that badly, why don't you just move down there? That's what you've wanted this whole time, isn't it?"

He winced. Gradually, her eyes widened.

"Oh. I'm sorry. You mean...?" She sat beside him on the edge of the bed. Drawing a shaky breath, she added, "It didn't even occur to me."

Her genuine shock rattled him all the more. That it wouldn't even occur to her only confirmed how deeply wrong the whole thing was.

She folded her hands in her lap, struggling, he could tell, to land on the right words.

"The last time this happened – three years ago – you went fishing with Frank for three weeks," she tried.

"That was during albacore tuna season."

"Well, Dungeness season starts up in a month or so."

"Mom, the point is, albacore season is in the summer. I'm in school right now. I can't take off for three weeks to go fishing."

His mother looked around his room again. "I get the impression you haven't been to class in a while, anyway."

His eyes strayed over to the bottom drawer of his dresser, where he hid his bong. Right about now, he could really use some more of Mike's exceptional weed, but he had smoked the last of it the night before.

"You may as well get out of the house and do something," his mother persisted. "Even if it's not school."

"I *am* getting out of the house, Mom. I'm still working."

She raised an eyebrow. "At Dunphy's?"

"Yeah...?" he replied, a bit defensively.

"So you're working at her father's restaurant. And this will get your mind off her... how?"

He frowned. Crossed his arms over his chest.

"Quit Dunphy's, Will. Frank could use a good deckhand right about now. I think he recruited his current one off the short bus. You've got to get out of the house and distance yourself from anything that reminds you of her."

"Thanks, Mom," he said curtly.

Her jaw tightened, but after a moment's hesitation, she rose to her feet. "Leftover pasta in the fridge. I used the San Marzano sauce."

He felt a pang of guilt, and something else more poignant. A little over three years ago, his grandmother had somehow coaxed San Marzano tomatoes from the foggy microclimate and sandy soil of the

Outer Sunset. She canned them, made sauce, then put a dozen or so containers in the deep freezer. He knew his mother had retrieved one of Nonna's containers in a last-ditch effort to tempt him.

But he only mumbled, "Thanks," and tried in vain to blot out the memory.

So instead, William picked up the phone beside his bed and called his brother's apartment. But of course Mike wasn't there, so he dialed MacGowan's next.

"MacGowan's." The music rampaging in the bar nearly overwhelmed the smoky female voice.

"Hey, um... this is Mike Quinn's brother. Is he there?"

A pause. "Jimmy?"

He flinched. "No. William."

"Well, that makes a lot more sense," she chuckled. "I didn't think they'd let Jimmy call from prison."

"Is he there?" William persisted. "Mike, I mean."

"That's him screaming on stage in the background. Can't you tell?"

Increasingly agitated, William rubbed his eye and pinched the bridge of his nose. "Yeah, okay... well, can you do me a huge favor and ask him to call when he finishes?"

"No problem."

But he lost patience after five minutes and dragged himself out of bed. Threw on some jeans and a thermal sweater, and over that, a plaid flannel shirt - what Mike derided as his "lumberjacket." But he felt too malnourished to walk the few blocks to the bar, so he changed into the black motorcycle jacket, instead.

He cast a dubious look in the mirror at the scruff sprouting on his face and ran his hand through his hair until it stood on end. At the moment, it gave a whole new and very literal meaning to the term "dirty blond." But there was nothing he was willing to do about that now.

He drove his motorcycle the few blocks to MacGowan's and flashed his fake ID at the entrance. Thankfully, the jukebox and the clamor of bar patrons had supplanted the jarring blare of his brother's heavy metal. He found Mike onstage with the other bandmates, stowing his guitar in its case. Rather than announcing himself, William jumped onstage and began wrapping up cords.

Not recognizing him, the other bandmates froze in shock. Finally, Mike spotted him and leaped to his feet, grinning.

"Hey, man! What the fuck?" He gestured to William's facial scruff. "Are you homeless now?"

"I tried to call you," William grumbled.

"Yeah, I know. Cindy told me. I just tried to call back. Mom was worried about you, and now I see why."

"I got impatient."

The silver piercings in Mike's lip, eyebrows, and nose flashed in the stage lights. He had graduated from black faux-hawk to black-and-green liberty spikes, and with the new gauge piercings in his earlobes, he looked more aberrant than ever. He clapped a hand on William's arm, turned to his bandmates, and shouted, "Guys, this is my kid brother, Will. I move out of the house, and he still follows me around like a little lost puppy-dog."

"William," corrected William, but no one heard him over Mike's guffaws. Mike steered him straight to the drummer, whose bass drum proclaimed IRONSHAFT in an aggressive red font. Aside from Mike, he was the only band member who hadn't stepped right out of a mid-eighties hair-metal video on MTV. In fact, with his sweater vest and close-cropped Caesar cut, he was downright preppy.

The drummer startled William by springing forward with a wide smile and a violent handshake. "Niall. Mike's told me a lot about you."

"He has?" William shot a suspicious look at Mike, who in turn slapped him on the back with his trademark cretinous laugh.

"Dude, we should all get a drink. Cindy says it's on the house."

"Not yet," William said aside to Mike. "I need to talk to you first."

"Sure, man. What's up?"

"Out back."

Mike scoffed. "Out back? What is this, a drug deal?"

William seized Mike's arm, encased in brightly-colored snakes, skulls, roses, and naked ladies, and steered him offstage.

"Jesus, chill out!" protested Mike. "Can I at least get my jacket? It's fucking freezing out there."

William waited for him to slide into his silver-studded black leather jacket, then led him out the back door into the dimly-lit alley behind

MacGowan's. Out here, it reeked of urine and rotting trash from the dumpster.

"All right, man," Mike said, shuffling back and forth and glancing around. "What's up?"

In a low voice, William said, "Have you got any on you?"

"Shit. You know, I was just kidding when I asked if this was a drug deal."

William fixed his brother with an earnest gaze.

"What – you mean *here?*"

"Yes, Mike. Here."

"Well…" Blinking a couple of times, he finally admitted, "Yeah. What do you need?"

William pretended to consider a moment. "All of it?"

"Fuck."

"You think you can just smoke me out?"

"Fuck you. Are you serious?"

"My next paycheck is Friday."

Mike gaped a moment longer, then heaved a big sigh. He reached into an interior pocket of his jacket and pulled out the weed.

"You know, the only reason I had this on me right now is because Cindy is a good friend. We light up all the time back here."

"Uh-huh."

William had brought his own papers, so Mike took one and rolled a joint. After lighting it, Mike took a couple of puffs before passing it over, then watched William take a couple of deep, bracing hits. "You lighting up with Julia now?"

Hearing her name gutted William all over again. To hide it, he blew a huge cloud of smoke, and said nothing.

Mike's face fell. "Aw, man. No way. For real?"

William turned away. Took another hit.

"You mean you've been going through all that shit by yourself?" Mike sucked his teeth and said, "Fuck it, man. Love is a myth. A social construct invented to sell greeting cards."

William enveloped them both in another shroud of smoke. "The Nobel Prizes you could win with that intellect."

"Shut the fuck up." Grinning, Mike snatched the joint from

William. "Well, listen, man. I'm getting a new band together with Niall, that Irish dude. Pub rock. We both want out of the heavy metal thing. I never liked it, even in the eighties."

While Mike took a puff, William asked, "What the hell is pub rock?"

"Kind of punk, kind of folk," Mike replied after the smoke cleared. "I'm singing lead and playing rhythm, but we need a lead guitar and a backup singer."

"No."

Mike sucked his teeth in chagrin. "Oh, come on; why not? Can you even imagine the sheer volume of poontang? With your looks and my raw charisma, we each make one-half of a stud. Together, we're unstoppable."

While Mike took another hit, William asked, "Is that why Niall said he's heard so much about me?"

Mike held his hit, and grinned.

"You've already committed me, haven't you?" William shook his head in dismay, but he couldn't help smiling a bit. "Bastard."

Mike simultaneously exhaled and laughed, and wound up choking. When he finally recovered, he said, "See? I knew that would make you feel better. That, and a bit of dank nug."

William lifted an eyebrow. "'Dank nug?'"

Ignoring him, Mike extinguished the joint. "Now, come inside and drink with me and Niall."

"Not until you swear to never say 'dank nug' again."

Jackhammer-laughing, Mike merely seized William's arm and steered him back inside, where the other bandmates were still helping Niall load the drums into his van. So Mike led William to the bar while they waited.

Cindy turned out to be the top-heavy brunette bartender, flirting with forty, spilling out of a tightly-laced green corset. And apparently, middle age wasn't the only thing she flirted with. As she pushed William's Irish Car Bomb across the bar, she glanced up and did a double-take. Tilted her head, and flashed him a coquettish smile.

"Well, aren't you a big, tall boy."

He froze. Turned away, and knocked back his drink to hide his scorching face.

"You cannot possibly be Mike's brother," she persisted, in her throaty voice.

Thoroughly tongue-tied, he looked helplessly to Mike.

"My brother is a man of few words, as you see," Mike offered, with his shit-eating grin.

"He shouldn't need very many."

Wide-eyed, William glanced back at her in dismay, and she winked before turning to mix Mike's drink.

Mike leaned into William and said in a low voice, "Poon."

"Come on. She's old enough to be our mom."

"Dude, middle-aged women are the bomb. She'll probably be so grateful, she'll let you fuck her in the ass. Put in a good word for me and we can spit roast her."

"Jesus; shut the hell up already," hissed William, looking around to make sure Cindy hadn't overheard. Before his brother could embarrass him further, he leaned in and said in a low voice, "The rest of it's in your car?"

"Dude, get your own fucking supply and stop mooching off me."

"I'm not mooching. I'm paying you for it. Friday."

"Yeah, but I didn't sign on to be some middleman."

Cindy pushed Mike's drink across the bar, and William studiously avoided her leer. After she bustled off to serve someone else, Mike added, "If I keep coming back at this rate, there'll be questions."

"Fine. Then who's your plug man?"

Mike chugged his drink and slammed the empty glass down on the bar. "I'm gonna go make a phone call."

William watched him disappear into the hallway leading to the restrooms and the pay phone. He seized a handful of nuts off the bar and was dodging Cindy's thinly-veiled innuendos on that point when Niall startled him with a hand on his shoulder.

"Hey, what's the craic?"

William blinked.

"Ah, come on now; you're gonna have to do better than that if you wanna join Act the Maggot."

"Act the Maggot?"

"It'll require a bit of authenticity, you know. But don't worry, I'll bring you up to speed."

William stared at him, flummoxed. Niall retrieved a pack of cigarettes from his back pocket and held it out to him. "Fag?"

William flinched as Jimmy's pock-marked face and reedy snarl flashed right in front of him.

I'm curb-stomping this little faggot! It's about time one of us did it.

Suddenly nauseous, sweaty, and out of air, William could only stammer out, "Wh-what?"

A resounding belly laugh yanked William back to the present. It was Niall's laughter; Niall's voice. Niall's good-humored face in front of him – not Jimmy's.

"I'm not comin' on to ya, man!" gasped Niall between spurts of laughter. "I'm offering you a cigarette. The Irish slang still slips out, even after a couple of years Stateside. I reckon it'll get me in trouble one of these days."

"Oh..." Niall had misinterpreted the cause of William's panic as much as William had misinterpreted Niall. Unable to locate his voice, William declined the offered cigarette with a shake of his head. Shrugging, Niall drew one from the pack with his teeth, which made William all the more glad he hadn't taken Niall up on his offer.

"Listen," Niall said after lighting up, "I've written a whole album of songs already, and Mike tells me you're a bit of a songwriter, yourself."

It dawned on William. "Act the Maggot is the name of the band?" The adrenaline was draining too slowly from his system. He prayed Niall couldn't hear that his voice still trembled as much as his limbs did.

"Yeah. Bollocks, right? It wasn't my idea, I swear; it was Mike's." The cigarette leaped in Niall's mouth as he talked.

"Act the Maggot... I don't get it."

"Well, yeah; it's like 'act the fool,' as you Yanks might say."

"Oh." William tugged at his fingers and knuckles to hide how badly his hands shook, but at least he could manage a smirk. "That does sound like something Mike would pick."

"I will say, it was better than his first idea – Craic Is Wack."

No one had been eavesdropping on their conversation, yet Niall's loud, infectious chortle spread to the other patrons at the bar, radiating outward in both directions from him. William caught it as well, and thankfully the laughter ushered the last of the panic from his veins. Before William knew what was happening, Niall slapped him on the back, hard, and shouted, "Bar wench!"

William's laughter caught in his throat as Cindy approached. She leaned over the bar, right in front of William, to refill the bowl of nuts he had emptied. She lingered over the task, her ample assets on full display to him.

"Niall," she said. "You're cute, in a Lucky Charms sort of way. But the only reason you're getting away with calling me 'bar wench' is because your friend here is cuter."

Her face was round, but pretty; her skin remarkably well-preserved for someone who had spent a career enveloped in tobacco smoke. She wasn't skinny, but she wasn't exactly overweight, either. Definitely curvy, in strategic places.

She lifted her eyes then, and William's snapped immediately to her face. But she had caught him red-handed, and her mouth twisted into a wry smile.

Thankfully, Niall rescued him. "Cindy, I'd like to buy my round."

"You mean for you and Mad Max here? Or for you, Max, and Mike?"

"The whole pub, Cindy. The whole feckin' pub."

"Go home, Lucky." But she pulled them both a pint of Murphy's, with a third one for Mike when he got back from the phone.

Niall pushed a twenty dollar bill across the bar and said, "Have one for yourself later."

In response, she lightly slipped her fingers around William's wrist, and turned his watch face up. "I get off in thirty."

"I'll bet you do," Niall replied on William's behalf, and unleashed another one of his contagious laughs. Then, after roundly abusing the quality of stout in America and lamenting the absence of Beamish, Niall demolished his entire pint in one gulp. Wiping his mouth on his forearm, he turned to William and said, "Listen, I want to get this in before the other guys come back. They don't know it's the end of days for Ironshaft. Cindy put in a word with the manager here, and we're in. Act the Maggot, every Friday night. It's ours for the taking. All we have to do is tell them when we start. And get a lead guitar, since my own brother moved back to Ireland last week for a girl, the plonker. Which is where you come in."

"Uh-huh. Where's that?"

Niall took a drag from his cigarette. "Can you come in tomorrow for rehearsal? I have a studio lined up and everything."

William sipped his Murphy's. Licked the foam from his upper lip, considering.

"I don't know if this is the best time for me," he said. "I've fallen behind at school lately."

"Fair enough. It's just, we needed to get moving on this *yesterday*. Maybe you can just fill in a short while? Until we find someone permanent?"

At that moment, Mike returned from the pay phone and, finding his pint waiting for him, slid it down the bar to Niall. "Thanks, man, but it's all yours now. Will and I gotta bounce."

William, in mid-gulp with his own pint, choked a bit. "Now?"

"Yeah, dumbass. When your plug says now, you come *now*."

William's bar stool scraped backwards as he rose without further ado. He felt a hand on his arm, and Niall said, "Rehearsal tomorrow?"

William zipped his jacket, considering. "Yeah, okay."

Niall patted him. "Good man. Mike will tell you where it is." With a smirk, he added, "I'll make your apologies to Cindy."

Rolling his eyes, William followed Mike out to Jimmy's old 1968 Camaro that Mike had restored himself and painted bright yellow. As he somehow pretzeled his legs into the passenger seat, William asked, "Where are we going?"

"Mission District."

William tried not to show his alarm. "At this time of night?"

Mike patted him on the knee. "Don't worry your pretty little head, Sis."

"Should we take my bike, instead?"

"Are you kidding? Look dude, I know Julia's not here, but I'm not sitting behind you on that thing and wrapping my beautiful long legs around you."

It was insensitive at best; below the belt at worst. Either way, it silenced William; and though Mike had never had the best judgment, William was desperate for a fix. So as Mike's stereo blasted The Dead Kennedys out the windows, and his Camaro blasted testosterone down Guerrero to 19th Street, William tried to shrink himself as far down in his seat as he could. Which, for him, was an exercise in futility.

Mike turned down a side street, and his car screeched to a halt in front of a faded turquoise house with peeling vermilion trim and bars on the windows. Mike flashed another one of his stupid grins and, whistling, led William up the steps to the front door. He knocked, and the door swung open.

William recognized the piercing hazel eyes of the woman on the other side, but for a few seconds, it wouldn't quite register.

"Haze?"

She blinked, apparently just as dumbfounded to find him there. "William? Is that really you?"

Turning back to Mike, he jerked his thumb over his shoulder. "*Her*?"

Grinning, Mike pushed past William and held his fist out to her. "What up, Haze?"

"You're not black, Mike." Haze stepped aside and waved them in.

"Mike," William began carefully. "Let me just make sure we're all on the same page. We're here for what we talked about at the pub, not tattoos – right?"

"Dude, are we at her studio?" Mike scoffed and looked toward Haze, as if to say, *can you believe this fool?*

But Haze did not look at William as if she thought he were a fool. Her restrained gaze put him at ease as he crossed the threshold into her foyer.

"Nowadays I only do this for a select few," Haze explained, closing and locking the door behind them. "Jimmy and Mike have been loyal customers for years."

"Of both enterprises, apparently," William observed.

"Jimmy and I have single-handedly kept her in business all these years," Mike quipped.

"In case you haven't noticed, there's a one-month wait list at the studio," she retorted. Fantastical creatures stampeded down her arms from somewhere beneath the short sleeves of her black peasant top. The décolletage above its neckline hinted at more.

She had never once removed her eyes from William.

"Mike didn't tell you it was me?" William ventured.

"No, he did. You just look... different."

He felt the familiar heat rising to his face, along with his old insecurities around women. Every instinct in his body commanded him to look away, but he forced himself to hold her gaze.

She blinked first.

"Make yourselves comfortable," she offered, gesturing toward the couch. She settled herself on the adjacent chair, at right angles to them. Her eyes swept past Mike's grinning leer in favor of William again.

"*Haze,*" he said. "And all this time I thought it was because of your eyes. Or because you were in Hayes Valley."

She returned his smile, circumspect. "After they tore the freeway down, the yuppies moved in. That's why I'm in the Mission now."

Her voice still bore traces of her Russian origins. A silver barbell septum piercing adorned her nose. She had deliberately streaked her long, shaggy dark hair and bangs with gray. She reached up with slender fingers to tuck a lock behind her ear, showcasing a scaffold piercing with an arrow-shaped earring.

She said, "How is your albatross?"

"I followed orders, and kept it out of the sun."

Her features remained Russian-stoic. "Are you ever going to let it out of its cage?"

"Right! What the hell is that about, anyway?" Mike chimed in good-naturedly. "And by the way, I'm still pissed you didn't let me ink you, Will. I mean, I drew the fucking thing."

Haze had a pair of grooves between her full, dark brows, grooves etched prematurely by deep concentration. The grooves deepened slightly at Mike's interjection.

"Don't say ink," she rebuked. "It's disrespectful."

Mike scoffed. "What are you talking about?"

"Tattoo is an ancient art form. In some cultures, it's a spiritual practice."

Mike held his hands up in mock surrender. "Hey, whatever you say."

Shrugging off his insincerity, she turned back to William. "When are you going to let me put that crab on you?"

"Crab?"

"Yes. We talked about this. You're a quintessential Cancer, and a crab fisherman. What could be more perfect?"

He smiled again. "Lately I've been thinking about a mermaid."

She tipped her head quizzically. "A mermaid?"

"Dude," Mike groaned.

William ignored him. "Can you do it?"

"Of course," she said. "Where would you want it?"

He shrugged. "I'm not sure yet."

"Any other pointers? What do you want it to look like?"

"Black and gray."

"And topless," Mike chimed in. "Come to think of it, this isn't such a bad idea, after all."

Haze ignored him, as William had. "Maybe have her sitting, like she's on the rocks? Turned away, looking out to sea, so all you see is her lovely slender back. And maybe just a hint of side boob?"

William laughed a bit. She came to sit beside him and took up his left arm. Touched her fingertips to the inside of his forearm.

"I've been doing some reading lately about chakras. They say the left arm is the receiving arm. And the inside of the arm is controlled by the heart chakra. Seems like a good spot to put your mermaid."

Her shrewdness left him speechless. The corners of her mouth turned up in a self-satisfied sort of way. She lowered his arm and returned to her own chair.

Abruptly, she said, "Don't you get couch-lock from that shit?"

"Um... what?"

"I mean, that strain is all well and good for Mike – no offense, Mike – but I thought you'd like something a little less... mind-numbing."

Sheepish, William replied, "Honestly, right now, I just want something to wind down with."

Haze shrugged. "Whatever you say." She rose again from her chair and ascended the staircase, leaving them alone in the living room.

Bemused, William looked to Mike, who nodded reassuringly. Sure enough, a minute later, the stairs creaked again beneath her footsteps.

She had already measured it out – only a half-eighth, by the looks of it – and held the baggie out to him.

"Actually, I was hoping for –" He stopped because Mike kicked him. Hard.

"Right on, Haze," blurted Mike. "We'll bounce now. Great seeing you."

But Haze peered at William – rather earnestly, he thought. "Try it first. You can always come back for more."

William knew then that she hadn't given him what he asked for. He was a bit peeved, but he was also utterly inexperienced at buying weed from a dealer. What little weed he had smoked in the past, he had always just bought off of Mike. So he shut up, nodded, and handed over the cash.

Without further ceremony, he and Mike rose from the couch and allowed Haze to see them out. As soon as they were back in the car, Mike seized his arm. "Holy shit, dude, you have got it goin' *on!*"

William raised an eyebrow. "What are you talking about?"

"Do you have any idea how many years both me and Jimmy have been trying to bang her? We thought she was a dyke, 'cause, you know – Russian chick, living in the Mission, working as a tattoo artist. But I have *never* seen her look at a guy the way she looked at you just now."

William waved his hand dismissively.

"Hey dumbass. You know how she only gave you a half-eighth?"

"Yeah; what was that about? I'll go through that by tomorrow night if it's any good, which – who knows, since it's not what I asked for."

"Dude. I can guarantee you it'll be the best bud you've ever smoked. That's why she gave it to you, and only a half-eighth – so you'd come back. As soon as possible."

Mike's theory landed like a jolt of electricity, and William's eyes drifted unfocused as he considered whether his brother might actually be right.

Granted, loving Julia still felt as necessary to life as breathing. He still thought of her every minute of the day; still craved her, body and soul, like an addict craves their drug.

Still, for the first time since Julia had broken up with him, his traitorous nether regions stirred. Haze had been his first crush – the star of his earliest nocturnal fantasies. She had never been any great love, and he knew she never would; but at least the prospect of getting off with her made him feel something for the first time in weeks.

Mike perpetrated his cretinous laugh, tearing William from his thoughts. "Aren't you a sweet, innocent little thing. You've got to play that up for us, man. Score us some free weed."

Dragging his attention back to his brother from more welcome thoughts, he retorted, "That strikes me as monumentally stupid."

"Free weed. Strikes you as stupid."

"Somehow, a female Russian tattoo artist, surrounded by Salvadoran gangbangers in the heart of the Mission, has access to the best weed in the city. Does that not strike you as odd?"

Mike clapped his hand on William's shoulder and shook him a bit. "Relax, bro! You think too much."

"Somebody has to," William grumbled, shrugging him off. But he was already thinking about those animal tattoos on Haze's arms, and the ones halfway concealed below the neckline of her shirt. Sort of tribal, but more delicate. He wouldn't mind getting a closer look at those.

"THE EAGLET FEASTS ON BLOOD."

May-gray had long since crouched on the Outer Sunset, swallowing the neighborhood's sights in fog and forcing William to turn inward to amuse himself. So, as he strolled home from the bus stop after school, he thought about Charles Baudelaire. Or, more specifically, about his poem, *L'Albatros*.

Or – even more specifically – about the skinny redhead with the orthodontic headgear who lisped her way through her reading of *L'Albatros* in class.

The pricks in French class whose parents could afford to send them to Holy Cross without scholarships called her Horsey Face, and Mosquito Bites. William supposed it was because of her buck teeth and flat chest.

But if they thought they could get under her skin, she quickly disabused them of that notion. "Take a picture; it'll last longer," she would retort. Or, perhaps, "I hate to break your hearts, boys, but don't start picking out curtains." Then she would toss her copper hair and flounce right past their desks, head held high.

He had to hand it to her – she might not be much to look at, but she made them all look like punks.

She almost certainly belonged to the couple who owned Dunphy's Restaurant, across the pier from his parents' fish processing plant. Nonna had told him their daughter would be going to Holy Cross, and Monsieur Laurent always referred to her in class as *Mademoiselle Dunphy*.

What was her first name, again? Jillian? He waffled back and forth between that and Jessica as he twisted his key in the front door lock. Between that and Nonna's stray cats, who came shooting out of the tunnel entrance at his approach, he never noticed the unfamiliar car parked in front of the house.

The voices drifting down the stairs snapped him back to the present. The first one belonged to Nonna, but it wasn't until he reached the landing at the top of the stairs that he finally recognized the second, just as its owner's face came into view.

William stopped short. "Andy!"

"Will," Nonna chided gently, with an apologetic smile at the youngish man in the clerical suit and collar, sitting on their sofa. Average build, bland generic features, close-cropped medium-brown hair. "It's *Father Molloy*, please."

"Sorry," Willam muttered.

Andy returned Nonna's smile with a reassuring one of his own. "It's okay, Mrs. Cardone; I told William to address me by my first name."

"Oh," Nonna said in breathless surprise.

A couple of years earlier, in a last-ditch attempt to persuade William to undergo Confirmation, she had connected him with Father Molloy. He was a brand-new priest in his late twenties, informal and relatable, but with a razor-sharp intellect. He eventually told William to just call him Andy. They had spent long hours debating the doctrine of original sin, theism versus deism, and the soundness of Thomas Aquinas' *Quinque viae*. In the end, Andy didn't convince William to undergo the sacrament, but he made William almost sorry not to have been convinced.

It wasn't until Mike teased him about his relationship with the priest that William realized how it might have been construed. But

Andy's attentions had only ever been earnest and appropriate. Unlike, allegedly, his predecessor, who transferred to another parish under a cloud of rumor and suspicion.

It was Nonna who found out about the scholarship to Holy Cross, but Andy wrote the letter of recommendation that clinched it for William. So it was with genuine respect and enthusiasm that William's face lit up in a grin. "To what do we owe the pleasure, Andy?"

"William," Nonna said, a little firmer this time. "Ix-nay the eekiness-chay."

This time, Andy bestowed his reassuring smile on William. "I came by to share some good news with your nonna. She thought you'd like to hear it, so she asked if I could wait until you got home."

William's eyes flickered to his grandmother, and he watched her struggle to compose her features. But her dark eyes sparkled, and a hint of rosiness spackled her weathered olive complexion.

His pulse quickened in suspense. "What is it?"

Andy patted the sofa cushions. "Sit."

William obeyed, and Andy regarded him with a complacent smile. "Will, your Nonna mentioned a few months ago that she was keeping her eyes peeled for college scholarships. You know I'm teaching a Religious Studies course at USF, right?"

"University of San Francisco?"

"That's right. And, well... it turns out they're offering a brand-new scholarship, starting next year. Full ride. Housing, books... the works. And I want to recommend you for it."

William barely caught his jaw before it hit the floor. "You want to recommend... *me*."

Andy chuckled. "Of course. You're the first one I thought of."

William had to steal another glance at his grandmother, just to reassure himself that Andy wasn't pulling his leg. The tears shining in Nonna's eyes and the way her lips trembled through her smile provided all the assurance he needed.

Turning back to Andy, he stammered, "But... why me?"

Andy gave a quizzical tilt of the head. "You don't think you deserve it?"

After yet another shifty glance at Nonna, William straightened. Cleared his throat. "I mean…"

"William," Andy began gently, "you're brilliant, scholarly, and gifted. I say all of this knowing it would give most kids your age an ego complex; but you're also thoughtful, diligent, and humble. Over-confidence is the least of your vices."

"Okay," William said slowly, genuinely moved by Andy's faith in him. "But surely there must be some catch to this scholarship."

Andy tipped his hand from side-to-side. "*You* might think it's a catch. Your nonna and I don't."

"Let me guess," William speculated drily. "I have to be a confirmed Catholic."

Andy grinned. "Bingo." In response to William's annoyance, he quickly added, "And don't blame your poor nonna for this – she had nothing to do with it. She's ready to accept your decision, whatever it may be, on one condition: that you spend one afternoon in conversation with me."

"Of course." In spite of himself, William couldn't suppress a smile. He knew beyond a shadow of a doubt that Nonna only wanted what was best for him. Maybe it was inconvenient that she believed what was best for him was Confirmation; but he could easily put up with that in exchange for the unwavering support, presence, and unconditional love she had always offered him.

"Will," Nonna began, "Did I ever tell you I graduated salutatorian of my high school?"

William's eyebrows shot up his forehead. "Really?"

"I was offered a full scholarship to the College of Notre Dame, in Belmont; but Papa wouldn't let me go. He said I didn't need a college diploma to be a wife and mother."

Outraged on her behalf, William frowned. "Nonna… why didn't you ever tell me that?"

"Because I never wanted anyone thinking I resented this life. I haven't; not even for a second. *But…* I do wish I could have had my cake and eat it, too."

Andy chuckled softly beside William, but William only pressed his clasped hands to his lips and frowned down at the rug.

"Will," Nonna proceeded, more quietly this time. "You remind me so much of me at your age, and also of my brother Vincent. He went to college and eventually became a bishop, you know; and I see that same potential in you." When William opened his mouth to argue, Nonna lifted her hand. "College, is all I mean."

"Nonna... I've always wanted to be a fisherman, like Uncle Frank."

Nonna sighed. "You may enjoy fishing with Frank, but you've been reading since you were three. You read *The Iliad* and *The Odyssey* when you were seven. *Seven*, Will. And you've devoured every book you could get your hands on since. You were writing sonnets when you were eight. You picked up a guitar when you were ten, and just played."

"Actually, Mike taught me," William balked.

"Will," Andy admonished, "just hear her out."

William slouched in resignation, waiting.

"Let me put it this way," Nonna continued. "My parents came from Sicily with nothing but the clothes on their backs, and each other. They defied their families to get married, you know – my mother was Arbëreshë," she added by way of explanation to Andy.

Andy glanced back and forth between William and Nonna. "Arbë-who?"

"Arbëreshë," William repeated. "They're sort of an ethnic sub-group in Sicily, descended from Albanians."

"So when they came here," Nonna added, "they were just completely on their own."

"How did they manage?" Andy marveled.

"They worked nonstop their whole lives," Nonna replied. "Besides fishing, Papa cleaned sewers, swept streets, dug graves... whatever he could get. Mamma peddled fish from a cart, up and down the hills of San Francisco, with all her babies in tow." Turning to her grandson, Nonna added, "And to all thirteen of us kids, they said the same thing: 'We're doing this so you don't have to.'"

"I know they made a lot of sacrifices," William replied, "but I'm sure they did that so their kids and grandkids would have choices, right?"

"Of course," Nonna conceded.

"And I do actually enjoy fishing, you know. I've never felt more like myself than when I'm out there with Uncle Frank."

"That's great, Will; I'm not trying to disparage that," Nonna assured him, "but right now, you're young, with a strong back and forgiving joints. Meanwhile, you've seen the toll it's taken on Frank."

William had no rebuttal for that. Frank looked at least a decade older than his forty-one years and groaned under the burden of slipped discs, sciatica, and carpal tunnel. At sea, he subsisted on a diet of ramen noodles, Twinkies, cigarettes, and sugar with a little coffee in it. On land, he swapped out the sugar in favor of Kahlua or Bailey's to cope with the havoc his frequent absences wrought upon his family.

"Your nonno tried to warn Frank," Nonna continued gently, and William knew that by *nonno,* she meant her long-dead husband – the grandfather William had never met. "He saw what it did to his own father. It's why Nonno invested everything he had into Cardone's. He didn't want that for himself or his kids."

Stumped for a response, William slouched in his seat, glowering down at the rug.

"Will," Andy ventured after a few moments, "it's obvious that writing poems brings you joy. You showed me some of them, remember?"

"The few ones Jimmy didn't get to, yeah." There were a handful that William had scribbled on notebook paper at school, then stuffed carelessly into his backpack, only to forget about them. He rediscovered them a few days after Jimmy decimated his last composition journal, then kept them hidden there until Jimmy was arrested two weeks later for carjacking.

After a lengthy silence, William finally lifted his eyes to find both Nonna and Andy watching him with something like pity. It soured his stomach.

They both knew William hadn't written anything since then, even though in theory, he had no one left to hide from. Jimmy had been incarcerated this whole time, and since it wasn't his first offense, he had no hope of parole any time soon. But Jimmy's past ridicule cast long shadows over the present.

Faggot.
Cocksucker.
Fudgepacker.

I'm gonna curb-stomp your fairy ass!

Nonna interrupted William's rumination with, "I told you earlier you remind me of my brother Vincent. He and I were the scholars of the family, and the whole family was always very musical – you and Mike come by that honestly." Her eyes suddenly glistened, and her chin wobbled. "Your parents and I tried to help Jimmy, and when that, um..." She glanced briefly at Andy, then seemed to choose her next words carefully. "...when that didn't work, I did what I could to protect the rest of you, but..." To William's dismay, a single tear spilled over onto Nonna's cheek. "I couldn't."

While Andy murmured reassurances to Nonna, William rushed over to sit beside her. His brows pinched with anguish as he grasped her hands. "Nonna, you're the only one who ever really tried to help." Despite Nonna's protestations to the contrary, his parents had not; that was for sure. Not even when they were around and not working. Not even when his father wasn't passed out drunk on the couch. And neither of those scenarios occurred very often.

Nonna withdrew one hand to swipe at her cheek. "And now here I am, making you comfort me." She forced a ragged laugh. "I'm sorry. It's just... Will, don't let Jimmy take the *you* out of you. Not to fit Jimmy's twisted ideas of what it means to be a man. It would break my heart."

William wiped his hands down his face and turned his eyes up to the ceiling. "It's not just that, Nonna. Even if I wanted to apply for a full-ride scholarship, my grades aren't competitive enough."

"Any minor blips in your grades," Andy interjected, "are only because of how hard you work, helping your family. You can explain that in your essay, and I'll reinforce it in my letter of recommendation."

William stared down at the rug again and tugged at his knuckles while considering Andy's offer. Finally, he lifted his eyes and said, "And all I have to do is undergo Confirmation, huh?"

Andy grinned. "Not my rules – USF's. But you do have to actually mean it, Will."

"Of course," William grumbled, a bit sardonically.

"Will," Nonna said, her tone carrying a mild warning.

But Andy chuckled. "Don't stress about it, Will. The only thing your nonna asks of you is an afternoon's conversation with Yours Truly. We've never had trouble finding stuff to talk about, have we?"

William shrugged. "Okay. When?"

"How about now?" Andy gestured toward the window. "The fog is clearing up. We can sit on the back patio."

"I'll turn on the patio heater and bring you some coffee," Nonna offered.

William blew out a sigh of resignation, and a few minutes later, he sat comfortably at the long, rectangular patio table that had hosted countless Cardone and Quinn family gatherings.

After an awkward silence, William opened with, "So."

"So," echoed Andy with another one of his disarming grins.

Despite his best efforts, William broke into a wide grin of his own and shook his head. "Andy, we've been over all of this, and nothing has changed."

Andy played coy. "Over all of what?"

"There's no planet on which I could sincerely go through Confirmation."

"Because you don't believe in all that stuff," Andy finished, succinctly summarizing what William had told him two and a half years ago.

"Exactly."

But Andy continued slowly nodding, as if waiting for William to elaborate.

"Do you still believe all of this is part of some grand plan?" William demanded.

"What do you mean, 'all of this?'"

William gestured all around himself. "*This.* The world. History."

"Well, I wouldn't be a priest if I didn't."

William's eyes narrowed. "So you honestly believe the Holocaust was part of God's plan."

"Will, did you ever read the Book of Job, like I suggested?"

William huffed. "Yeah. A few dozen chapters of Job moaning, 'Why me?' followed by God replying, 'What the hell do you know?'"

To William's surprise, Andy tossed his head back in a guffaw. "That's a bit of an oversimplification, but actually... you're not far off."

"So, what? We're just supposed to accept that we'll never understand why God allows babies in ovens to happen?"

Andy folded his arms on the tabletop and leaned in. "What about *Man's Search for Meaning*, by Viktor Frankl? I suggested that one, too. Did you ever read it?"

Blanching, William admitted he had not.

Andy sighed and sat back again in his chair. "Don't get me wrong, Will; I'm with you. I can't grasp how something like the Holocaust fits into the plan of any benevolent, omnipotent God. But our power lies in our response. Just because God is all-powerful doesn't mean we're powerless."

"But if God really were all-powerful, He could have made a prefect world."

"Maybe this *is* a perfect world," Andy posited. "Maybe it's the most perfect world possible."

"That's depressing," grunted William.

"If you choose." When William merely blinked, Andy added, "There's a line in Job where God basically says, 'The eaglet feasts on blood, and wherever the slain are, there it is.' But you know, the same eagle that preys on livestock also keeps rodents out of fields and silos. Maybe God made a perfect world, a world of natural balance and order where we still have the power to choose; and we're the ones who keep screwing it up with our terrible choices and our lousy attitudes."

William leveled Andy with a dubious look, but at that moment, Nonna emerged with the coffee. After pouring a cup for both of them and leaving the cream and sugar, she didn't linger. William supposed she didn't want to disrupt any momentum Andy had established.

As he poured cream into his coffee, William set his jaw. "Andy... I enjoy our conversations. I'm very grateful for your friendship and your confidence in me. But if I go to college, I'll have to find a different scholarship, because I can't go through with Confirmation."

"You know, Will," Andy said tentatively while stirring his coffee, "we can make this an ongoing dialogue. We don't have to limit it to just this afternoon."

But William shook his head. "I won't change my mind."

Andy said nothing; he just peered up at William from beneath his eyelashes and continued to stir his coffee. William couldn't get a read on his expression. Sad? Frustrated? Disappointed? Maybe all of it.

Finally Andy yielded, and they spent the rest of the afternoon talking about poetry, sports, and school.

"HIS GIANT WINGS KEEP HIM FROM WALKING."

The irony was, when William was eleven, he actually dreamed of being a monk. A life of solitude, scholarship, and quiet reflection sounded perfect to a nerdy little introvert like him.

Then, when he was twelve, puberty hit.

Not long after, Jimmy ripped up his composition notebook for the first time, and the regular brutalizations began. The random "inspections" of his bedroom for contraband "homo shit," like poetry. Breaking the door down if William had bothered to lock it. Pinning him to the bed or the floor, just to assert his dominance, until William's limbs went numb. Forcing him to drink until he finally pissed himself. William would have done it voluntarily just to put an end to it, but his terror was so great that he couldn't even relax his bladder. And when the pain finally overrode all bladder control, Jimmy would rub William's nose in it as if he were a dog, then hover menacingly in the doorway while he made William clean up after himself.

This particular torture only occurred when everyone else was out of the house. Perhaps Nonna was grocery shopping, or shuttling Kelly to and from her soccer games. Mike would be out somewhere, raising hell. His parents, as always, were at work.

But there were other, more brazen torments, too. Random sucker punches to the stomach or nuts as they passed each other, right outside the kitchen where Nonna was cooking. William learned to swallow his screams, or else he'd get even worse the next time. If anyone discovered him in the immediate aftermath, doubled over in pain, he blamed it on diarrhea or constipation.

He couldn't predict when it was coming, so he learned to hide. Shrink. Lock himself away.

And then, of course, when he was fourteen, Jimmy decimated his second composition notebook. That same day, William met Haze. From then on, despite all the prayers and hours spent in confession, his carnal urges remained firmly in the driver's seat.

He had to find some way to release the tension – the relentless hypervigilance, even in his sleep. The masking; the prosaicism of his life now. He released the tension every night in the shower, since he could no longer release it in the form of poems and songs. Jimmy had irrevocably robbed that from him. So instead, he stood under the spray of hot water, screwed his eyes shut, and imagined how much better his release would feel surging into a woman's receptive body, instead of down the drain. No amount of prayer had ever brought him that kind of relief.

But poetry once had.

Now, two and a half years on, cloistered in what had once been Jimmy's meth den but was now his bedroom, William opened his French textbook and re-read *L'Albatros*.

After dissecting the poem at length and allowing its cadence to settle over his students like a warm blanket, Monsieur Laurent had lectured on how rarely translations do justice to the original. How the translator sacrifices the original beauty or meter to preserve the meaning, or vice versa. To drive home the point, M. Laurent assigned them to conduct their own translation of *L'Albatros*, without consulting existing ones.

The entire class groaned, except William. Sparks crackled along his skin for the first time in two and a half years.

> The Poet is like the prince of the clouds,
> Who haunts the storms and laughs at the archer;
> Exiled on the ground amid jeers,
> His giant wings keep him from walking.

"How true," William murmured aloud to his empty bedroom after translating the final stanza. Not just true of his own experiences, but of his clunky translation, as well.

But maybe Nonna and Andy were right. Maybe it was finally time to stop limping in the shadow of a cruel tormenter who had once tried to clip his wings.

"TI VUGGHIU BINI."

A few weeks later, as William made his usual trek home from school, the June-gloom cleared long enough for him to spot the redhead from French class.

Her name was Julia. He had finally learned it back in May, after her virtuosic reading of *L'Albatros*.

She was clearly oblivious to her audience as she danced down the sidewalk, headphones over her ears, singing along badly to some song. He didn't mean to be a creeper, but his eyes couldn't help lingering. Her waist-length curtain of copper hair bounced and swayed along with her from beneath the brim of her bowler hat.

A week or two ago, she had finally shed the orthodontic headgear. She was still skinny; still flat-chested. Still wore long, baggy dresses that looked like something out of *Little House on the Prairie*, paired with vests and hand-crocheted cardigans and granny boots.

But that smile...

Despite the orthodontic treatment, her smile still betrayed a hint of an overbite. Even so, there was something about it. Luminous. Irrepressible. A bit mischievous. As if sharing some private joke with herself, it often warmed her features while she daydreamed in class, wrapped up in her own private Idaho.

She clearly didn't require anyone's approval. She seemed not exactly oblivious, but actually *impervious* to the taunts of their peers.

Watching her skip and twirl ahead of him, William couldn't help wondering where people found that kind of confidence. A poignant ache squeezed his chest, but before he could analyze it, she turned down a street three blocks from his own and vanished back into the fog.

He was still thinking of her when he unlocked the front door to his house, shooing away one of the more domesticated of Nonna's strays, who tried to dart past his ankles into the house.

Once William made it inside, he kept the front door open a crack to peer back out at the orange tabby, who protested with a plaintive mewl. But William good-naturedly said, "Better luck next time, buddy."

He still felt a little guilty, even though he knew Nonna's feline street urchins suffered not at all under her attentions. But then a warm, spicy aroma, redolent of the ocean, drove all thought of cats, Julia, or anything else from his mind.

Cioppino.

After dropping his backpack in the in-law unit, he made a beeline upstairs to the kitchen. Sure enough, he found Nonna in her well-loved, green-and-white-checked apron, stirring something in a pot over the stove. She had tamed her unruly salt-and-pepper coils of hair beneath a matching green-and-white-checked kerchief. As he approached, she greeted him with a smile, her glasses fogged up a bit from the steam.

"Surprise!" she sang out. "Happy last day of sophomore year!"

"You made cioppino for me?" He came closer and peered into the pot at the beginnings of the luscious seafood stew. His favorite.

"You bet I did."

William made a *tsk* sound. "That's too bad. I was going to McDonald's for dinner. Guess you'll have to feed my share to your freeloading strays."

Laughing, William tried to dodge the clean wooden spoon she snatched from the countertop, but as usual, she was too quick – it swatted him on his backside. It was a playful, affectionate little gesture she had administered for as long as he could remember. That was also about how long he had been cooking with her – as long as he could remember. And despite her age and the plump build of a grandmother whose love language was food, she was still spry and feisty.

Once his laughter subsided, he inquired, "Where did you get Dungeness crab at this time of year?"

"Oh, I have connections," Nonna replied with a cheesy grin and a wink.

William supposed she was referring to Uncle Frank. As she got back to work, he told her about his plans to spend three weeks this summer albacore tuna-fishing with Frank – until he spotted the tight line of her mouth.

Tentatively, he ventured, "I'll make a ton of money from that trip, you know. I can put it in my college savings account. The one you opened for me."

With a nearly inaudible gasp, Nonna turned to gape up at him. "Does that mean you're considering it? Going to college?"

William nodded, smiling faintly, and watched her eyes suddenly glint with moisture. She set the spoon on her favorite eggplant-shaped spoon rest and turned to grasp William's hands in her own spotty, wrinkled ones. The strength of her grip belied her four-foot-ten-inch stature.

"I am *so* proud of you," she said, craning her neck far back to see him, her voice cracking a bit as she enunciated each word. "You'll be the first person on both sides of your family to go to college, besides my brother. Did you know that?"

A strange chokehold suddenly gripped William's throat, and all he could do was nod.

"You'll have a great life, Will." She squeezed his hands, her watery eyes flitting back and forth between his. "The sky is the limit for you. I have no doubt."

"Only thanks to you," he managed to choke out. "I mean, it's not like anyone else in this family would have given me a writing journal, or entrusted me with a Nikon camera when I was only six, or found me a scholarship to the best high school in the city."

"Will, a nonna isn't supposed to play favorites, so I'll just say this – I always knew you were different, in the best possible way. All I did was plant a few seeds, but you are the one who tended them into a bountiful harvest."

With that, she tugged him into one of her signature bear hugs, and a tear escaped from him unbidden when she whispered, "Ti vugghiu bini, niputeddu miu."

"Love you, too, Nonna," he whispered in return.

When she finally released him, she held him by his elbows a moment and smiled, her lips still trembling, eyes still shimmering up at him. "Now come on – it's time for you to learn my secret."

"What secret?"

"The secret of what turns a good cioppino into a *great* cioppino, of course!"

A rare, wide grin snaked its way across his features. "You mean you're finally going to divulge the top-secret classified ingredient? The one you've been holding out on me all these years?"

"The very one," she chirped, giving his elbows a final squeeze before turning back to the stove. "You're ready."

That night, his belly and heart both full, he picked up the phone on his bedside table and dialed Andy's number.

"Will," Andy greeted. "This is a surprise. I thought you'd be celebrating your last day of school."

"I already did."

"Well, then. Quoting you, 'to what do I owe the pleasure?'"

William chuckled, emboldened by the warmth seeping through his veins from the rare glass of wine Nonna had poured him at dinner. A peppery Zinfandel to complement her zesty cioppino.

"Is it too late to start Confirmation classes?"

"NEVER LOOK A GIFT HORSE IN THE MOUTH."

June-gloom melded seamlessly into no-sky-July, and William spent his days either working at Cardone's for his parents, or on Uncle Frank's boat. Sometimes, while hoisting totes of fish or crabs to the pier, he spotted Julia Dunphy. She would emerge from her parents' restaurant and linger for about fifteen minutes, contemplating the boats, the bay, and the Golden Gate Bridge. Other times, she would read books he couldn't make out the titles of, her lips moving silently along with the words. It made him smile, for some reason.

She was still all sharp cheekbones and elbows. She still dressed like Mimi from *La Bohème*. Of course, he wasn't much to look at, either. Over the past couple of years, he had grown so much and so fast that his bones ached constantly. These days, when he looked in the mirror, an unrecognizable stick insect stared back at him through disproportionately large eyes.

With a sigh, he tore his gaze from Julia and re-focused on the job at hand. Nonna had asked him what he wanted to do for his birthday, and he had told her, "Go fishing with Uncle Frank."

With a tight smile, Nonna had replied, "I think it might be good for you to spend a couple of weeks out there with him. See what it's *really* like on that side of the hoist." But William knew his ongoing fascination with fishing worried Nonna a bit less, now that he was actively contributing to his college savings account and talking to Andy about Confirmation.

If he was being honest, he still didn't buy this stuff, but he claimed he did. It made it all worthwhile when William saw the tears of pride shimmering in Nonna's eyes each time she caught sight of him and Andy, seated in conversation at the dining table. He adored his grandmother and would do anything to make her happy. If that meant undergoing Confirmation, then lying to do so was a small price to pay.

After all, he didn't *really* believe in hell.

As he accompanied Frank back to the slip and tied the boat to the pile, he remembered that Nonna had called that morning to say she had another one of her headaches. She insisted they were migraines because she got blurry vision; though admittedly she hadn't had migraines since menopause. But clearly they were back now, and they troubled her more and more; so she had stayed home today to rest.

William decided to help his parents by cooking dinner. After ducking into the processing plant to inform them, he walked all the way to the Italian grocer in North Beach, gathered the ingredients for chicken marsala, then caught the next bus home with his haul.

But to his surprise, when he unlocked the front door, heavenly aromas wafted downstairs to greet him. He stopped short, the grocery bag still in his arms.

"Hello?"

"It's me," Nonna called from upstairs.

With his long legs, William scaled the stairs two at a time and hurried into the kitchen. Sure enough, Nonna sliced eggplant at the counter.

"What are you doing?" he demanded, setting the groceries on the kitchen table and coming to inspect her.

She turned to lift an eyebrow. "What does it look like I'm doing?"

"Not resting at home," he retorted.

She pointed to her head and grinned. "Not suffering from a migraine."

"That was fast," he observed. "Don't they usually last longer?"

"Never look a gift horse in the mouth." She nodded over to the bag on the table. "What's that?"

William took that as his cue to start putting away the groceries. "Dinner tomorrow. Chicken marsala. You're invited."

She gaped at him a moment. "You were going to make that tonight, weren't you?"

He shrugged. "I'll make it tomorrow, instead."

"I'm sorry, Will. If I had known–"

"It's fine," he chuckled. "I'm glad you're better."

Smiling warmly, she wiped her hands on her checked apron and came to meet him at the refrigerator. "You're such a good boy, but you had better quit growing, or I won't be able to do *this* anymore." Standing on her tiptoes and reaching as high as possible, she managed to give his cheek an affectionate pinch.

Warmth flooded his chest, and he stooped to kiss her cheek. "I make no promises, Nonna."

She laughed. "Let me help you put those groceries away. Then I'll show you how to sweat the eggplant so it doesn't get soggy."

Over the next few minutes, they salted and pressed the eggplant slices, leaching the excess moisture. As they worked, William's mind drifted back to a certain girl on the pier.

"Nonna, does the Dunphys' daughter work at their restaurant now? Because I keep seeing her over there."

"Which daughter?"

His eyebrows lifted in surprise. "There's more than one?"

"There's two, actually."

"Oh... well, I'm talking about the redhead. Julia."

Nonna gave him a sidelong smirk. "Has she caught your eye?"

His neck suddenly felt hot, and his scoff of denial was too vehement. "She seems... a little quirky."

She hummed. "Well, I have no idea if Julia works there now. That would be a better question for your parents." Shooting him another impish grin, she added, "Or for *her*."

He shuddered at the thought of actually speaking to Julia – not because she repulsed him, but because he shuddered at the thought of speaking to *anyone* outside the family. It's why he had no real friends to speak of.

Their conversation paused as they flipped the eggplant slices, placed them between two clean dry dish towels, and re-stacked the heavy books on top. But afterward, while they waited, Nonna seemed preoccupied.

"Is your headache coming back?" William speculated.

The furrow between her brows smoothed out, and she smiled gently. "Thank heaven, no."

Another few minutes of silence followed while William used Nonna's rolling pin to crumble stale bread. Then he watched as Nonna mixed the crumbs with dried herbs and spices.

"Will..." she began tentatively. "If you ever fall in love with a woman, don't degrade her by living in sin."

William's entire head and neck flooded with heat, and an involuntary guffaw escaped his throat. "Wha...?"

She peered up at him again, even as she continued sprinkling oregano into the crumbs. She didn't need to measure – she knew how much to add by instinct. "I mean it, Will. You have a big heart, and one day you're going to fall in love. You feel things deeply, even if you don't wear your heart on your sleeve; so when you fall, you'll fall hard. You'll be tempted to move quickly, but there's no need to rush."

"Nonna..." Mortified, William coughed out a laugh. "If this is because of me asking about Julia–"

Nonna cut him off with a dismissive wave. "It's just... you're nearly a man now, and you're also on the path to Confirmation. I want you to be happy, and sticking closely to what you're learning from Andy will serve you well in all areas – including romance."

His cheeks still radiated heat, and he couldn't look her in the eye. The only response he could offer was an awkward, "Um... okay. I'll bear that in mind."

"Good. I said my piece," she declared, whisking the dish towel from the eggplant slices with a flourish. "Now, grab the flour and the eggs – it's time to get messy."

Chuckling, he shrugged off the last of his embarrassment and happily complied. Ever since he could remember, he had loved getting his hands messy with food. He had never outgrown the fun of breading eggplant. That's when it dawned on him – cooking brought him the same contentment he had only ever known from fishing and poetry. Especially cooking with his feisty, hopelessly behind-the-times nonna. And as with his poetry and songwriting, his family ribbed him endlessly about it.

But maybe the joke was on them. Maybe one day, the skills Nonna had passed down to him would pay dividends. It was one more gift he could never repay, even if he had forty lifetimes.

46

SEPTEMBER 1995, PART II

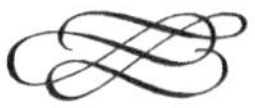

William had an exam on Wednesday morning, then worked the lunch shift at Dunphy's. After that, he kept his word to rehearse with Act the Maggot. To his own surprise, he actually felt good about it all; but the end result was, he didn't get the chance to try Haze's product sample until Thursday.

That night, he picked up the phone and dialed Haze's number, all the while convinced she couldn't possibly be home. She was a cool girl; surely she would have found something cool to do, with someone cool, even if it was only a Thursday night. Something that didn't involve sitting at home, selling weed to losers like him.

"Hello?"

"Oh. Hey. Uh... this is William. Quinn."

"Oh, hey." She said it at the same moment he said Quinn. She hadn't needed the clarification.

"Hey. Um... can I meet you somewhere?"

"Sure. Come through."

"Oh. Okay." He scratched his nose. Felt a bit sweaty. "Where?"

"My place."

"Oh. Yeah, okay."

He hung up, and opened his wallet to make sure he had enough cash. Checked his face in the mirror. She seemed to like him just fine last time, when he was scruffy. He took a whiff of his armpits. Doffed his clothes, and took the quickest shower of his life.

He scanned the few remaining clean clothes in his closet. Pulled on a Led Zeppelin T-shirt. Located a pair of jeans he hadn't worn more than once without laundering. Zipped his motorcycle jacket, and surveyed himself one last time in the bathroom mirror.

He drove across the city to the Mission District and parked in front of her house. Haze opened the front door even before he knocked, as if she had been watching for him.

But she shattered that misapprehension by saying, "I would have expected a noisy arrival from Mike, but not from you."

"Oh." He cringed inwardly at his own self-delusion. "It was Mike who tricked this bike out for me. I had no say in the matter."

He crossed the threshold into her foyer, and without any further niceties, she led him into the living room. She gestured to the sofa, and he took a seat. Her black cropped tank top drew his eyes to her waistline. The tank top had a white coat of arms with a double-headed eagle, and Cyrillic writing: Россия. The hem of her red floral broomstick skirt brushed the tops of her Doc Martens.

She sat in the same chair as before, at right angles to him. She peered at him, matter-of-fact. All business.

"How did you like it?"

"Well," he said, shrugging a shoulder. "I'm back."

A scale, a wooden box, and some baggies sat on top of the coffee table. "How much, this time?"

He could easily go through a full ounce, but that would sustain him for too long in between visits. "A half-ounce?"

Without another word, she got down to business. With no sleeves on her shirt to impede his view, he had a clear view of the tattoos on her arms. Her left shoulder sported a bucking deer with a griffin's beak. Its head sprouted ram's horns and what looked like a bouquet of flowers. A panther prowled across her right shoulder. Other hybrids of griffins with sheep, goats, and birds cascaded down both arms.

She caught him looking, so he quickly said, "Those are new since the last time I saw you. Three years ago, I mean – not on Tuesday. I saw them on Tuesday, of course." He winced at his own rambling.

She said nothing, and her expression never changed. Cold. Totally different than Tuesday.

He tried again. "I always thought it was odd – a tattoo artist with no tattoos."

"No visible ones," she pointed out. Still aloof. But her eyes flitted to his briefly.

"True," he conceded, his dick waking up a bit, rendering him mute. He sucked so hard at this. The only reason he had ever gotten laid was because Julia was happy to do most of the talking.

He reached into his jacket again and retrieved his wallet. Held out the cash to her. She looked at it and said, "It's one-forty for a half-ounce of this."

He felt his stomach drop at the price, but reached into his wallet for another forty dollars. She held the bag out to him, and he tucked it inside his jacket.

She rose from her chair then. He rose too, and without so much as another word, she led him to the foyer. Stepped aside, and held the door open for him.

Clearly, Mike had been completely wrong.

"I'm sorry about Mike," he blurted.

Her eyes snapped up to his, widening. At least her expression had finally changed.

"He's such an idiot," he continued. "But... Well. I don't have to tell you. You were there that day."

The hardness in her gaze unfurled somewhat. He could tell she knew – he wasn't talking about Tuesday.

"Yes, I was," she acknowledged.

They peered at each other a moment longer. Then he patted his jacket, over the spot where he had concealed the weed.

"Well. Thanks," he said, and turned to go.

"But that was six years ago."

He turned again. "What?"

"You were just a kid. And Mike was just doing the right thing - protecting his little brother. But that was six years ago, and you're not your brother's keeper."

"I know that. But I have no doubt he saved my life that day. So watching his back these days feels like the very least I can do."

She put her hand on his arm. "I'm sorry."

Startled, he said, "For what?"

"I've had a really hard time forgiving myself for the part I played in what happened that day."

He gaped at her in disbelief. "What are you talking about?"

"Letting you believe the wrong thing about what happened that day, for starters. I let you believe it because I didn't want to go to prison, myself."

Thoroughly confused, he arched his brows.

"He was trying to get more crystal off me," she explained. "He didn't believe I didn't have more. He had already been awake for three days straight."

William shifted his weight. "Oh."

"I used it with him back then. Him and Mike. And I was the cook."

So many things were falling into place now. He probably could put two and two together if it happened today, but his fourteen-year-old mind's interpretation had long since become canon.

"I'm not involved in any of that anymore," she added quickly. "I went to rehab right after that, like Mike did. I had really spiraled. You know – my mom died. But that doesn't excuse anything. I fed their addiction, and by feeding it, I nearly got you killed."

"No you didn't. You were the one who went for help. Jimmy is the one who nearly got me killed, and who knows what he would have done to you."

"Will." She had never called him that before. Her hand was still on his arm, and his pulse quickened. "That day... did..."

"What?"

Her hazel eyes flitted back and forth between his, and he saw her throat work with a swallow. "Did he hurt you?"

Bemused, he said, "Not really. I mean, a little... you were there."

She peered at him a moment with those keen eyes of hers – brown, with flecks of green and amber. Then, apparently satisfied with his response, her face relaxed. Stepping backward, she withdrew her hand from his arm, and he immediately missed its anchoring presence.

"Mike isn't the reason I was unfriendly in there a minute ago," she admitted. "I just... I have a lot on my mind today. Sorry about that."

"It's okay."

She gestured to his jacket. "Enjoy."

He nodded, and turned to go.

"JUST BE YOURSELF."

He liked to put on Pink Floyd when he was smoking his bong. Not exactly original, he knew; but as his visionary father would say: "Stick to what you know."

There was what his body and brain knew, and then there was the little matter of his heart.

He glanced over to the corner of his room, where he kept his guitar case.

"Just be yourself," Julia had told him after he played and sang *Wish You Were Here* to her. "You don't need me or anyone else to give you permission."

That was easy for her to say. Being himself had nearly destroyed him twice already.

Well. Since she wanted him to be himself, he would go right ahead and be himself. She wasn't there to give or deny her permission, anyway. But maybe Haze could be there, if he wanted her to be.

Haze.

The bedroom in the in-law unit, where he had lost his virginity to Julia and where he now smoked Haze's weed, was William's space. But before all of that, Jimmy ruled the in-law unit.

And Haze. She was there.

The bowl was cashed, and all surreal twenty-three-and-a-half minutes of *Echoes* had unspooled. The needle bumped against the record label and popped back into the dead wax, again and again.

William set the bong on his bedside table and returned the record to its sleeve. He glanced again toward the guitar case in the corner of his room.

Against his better judgment, he dropped *Wish You Were Here* onto his turntable.

It was night-time now, but it had been early morning the day Julia resuscitated him. Maybe not from a literal, physical death, but certainly from a metaphorical one.

The December sun poured through his blinds, foiling their plans to sleep in together every morning of winter break. She had woken him up, as she nearly always did, with her hand wrapped around his morning wood.

Good times, for sure.

But that wasn't what he remembered most about the day. Nor even the way he had later given her the mermaid necklace at the top of Turtle Hill.

What he remembered most was the way she sat up in his bed, utterly unashamed of her nakedness, like a pre-fallen Eve. He too sat on the edge of the bed, stark naked, and played *Wish You Were Here* on his guitar. It was the first time he had allowed her to hear his singing voice. He did it because she had threatened to never join him in his bed again. And even though he knew she was only teasing, he also knew it would make her smile. And God, what *wouldn't* he have done?

"Just be yourself," Julia had said afterward, as he traced the faint blue veins beneath her skin with his fingertips. "You don't need me or anyone else to give you permission."

That was Julia.

He liked Haze, a lot. He admired her keen spark of intelligence and her formidable life force. He liked her tattoo suit, the bump on the ridge of her nose, and her low, dark, heavy brows. He liked how it made him feel to know that he had pierced her armor of enigma and wariness.

But there wasn't enough weed in the world to blunt the memory of Julia, sylphlike in his bed, smiling at him with her whole face, giving him permission to be himself for the first time in four years. Even if no one else gave him permission. Even if *she* didn't.

He looked toward the closet. Considering. Resisting. Finally, he got up and opened the closet door. Pulled out an old shoe box. Set it on the bed beside him, and slowly lifted the lid.

He hadn't looked in here for nearly a month. Not since shortly after he visited her in Santa Barbara and allowed his jealousy to hammer the final nail in the coffin of their relationship.

He reached inside. Pulled them out, one at a time. Poems and songs that he had written about her, chronicling his growing feelings over the entire two years they had known each other. In all that time, he had never once shown them to her.

One after another, he read them. There was no sap or sentimentality to them. An outsider reading them might never have guessed what they were about. But he knew.

Beneath the poems and songs were the photos. Copies of the ones he had given her when they were together, and ones that she had never seen before. The one he had taken of them together at Año Nuevo. The ones she had snapped of him alone at Julia Burns State Park. The ones he had taken of her, just before he proposed.

"I'm not going to stalk you, Julie," he told her when she broke up with him. "If you want me, I'm here. If you want me to come to you, just say the word."

He hadn't heard from her since.

Her sleep-mussed copper hair, her un-made-up freckled face, her stinky morning breath. Even in his memories, her entire being overthrew him.

The next morning, he retrieved some packing tape from the cabinet in the den and secured the lid firmly atop the shoebox. He walked down Taraval all the way to the post office, and addressed a shipping label to her at Anacapa Hall.

He wasn't stalking her, he told himself. He was just returning what had always been meant for her, anyway.

He had to make one last Hail Mary pass. If he still didn't hear from her, he'd have his answer.

He had his answer soon enough. Every day that the phone didn't ring, that the mailbox revealed no letter from her, was another turn of the screw.

JULY 1993

"I'LL THINK OF SOMETHING."

"**W**ill! Dunphy's order!"

His mother's sharp bark, hurled through the open door of the storefront into the depths of Cardone Fisheries, shattered William's last reserve of calm. He straightened reflexively and dropped the knife with a clatter onto the filleting table. Abandoning the half-gutted salmon, he practically sprinted to the walk-in to retrieve the totes of fish.

For the second summer in a row, Julia was working at her parents' restaurant across the pier. And this summer, her parents were sending her over to Cardone's each morning to pick up their daily order.

The first time she came in, he recognized her immediately, of course. She stood out like a sore thumb, as always. This summer, though, there was something different about her. She still hid her figure under all those baggy layers, but her face had filled out somewhat, softening its sharp angles.

Also, she had taken notice of him.

Every morning, undeterred by his laconic replies, she forced her

54

cheerful snippets of conversation on him – framed, of course, by that wide, radiant smile of hers. She was a burst of sunlight piercing through fog, and he caught himself looking forward to her arrival each morning.

A week ago, he had finally worked up the nerve to cross the pier to Dunphy's. As they loitered near her post at the hostess' station, waiting for the Fourth of July fireworks to start, Julia kept him in stitches about everything from bad eighties TV shows about lizard people, to her short-lived conversion to Islam at age thirteen. He learned she kept salt-water aquariums, including the giant one in the lobby at Dunphy's – a skill she had picked up working at her uncles' aquarium shop. She, in turn, pried it out of him that he enjoyed photography, and demanded he bring proof next time. And of course, they compared their favorite books and poets.

In the end, as they stood on the pier watching the fireworks, he had come tantalizingly close to kissing her, before chickening out.

Adding to his regrets, Julia left that very next week for some marine biology summer camp; so for the past seven days, he had endured her crazy sister Alison coming in to pick up the Dunphy's Restaurant order, instead. Same oblong face, same slight overbite. No freckles. Peroxide-blond hair.

To make matters worse, Julia's absence coincided with the one-year anniversary of something he had been trying very hard to forget. Without her burst of sunlight to distract him, the anniversary came and went in the most dismal fog.

He had given up fighting it, and let himself count the days until Julia's return. Seven, six, five, four...

Yesterday, he rounded the corner into the processing plant's tiny storefront, his legs rubbery with anticipation – and felt his stomach drop.

"She's on the schedule to work tomorrow," Alison explained with her cheeky grin.

It had ruined his whole day.

But that was yesterday. And today, as he pushed the hand truck through the swinging door to the storefront – there she was. With her goofy little two-tiered service cart.

She had buttoned a black vest over a shapeless long dress, rust-red with a small floral print. She wore black lace-up granny boots, and a voluminous mustard-colored scarf overwhelmed her shoulders. Knowing her, she had probably crocheted it herself. She had curled her copper hair and pinned on a miniature black top hat a jaunty angle.

Good God. What was it about this bizarre Dickensian waif?

She didn't keep him waiting long for the answer as she greeted him with her usual bright smile. "Hi, William."

"Hey, Julia." He didn't think he had ever said her name out loud before. He had turned the three syllables over and over again in his mind during the past week. Strange how prosaically flat they fell from his mere mortal voice.

He pushed the hand truck around the front counter, currently displaying rockfish, sole, and prawns on ice. Around the live crab tanks, empty and drained now, to where she stood just in front of the shelves.

He swung the totes onto her rolling cart, one at a time. Slower than usual. He pointed to the last remaining tote.

"This one's a bit heavy. I'll carry it over for you."

It was an obvious lie, but she smiled even more brightly and said, "Thanks!"

He followed her and her cart out the open bay and onto the pier. They dodged the processing plant workers and the deckhands, hoisting their totes of sablefish, skate, and salmon from the boats.

Everything he had planned to say to her – gone.

When they finally detangled themselves from the crowd, he strode to catch up and walk alongside her. She smiled up at him hopefully. At least that's what he hoped that look meant – that she was hoping he would say something first, for a change. She was walking very slowly. Too slowly.

"How was your marine biology camp?" he blurted.

"Great! Though I didn't get to help document whale fecal plumes, after all. Their full-color brochure lied."

The whale fecal plumes. Yes. Waiting for the fireworks, he had laughed at the absurdity of it with her.

"That sucks," he offered.

Surely he had something more. Some joke, some mild sarcastic remark. Some sparkling gem of his wit and intelligence. But her beautiful proximity, after more than a week's separation, stupefied his senses.

As usual, his reticence didn't deter her in the least. "It's okay; I think I'll give it a week before I sue them for false advertising. You know – give the raw feelings a chance to mature into a nice ripe apathy. I don't want to do anything too rash." When he still said nothing, she persisted, "But, on the plus side, I did conduct an otter trawl for plankton. And I practically ended up teaching the unit on aquariums myself. They had foisted some hapless grad student on us who kept aquariums as a hobby, and not even saltwater aquariums. My Uncle Rob will be proud of me when I tell him."

Her uncle. Of course. "How is he doing?"

"Not good," she admitted, her smile straightening as she turned her eyes down to her cart; and he instantly regretted the question. "I saw him on Sunday, when I maintained his aquarium. He's too weak to take care of it anymore. He lost a lot of weight in just one week."

"I'm sorry." Was that really the only response he could find? *I'm sorry*? Her uncle had practically raised her and was near and dear to her heart. There were so many questions he could ask, but he didn't want to seem intrusive.

To William's dismay, they were already at the back door of the restaurant. Still tongue-tied, he followed her to the walk-in. It didn't help that the frenetic pace and noise of the kitchen dazzled his senses even further. The prep cooks and line cooks shouting to each other in Spanish. The metallic crash of cookware, the roar of vent hoods. The electric buzz of the walk-ins and the reach-ins. The pastry chef – Julia's sister – plating panna cotta while rebuffing a waiter's advances.

Julia's father, blustering into the kitchen, hot on Julia's heels. "What the hell took you so long? Where is your mother?"

Julia swung open the door to the walk-in. "Hi, Dad! Nice to see you, too!"

"Get that shit inventoried and distributed so we can actually start service on time tonight. It's bad enough that we're down two cooks without you pussyfooting around like you work for the government."

William knew that Paul could see him there, and he had known Paul for years from working at his parents' processing plant. But Paul was too fired up to acknowledge his presence. He was already gone, rough-handling the grill in the absence of its proper occupant, demanding to know where the hell everyone was today.

"He's a chef," Julia stage-whispered to William, as if that explained everything. Thoroughly unruffled, she turned to smile. "Welp, I guess I'd better get started."

A burst of inspiration struck him. "I can help you."

Her eyebrows lifted. "Do you mind?"

Did he *mind*? "What do I do?"

She gave him a quick once-over that he felt in every cell of his body. "You don't have a coat."

"Neither do you," he pointed out, gesturing up and down the length of her. It gave him a welcome excuse to reciprocate her once-over.

She tugged at a couple of toggles on her bulky scarf. The loosened fabric tumbled down her torso, revealing itself as a waist-length turtle-neck shawl, crocheted from thick woolen yarn.

He shrugged. "I'm warm-natured."

She lifted a finger. "Wait here."

He watched her trot down the hall to her father's office and emerge a moment later with a triumphant grin and her father's coat. William shot an anxious look at the grill, where her father was too preoccupied to notice her theft.

"I can't wear that," he balked when she caught up to him.

"He never wears this one, anyway," she said cheerfully, swinging open the walk-in door. He opened his mouth to protest again, until she shut it by seizing his hand and yanking him into the walk-in.

Safely inside with the door closed behind them, he waited breathlessly in the cold to see what she would do next. He had heard rumors about things that went on in the walk-in at Dunphy's.

But all she did was hold up the coat with a grin, inviting him. Sheepishly he squatted and let her help him into it, his pulse quickening a bit at the brush of her hands against his sleeves and shoulders.

Afraid to look stupid in front of her, he listened carefully as she versed him in the peculiarities of the restaurant's inventory system. Her mother, she explained, had made it nearly incomprehensible so she'd never be out of a job.

Once he felt comfortable enough to begin logging the inventory on her mother's convoluted charts, they fell into a quiet rhythm. She tucked her red curls behind her ear, but they would not be subdued and escaped to tickle her cheek. She blew on her hands and rubbed them together, trying to warm them. He had a sudden, palpable urge to warm them around his waist, inside her father's coat.

He said the first thing he could think of. "Did you make that yourself?"

Startled, she followed his eyes to her shawl. "This? Do you like it? My uncle told me he used to crochet ones just like it for his girlfriends in high school. Before he came out of the closet."

He wanted to reach out and touch it, as he had touched the crocheted flower atop her hat on the Fourth of July. But that had felt so natural at the time. He wasn't as uninhibited today. And of course, he could think of nothing more to say.

So, as usual, she picked up the slack. "Speaking of hidden talents, when are you going to let me see those photos you bragged about on the Fourth of July?"

"I can bring them tomorrow. If you're working, I mean."

She smiled, scrawled something on her clipboard, and shelved a tote of sanddab. "You're on."

The door to the walk-in swung open, and the plump fifty-something woman who came through it flinched a bit to find Julia there.

"Oh, there you are," her mother said to Julia, adding, as a groove notched itself between her brows, "Oh... And you too, William."

"Hi, Karen – I mean, Mrs. Dunphy." He cringed inwardly at his faux pas.

"Isn't that Paul's coat?"

Julia rushed to the rescue. "William delivered a heavy order for me."

"Really? I don't think I ordered any more than usu–"

"And then Dad yelled at me because you weren't here," Julia swiftly cut in, "so William kindly volunteered to help."

"It was taking so long that I went to look for you," Karen explained. "I guess I went out the front door just as you were going in the back."

"I think we have it under control," offered Julia. "Do you need to update the schedule?"

"I updated it this morning." Turning her frown back on William, Karen added, "But thank you, William, for your help. I think I can take it from here."

William's heart plunged to his toes, as it had the day before when Alison showed up instead of Julia. He quickly wriggled out of Paul's coat and handed it to Julia.

"See you tomorrow," he murmured.

She lifted a hand in farewell. "Don't forget the photos."

Oblivious to his surroundings, he berated himself as he pushed his hand truck back down the pier to Cardone's. Why could he never remember anything he planned to say to her when he finally had the chance? What had he planned to say, anyway?

Why did he still seize up like that sometimes?

He was aware of a familiar masculine voice intruding on his consciousness. "Ground Control to Major Will. This is Houston; do you copy?"

"Oh, hey, Uncle Frank. Sorry."

Frank shouted at him from the deck of his boat, tied up at the pier. A stocky man with a mustache and black hair well-streaked with gray, he looked at least a decade older than his forty-three years. With his straight white teeth that didn't quite match his craggy face, he bore a strong family resemblance to William's mother.

His son Tony struggled with the hoist on the pier. They were nearly finished offloading salmon, which meant they had clearly been there for some time.

"Jesus, kid," Frank said, "you almost walked right past me again. Of course, I didn't bother you the first time, since you were with a cute girl."

William didn't quite know how to respond to that, but it intrigued him that someone else besides him found Julia cute. Until this summer, when she started coming into Cardone's, he had never supposed her to be all that attractive, but over the past year, she had kind of grown into her looks.

And so, he supposed, had he. At least he hoped that's what her furtive glances meant, when she thought he wasn't looking. As well as her heart-stopping smiles when he was.

Tony stopped struggling with the hoist long enough to mumble a greeting to William. Tony was a short, skinny mope who lately insisted on being called Anthony and only worked on his father's boat when he was home from Juilliard. William's mother dismissed Tony as "more useless than tits on a boar."

Frank said, "Hey, come on down, Will. I have a business proposition."

William abandoned his hand truck and climbed down the ladder from the pier to the deck.

"Hey, buddy..." Frank clapped his arm around William's shoulders and steered him into the cabin. "Mighty Mouse up there just told me he's taking off to go paddle boarding in Tahoe with some friends."

"Oh. That sucks. I hear the salmon are really biting."

Frank reached into the little fridge and handed William a can of Coke, which he accepted. As he popped the top and took a swig, it dawned on William.

"You want me tomorrow."

"It's just for the day, if your parents can spare you. We'll be back before dark."

William wasn't sure if his parents could really spare him, but they knew he could never turn down a chance to go fishing, and they always humored him. He agreed to meet Frank at the slip at four in the morning, and it wasn't until he was back inside Cardone's at the fileting table that it struck him – if he went fishing, he wouldn't see Julia the next day. He had promised to bring his photos.

So, when the plant wrapped up operations for the day, William wandered to the storefront. He told his mother he wouldn't be there the next day, and his mother *tsk*ed at his account of Tony running off to Tahoe.

"Running around with his hoity-toity friends from Pac Heights. Not even bringing his girlfriends home to meet his own father." She sprayed Windex on the display case glass and wiped it down with a vengeance. "Frank worked his ass off, paying for that turd's private education. Not a grateful bone in his body." Then she froze, Windex bottle in mid-air. Casting a sidelong glance at William, she hastily added,

"Not that there's anything wrong with going to private school, of course. Or college."

William smirked to himself. "Hey, Mom. Would you do me a favor?"

"Name it."

"When Julia comes in here tomorrow for the Dunphy's order, would you let her know that I had to go help Frank on his boat? I told her I was going to show her some of the photos I took."

His mother looked up at him in some surprise. He watched her expression slowly change as she connected the dots.

"Sure, Will."

"You won't forget?"

He detected a smile playing at her lips. "I'm pretty sure the second I lay eyes on her, it will remind me of this conversation. But Will, have *you* forgotten? Tomorrow's your birthday."

William couldn't think of a better way to spend his birthday than going fishing with Uncle Frank. Unless, later...

"He said we'll be back before dark. We'll still have time to do something."

"What do you have in mind?"

His eyes wandered down the pier to Dunphy's. "I'll think of something."

"NOSTALGIC IS GOOD."

That evening, after agreeing to show his photo portfolio to Julia, William let himself into the in-law unit and flipped the light switch. The indolent fluorescent ceiling lights flickered, then decided to stay on. He listened to them buzz as he retrieved a banker's box from a cabinet and brought it over to the sofa.

He lifted the lid and pulled the photos out one at a time, trying to figure out which ones Julia might like. What did he know about her, from their handful of conversations at Cardone's and the couple of hours they had spent together on the Fourth of July?

She loved the ocean, as he did; and she also loved marine mammals. He set aside photos of humpback and gray whales, and porpoises. Of fishing boats anchored on the horizon at sunset during Dungeness season.

She loved tropical fish, and aquariums. He wished he had been to the Monterey Bay Aquarium, but he had never traveled further than fifty miles from home – at least not by land. He considered sneaking over to take a photo of the enormous tropical aquarium she maintained at Dunphy's, but he quickly dismissed that idea as too stalkery.

She loved sewing, knitting, and crocheting. He set aside a photo he had snapped in a Guatemalan textile market in the Mission District, the multi-colored fabrics all waving from the ceiling like curtains in the breeze from the open door.

She loved the Farallon Islands, where her uncle used to accompany her on whale-watching excursions. He set aside photos of the islands' sea lion-strewn beaches, the rocks transforming the waves into white fans and silver beads.

She loved her Uncle Rob. He didn't quite know how to interpret that in photo, and he'd have to be pretty careful since her uncle was dying of AIDS. She had put on a brave face, but it had clearly been a painful subject.

She told him once that her uncle and his partner used to keep an aquarium shop in the Castro. That in fact they had practically raised her and Alison there.

William had once gotten lost at night, and had stopped his motor-cycle in front of the Castro Theatre just long enough to get catcalled, and to snap a close-up of its illuminated façade.

He set that one aside for her.

He reached into the cabinet again. Retrieved a five-by-seven photo mailer and filled it with his selections.

Well before dawn the next morning, William dropped the photo mailer in his backpack and drove to Fisherman's Wharf. He parked near Frank's slip and boarded the boat. He found Frank already on the deck, chopping bait.

"Good morning," Frank growled. For a career fisherman, he was a remarkably lousy morning person. William knew better than to attempt conversation this early. Instead, he sat silently on deck to bait hooks.

Later that morning, on the fishing grounds, six lines trolled through the water as they cruised along, mimicking a school of fish. Soon enough, the springs on top of the outriggers bounced, signaling a catch.

"Wow, you weren't kidding," William remarked. "They're really biting."

But there was no time for chit-chat. As soon as he gaffed a fish, he slammed its head against the gaff hatch to kill it, ripped its gills out, and bled it.

"Don't gut it," Frank grunted, too preoccupied for niceties. "Fishing's too hot. We'll dress 'em later."

So, William bled the salmon and dropped them right into the slush tank. It was a brutal, smelly business, but they had it down to an art form. The seabirds were having a field day overhead. Occasionally there was enough of a break in between bites for William to catch his breath and notice the whales in the distance and the porpoises flanking the boat.

"This is the life," he remarked out loud. He could do this every day; just follow the path of his ancestors. Chapped skin and carpal tunnel and the constant threat of a watery grave – he would take it all in the bargain for the chance to inherit this boat, if Frank's sons didn't want it.

"Don't get attached," Frank grunted.

William re-baited the hook, and said nothing.

Frank added, "Sorry to rain on your parade, kid, but this life is going the way of the history books. I wouldn't want to see you trying to make a living at this. Nothing but heartbreak; I don't even want that for my own sons. I'm on my third wife now, you know."

Well anyway, there was no better way to spend his birthday. Unless, maybe, later...

"Watch it!" bellowed Frank.

"Oh, shit. Sorry." William had nearly plugged Frank with the outrigger line.

"That's not like you. You pulled a Tony," Frank laughed good-naturedly.

Determined not to make any more absent-minded mistakes, William forced all thought of Julia from his mind. That evening, as they drove under the Golden Gate Bridge and into the bay, Frank said, "Go up to the top drive. She's all yours."

Touched by his uncle's vote of confidence, William climbed the stairs from the back deck to the second steering station. He maneuvered the boat alongside the pier in front of Cardone's and watched as his uncle, instead of him, tied it to the pile.

It was seven o'clock before all the salmon were offloaded, weighed, and paid for. As usual, William's father and uncle put on a show of arguing over the price. Often the argument went far beyond show, and later William's father would grumble, "Most fishermen have never been on this side of the hoist."

But today everyone seemed to understand that there was no time for arguments. While his father went to write Frank a check, Frank clapped a hand on William's shoulder.

"Your mom tells me it's your eighteenth birthday, you little shit. So not only are you wasting your first day of manhood with me, but I just got paid thanks to you. There's no way I'm not taking you out to celebrate."

William smiled sheepishly and shrugged his assent.

"Well, where are we going? It's your call. Just remember – Uncle Sam says you're man enough to go to war, but he still won't let you take a drink." Frank waited until William's mother nodded her approval and retreated back inside the plant before leaning into William's ear and whispering, "But Uncle Frank will."

William chuckled, but his eyes drifted across the pier to Dunphy's. "Honestly, I'm kind of tired. Can we just eat over there tonight?"

"You got it."

William's father had strategically outfitted the processing plant with a shower, and William had stuffed a change of clothes into his backpack, along with the photo mailer. William shed his foul weather gear and made short shrift of cleaning up. Within twenty minutes he joined his parents and his uncle again on the pier.

But in the meantime, Uncle Frank's whole demeanor had changed. A phone call right there at the processing plant from his wife had informed him that his younger son Dom was in some kind of trouble with the cops. Frank tried to force all of his cash on William's parents for the birthday dinner, but they insisted he save it for Dom's bail, instead.

Frank's hand was on William's shoulder, and he fixed him with an earnest look. "Another time?"

"Yeah, sure."

As they ambled down the pier toward Dunphy's, William and his parents watched Frank hop aboard his boat and steer it away toward its slip. Once the boat was gone, William's mother said, "Poor Frank. Such a couple of losers he has for sons."

William's father merely nodded in assent, and William couldn't help smiling to himself at the irony, considering how their own two oldest sons had turned out. But he listened to his mother expound upon the inevitability of an aspiring rapper like Dom winding up in jail.

"Maybe Tony doesn't look so bad anymore?" William offered good-naturedly, and she laughed and jabbed him with her elbow in response.

It was good timing because it made him smile, and they were at Dunphy's now. Julia, leaning against the hostess' station in front of her enormous, brightly-colored tropical aquarium, caught sight of him through the glass of the front entrance. She straightened in surprise.

"Hey!" she chirped as his father swung open the door. "What brings you guys here on a Wednesday night?"

"Today is Will's eighteenth birthday," Ann replied, squeezing William around the shoulders. He smiled sheepishly at Julia in response, but his legs felt as if they were coming out of his hip sockets and his knees were separating at the joints.

"What? I had no idea! Happy birthday!" she said warmly to William.

"Thanks," he replied. His voice sounded far away.

"Why didn't you tell me?" She rebuked him with a light swat on his arm, and his pulse rioted at the fleeting touch. "Luckily I still have a great table left for you."

William's eyes swept the length of her as she led them around the aquarium and into the dining room. He couldn't help it. Today, she wasn't wearing her usual slouchy thrift store finds and homespun accessories that hid her shape. Between the fitted bodice and shorter length of her babydoll dress, it struck him like a thunderbolt that the skinny waif in sophomore French had filled out into a tall, willowy seventeen-year-old.

Julia led them to a table with one of the best views in the smoking section, since William's parents both smoked. William peered attentively at her, in her canary-yellow cloche hat, as she distributed their menus. Today, her hair hung straight from beneath its brim.

"My parents will be so mad that they didn't know you were coming!" she admonished them. "They would have had something special ready."

"We didn't know we were coming either, until the last minute," explained William's mother, with a knowing look that William feared was all too obvious.

But if Julia noticed, she didn't let on. She just smiled her usual bright smile and informed them that their waiter David would be right with them.

As she sashayed toward the kitchen, William suddenly remembered the photos in his backpack. He hoped he could somehow slip them to her in a way that wasn't too obvious or desperate. He had taken so much care in selecting them that he now felt impatient to share them with her, and he wasn't sure if she would be working tomorrow.

A new iteration of Julia's father, less irascible than yesterday's version, emerged from the kitchen to wish William a happy birthday. The waiter poured wine from a complimentary bottle that Paul brought out, and William's father protested the indulgence.

"Nonsense! You only turn eighteen once." Paul surreptitiously slid a second empty wine glass next to William's father, for William. "It's the least I can do for you guys."

Amid the din, William spotted Julia again, smiling at the spectacle while she seated some more smoking patrons. He realized that she had gone into the kitchen to inform her parents that they were there. William suspected that Paul would comp their entire bill. Not only did Paul and William's father have a great working relationship, but they grew up only a couple of blocks apart and were good friends, in their mutually grumpy way.

As the evening wore on, Paul sent out course after course and another entire bottle of wine to the Quinns' table. A tureen of cioppino. A plate of fish cakes. Karen came out and chatted at the table with them for a long time.

When they had already been there for an hour and a half, William heard Alison's voice in the dining room and watched her deliver an entire platter of desserts to their table. Alison lit a candle atop his tiramisu and performed an uncanny impression of Marilyn Monroe singing happy birthday to Mr. President.

It must have been clear to Julia from the too-loud laughter erupting from his parents that they were having a great time. But each time she came into the smoking section to seat a new table, she could never linger. As a result, he wasn't having quite as great of a time, until at long last, things died down enough that Julia could join them. It was almost closing time. She emerged from the kitchen, balancing three coffee cups and a pot of coffee on a tray. Setting the tray on their table, she said good-naturedly, "I hope you guys aren't driving home."

"I don't know if they'll let us on the bus in this condition," snorted William's mother.

Julia poured them each a cup of coffee. She handed him his cup and then – finally! – she sat beside him at the table.

"If you need someone to drive you home in your car, Alison can do it," she offered to William's parents.

For good form, William's parents protested the inconvenience to Alison, and Julia reminded them that it was only a short walk from the Quinns' house to the Dunphy residence. After a few more halfhearted protests, William's parents acquiesced.

William felt his stomach drop again, as it had two days ago when Alison showed up at the plant. As it had yesterday, when Karen kicked him out of the walk-in.

And then Julia said, "We can bring William home later."

William's parents exchanged knowing looks, and a few minutes later, William watched complacently as his parents lurched their way to the front, trailed by Alison. When they were gone, Julia resumed her seat beside William. She rested her elbow on the tabletop, propped her fist on her chin, and gazed at him with those impish gray-green eyes.

William wasn't exactly drunk, but the wine had loosened him up, and his smile was uncharacteristically easy. Every time he drank alcohol, he wondered if *this* was what normal people feel like.

"That was clever," he said. He never would have dared to say it, without the wine.

A silence ensued and, for a change, William felt no compulsion to avert his eyes. Her lips twisted themselves into a softer, sleepier smile than she had given him before.

He said, "I hope my mom told you why I wasn't there today."

She nodded. "You had to go fishing with your uncle."

He lifted his backpack from the floor and retrieved the photo mailer from its interior.

She said, "Is this your grand portfolio?"

"I don't know; I'll let you judge how grand it is."

She reached into the photo mailer and examined them, lingering over each one for quite some time. She asked him questions. Was he in Guatemala when he took this one? Was it sunrise or sunset that created such light on the boats? What kind of camera did he use to freeze the waves in action like that? How did he feel when he saw whales on his uncle's fishing boat?

She arrived at the last photo. The Castro Theatre, at night. She stayed with it the longest of all. She didn't get choked up – there were no tears in her eyes. But some powerful emotion clenched at her throat, her jaw. Her face, normally such an open book, was now inscrutable.

He was sobering up in a hurry.

Finally, she turned a wistful smile on him. "You made me nostalgic."

"I'm sorry," he said quickly. So stupid. How could he have been so insensitive? He should have avoided any reminder of her uncle whatsoever.

But she shook her head. "Nostalgic is good." She peered at him a moment and said, "Have you ever seen a movie with a sad ending, but you felt like a better person for having seen it? That's how I feel about my uncle."

He nodded. He would have to try to remember that when he thought about his Nonna.

"And you told me you had no hidden talents." She gathered up the stack of photos. "Would it be super-rude if I asked to keep these?"

"Of course not," he blurted.

"I'll pay you for them."

He waved away her offer. "No charge."

"Okay, but you should totally go pro with this photography thing. Sell them at art festivals, and on postcards, and things like that."

He shrugged. "I'm not sure it's something I want to make a living out of. You know how it goes – once it's a job, it's not fun anymore."

"Well, if you ever change your mind, you'll have at least one customer. I've been making these fabric-covered photo frames lately, so I need something to fill them." She tucked the photos back into the photo mailer. "You have the Asian flush."

"The... what?"

"Asian people get it when they drink."

He laughed. "I think it's an Irish thing, too."

"Oh, okay. The Irish flush, then." She beamed at him with that broad smile of hers. It occurred to him then that her smile was toothsome in every sense, both literal and figurative. His heart stuttered at the sight.

Before the alcohol wore off completely, William took his shot. "I know a late-night diner we could go to, to sober me up."

"Are you trying to say my coffee wasn't strong enough?" she teased.

He smiled. Her coffee *was* too weak, but he wasn't going to admit it.

"I really wish I could," she added, "but I've got to stay and help here. And we won't get home until almost one o'clock as it is. But I'll totally take you up on that another time."

She kept him company there in between bursts of helping her parents and until the rest of the staff had gone home. But the alcohol had really worn off now, leaving him more uptight than ever.

She had shot him down. He was sure of it. What other interpretation could there possibly be? Maybe she was nice about it – she had tried to soften the blow – but she had shot him down all the same.

"I'VE HAD BETTER."

Early the following Sunday, when William arrived at Cardone's, his father was already on a tear. Even from all the way in the back of the plant, William could hear his father bellowing in the office. The plant workers who had already arrived traded apprehensive glances with each other, and with William.

"I leave for one day, and you buy ninety pounds of sanddab? What the hell am I supposed to do with all that sanddab, Ann?"

"Sell it?" William's mother retorted just as loudly. "Freeze it? Offer some to Paul? I can put it in the display case. People love sanddab, Jim. It'll sell."

The office door swung open, and as he burst through it, William's father shouted over his shoulder, "Tell your brother to pawn his sanddab off on someone else next time." Spotting William there, he ordered him to retrieve a couple of totes of sanddab from the walk-in and carry them over to Dunphy's. "Offer them to Paul for a dollar fifty a pound."

"Two-fifty," William's mother interjected, hot on her husband's heels. "It's fresh clean sanddab. He'd be crazy not to take it at two-fifty and make it a special of the day."

William's father swore under his breath and went to take it out on some hapless forklift driver. William's mother grinned and winked before retreating back into the office.

William wondered just how much his mother really knew, or suspected, of his feelings toward Julia. He wondered if that was in fact part of the conspiracy at hand. It was hard to tell, with his mother. She rarely spoke about tender things. William had only ever seen her cry once.

"You're a good man, Charlie Brown," William's father either praised or upbraided her, as the occasion or his ego suited.

In any case, it didn't matter what William's mother suspected. Over the past four days, William had successfully pushed all thought of Julia from his mind. When she came into Cardone's to pick up the Dunphy's order, he gave clipped answers to her questions. He didn't offer to carry any more totes to the restaurant. He hadn't re-invited her for coffee. He didn't believe she really meant it when she invited him to ask again.

He had forgotten how she read her encyclopedias until they fell apart and she had to keep them together with a rubber band. How she had converted to Islam for two days, and stole a little prayer rug for her bedroom. How she dressed and spoke like a poet from another era.

He had forgotten her long slender legs in black tights that she crossed, knee over knee, as she sat beside him on his birthday. Forgotten the constellations of freckles on her face and collarbones, and the way the skin bunched up around her eyes as she smiled. How she kept turning that smile on him, though he rarely gave her any good reason to persist.

He was quite proud of himself, how thoroughly he had forgotten all of this as he braced the hand truck with the totes of sanddab against his side and pressed the doorbell at the back door of Dunphy's.

The door flung open – and he remembered it all.

He forced himself to look away. Shifted his weight. Cleared his throat.

"Special delivery," he croaked. He had planned to say it, but it sounded so lame now. "A load of sand dab, right off the boat this morning. My dad wanted to see if your dad was interested."

"Normally probably so, but I warn you, we got a less than glowing review in the *Chronicle* this morning."

"Oh." He allowed himself one peek at her, and found his eyes lingering. She wore no hat. She had simply parted her hair at one side and pinned a teal-colored silk flower into it. The light illuminated the hair at the crown of her head like a copper halo. "What did it say?"

"Well, it compared our cioppino to something from a can of Chef Boyardee, for one thing. And it said something about the restaurant being apparently past its prime, like its owner and head chef."

"Ouch."

"Yep. Of course, I think my dad is the only one around here who's surprised by any of this. I remember all too well the time at school when I overheard a guy ask who I was. Someone told him that my father owns Dunphy's, and he said, 'I hate that place. It smells like old people in there.'"

William smiled but said nothing. The rest of her hair tumbled in luminous waves halfway down the embroidered bodice of her Mexican-style sundress. A bodice with definite signs of curves that he quickly diverted his eyes from.

Julia waved him down the hallway toward her father's office, where Paul sat uncharacteristically idle at his desk, the newspaper spread out before him. It took him a few moments to notice them standing there, but when he spotted William, he dragged himself to his feet to shake his hand.

"William. How are you? I hope you had a great birthday dinner here with your family the other day."

"We did, thanks. The food was great," William added kindly.

Paul sank back into his seat. "William, let me ask you something. You had the cioppino the other night. What did you think of it?"

William's stomach lurched. He shifted his weight and glanced back at the load of sanddab he had brought with him, considering. He was all too keenly aware of Julia's continued presence behind him. But he steeled his nerves, looked her father in the eye, and said, "I've had better."

He watched outrage and mortification wage battle on Paul's face. William had literally stunned him to silence for a few moments. When Paul finally recovered his powers of speech, he spluttered, "Oh really? Where?"

"My grandmother's."

Paul nodded, apparently spying an opening. "We all like best what we're used to."

William said nothing, and Paul demanded, "Well, what can I help you with? You came here; you obviously wanted to see me about something."

William mentioned the sanddabs, which Paul inspected, somehow managed to find fault with, and dismissed brusquely.

Great, William thought as he pushed his hand truck back down the pier. His parents would be pissed that he hadn't managed to foist the sanddab off on Paul. They would argue with each other; he could just hear his father gloating, "I told you so!"

And on top of all that – he was in love with Julia.

He had no control over his thoughts or feelings. There was no point fighting or denying it anymore. When and how could he see her again? His mind seized upon any excuse it could find.

The other day, when he delivered the tote of fish to Dunphy's, her father had mentioned they were short-handed in the kitchen.

He had already pissed off Paul by suggesting that his cioppino sucked. Of course part of the problem with Paul's cioppino was that it contained no Dungeness crab. And any San Franciscan worth their salt ought to know that cioppino without Dungeness crab wasn't cioppino at all; it was just seafood stew.

It was harder to come by Dungeness in July, but as Nonna had taught him, it wasn't impossible. Not if you knew who to ask.

William knew that if he made Nonna's cioppino and offered that as his job application, it could bruise Paul Dunphy's ego and put him out of his good graces permanently. Or it might possibly – if he was really lucky – earn him a job there at Dunphy's.

With Julia.

On his way home from work that evening, he went by the Italian grocers in North Beach that he used to frequent with Nonna. He bought the stewed San Marzano tomatoes, the vegetables, and the seasonings. He bought a package of rigatoni and a loaf of sourdough bread. He would make the clam juice himself, and he had already asked his mother to bring home the seafood. He told her he would be cooking dinner on Monday night.

The next evening, while his sauce finished simmering and his mother chopped the halibut, he retrieved the live crab from the bucket his mother had brought home.

"What turns a good cioppino into a *great* cioppino?" Nonna had once quizzed him.

By now, he had long-since memorized the answer: "Live crab."

He cracked them open one at a time, still wriggling, and removed the bodies from the shell. He dumped the meat into the sauce, along with the rest of the seafood and the rich but nauseating golden innards that Nonna called "crab fat." When the clams opened, he knew the cioppino was done.

He spooned it over cooked rigatoni and served it to his family with a salad and the sourdough bread.

It was only the second time he had seen his mother cry.

The next morning, William appeared again at Dunphy's kitchen door, ostensibly with another special delivery for Julia's father. But on top of the tote of fish sat a round container. After Julia accepted the delivery, William turned to Paul.

"I also brought you some of my grandmother's cioppino."

At least he had the wisdom not to do it in front of any of the kitchen staff. Her father accepted the container, and said, "Of course you did."

As William passed Julia on the way out the back door, she gave him a deer-in-the-headlights sort of look. But she stifled a laugh.

William made sure to return later that afternoon on some trumped up business for his father. Julia handed him back his clean container and whispered, "It was amazing."

Spotting him while slicing leeks, Paul said cooly, "Give my compliments to your grandmother."

His stomach plummeted to his toes. "I would, but she's dead."

The knife slicing the leeks slipped, and Paul narrowly avoided amputating his own fingertip. "But... you said it was your grandmother's cioppino."

William nodded. "It's her recipe."

"Who made this, then?"

"I did."

Paul slowly lowered the knife to the countertop. "Bullshit."

Minutes later, William stood in the kitchen in coat and hat with Mark, the sous chef, who frowned and sniped. William wasn't quite sure what had crawled up Mark's ass and died, but his resentment cooled quickly under William's humility. William either did not know or pretended not to know certain little tricks and seasonings that Mark obligingly filled in for him, and in short, William played the part of the grateful student. By the end of the afternoon, they had a pot of cioppino that was superior even to what William had brought in.

Paul folded his arms across his chest and glared suspiciously at William. "You said your grandmother taught you this?"

William nodded. "I mostly learned by watching, then doing. The whole family cooks together, when we can."

"And your grandmother was Italian?"

"Her parents were from Sicily."

Paul scratched his nose. Considered. "What else can you do?"

"Pretty much anything my grandmother could do. Or at least three-quarters of it."

By the time William left that night, he had a new part-time job as a dishwasher at Dunphy's. Paul had offered only the vaguest promise that it could lead to prep cook in the future, and William would have to give up much of his work at the plant and on his uncle's boat. But if he had any doubts about accepting, Julia assuaged them as he wriggled out of his chef's jacket and tossed it into the hamper.

She rounded the corner and leaned up against the wall. She crossed her arms over her chest in mock severity.

"I thought you said you have no hidden talents."

"If I told everyone about them, they wouldn't be hidden," he replied.

She flushed, and her mouth twisted itself into a coy smile. He answered it with a shy one of his own, his pulse tripping all over itself; then rounded the corner to leave.

OCTOBER 1995

"READY FOR ME TO RUIN YOUR CHILDHOOD?"

To William's dismay, female voices filtered out to him as he ascended into the living room. It had been a brutal day; his Foodservice and Hospitality Management professor had marked his most recent exam with a big red F. And then tempers had flared at the Act the Maggot rehearsal because they wanted him to be a permanent band member, and he didn't.

Instead, he was going to have to put his nose to the grindstone. The last thing Julia needed to hear about him from her dad or anyone else was that he flunked out of college. He had been psyching himself up all afternoon to come home and study. And now it looked like he'd have his sister and her friend rattling around in his brain all night, instead.

When Kelly's bedroom door swung open, the voices got louder. They were saying something about slutty Halloween costumes, and how no one would be surprised to see them dressed as dykes.

An Amazon warrior princess emerged in a black leather corset, a breastplate, and a fringed miniskirt. Whoever she was, she dwarfed

77

Kelly, nearly unrecognizable in a blonde wig, brown miniskirt, and dark green sports bra.

Kelly froze to find William there with the guitar slung over his shoulder. Her friend's enormous dark eyes locked on William.

Kelly snorted with laughter, and made the introductions. "Will, Xena. Xena, my brother Will."

"William," he corrected. "Your name is Xena?"

"No, you idiot," Kelly scoffed. "She's dressed as Xena. Can't you tell?"

He gave her a blank stare.

Kelly sucked her teeth in dismay. "Xena? Warrior Princess?"

"It's a TV show," explained Xena. Draping her arm around Kelly's shoulders, she added, "And this is Gabrielle, my trusty sidekick."

"Nice to meet you, Xena," said William, and she humored him with a short laugh. Her sleek dark hair fell halfway to her waist. "What's your real name?"

She lifted her chin, tossed him an impudent look. "Marisa."

Her legs below the miniskirt stretched for a mile. "Have fun tonight, Marisa," he said casually, already moving toward the kitchen.

Lucky Kelly, he reflected privately as he retrieved a beer from the fridge. He had always half-suspected that his sister was a lesbian, and now he knew. He would have to congratulate her on her excellent taste.

He closed the refrigerator door, and flinched as he nearly ran smack into Marisa. She said, "I wouldn't mind having one of those."

To his astonishment, she stood nearly at eye-level with him. He only noticed because he was so used to looking down on women – literally. But even without her boots, Marisa must have been six feet tall. She could have been anywhere from fifteen to twenty-five.

He said, "Aren't you a bit underage?"

"Aren't *you*?"

With a smirk, he used the kitchen counter as leverage to knock the cap off the bottle, then held it out to her. She took a swig, and he could tell by the way she grimaced behind the cover of the bottle that she wasn't used to drinking beer.

She said, "I hear you have a fake ID."

"You can tell Kelly I'm not making a beer run."

"Fair enough. How about a Boone's Strawberry Hill run?"

"Fruit-flavored piss? I couldn't do that to a friend of my sister's."

She stuck her tongue out at him before rejoining Kelly in the living room. He watched her go, with those legs, then retrieved another beer for himself.

Downstairs, he stowed his guitar case in the bedroom, then spread his textbook on the coffee table in the den. *Introduction to Foodservice and Hospitality Management.* He opened his binder to take notes, but his attention wandered to the muffled voices of Marisa and his sister upstairs. He drank his beer, and listened carefully to see if he could discern any of their words.

An image intruded into his consciousness of Marisa and Kelly lying naked in bed together. His response to the image was visceral, and involuntary. Disturbed with himself, he shook his head, trying to dislodge the thought.

He got up and went into his bedroom again. Retrieved the bong from the lower shelf of the dresser, and reached into the box where he stashed his weed. But he only scraped up seeds and stems.

Kelly and Marisa spilled downstairs, past the in-law unit and out the front door. He listened to their voices fade down the street and into the distance. No doubt off to some illicit shindig somewhere. Perhaps in St. Francis Wood, at the home of some Holy Cross kid's unsuspecting parents.

Just like the party he had attended, two years ago.

Against all reason, since he knew there was one and only one place he kept his stash, he scrounged a bit more in the bottom drawer. He slammed the drawer shut with a huff of frustration when, of course, he still came up short. He went to lie on his bed and stare up at the ceiling a while.

Two years ago today.

He went upstairs and eyed his father, already passed out on the couch. As per the usual routine, his mother had already plucked the burning cigarette from his hand, covered him with a blanket, and cleaned up the liquor he spilled. William stepped into the hallway leading to his parents' bedroom. No light escaped from underneath the door.

So he found the key to his father's liquor cabinet. It wasn't a state secret – Mike had once showed him where it was hidden. He unlocked the cabinet, and as his father sawed logs on the sofa, William helped himself to a bottle of Jameson.

Downstairs again, sufficiently warmed, he opened the drawer of his bedside table and retrieved his address book. Thumbed to the T section. *Temkina, Serafima.*

He lifted the receiver, and dialed Haze's number. Listened to the ringback tone – once. Twice.

It was Halloween. There was no way she was home.

"Hello?"

"Oh. Hey."

"Hey."

"Hey." Silence. "Ah – this is William."

"Yeah, I know."

"Really?" Silence. "I didn't think you'd be home." So stupid. Maybe she didn't *want* to be home alone on Halloween, and there he was, rubbing it in. Or – maybe she wasn't alone. "Hey. Uh – can I come over?"

"Sure."

She hadn't said, "Sure; come through." She had just said, "Sure."

He tore out of the Sunset on his motorcycle, dodging trick-or-treaters along the way. Took a roundabout way to the Mission District in order to steer clear of the Halloween shenanigans in the Castro. The Mission District, though already festooned for Día de los Muertos, was relatively quiet tonight. At the moment, his souped-up motorcycle was the most raucous thing in the neighborhood.

Once again, Haze's front door swung open, this time even before he had finished swinging off the motorcycle. And this time, she didn't deride all of its noise.

"Where is everybody?" he wondered aloud, glancing up and down the street as he ascended the front steps.

She cast him a wry smile. "Give it a couple of hours."

He followed her into the living room and once again found the scale and the stash box already on the coffee table. He assumed his usual seat. This time, her black T-shirt had a white torso skeleton on the front –

ribs, spine, collarbone – all corresponding in placement to her own. She wore slouchy ripped jeans with the cuffs tight-rolled halfway up her calves. A couple of inches of skin above her Doc Martens bore evidence of more tattoos.

She removed her black bowler hat, mussing her hair in an appealing way, and tossed it aside. "How much, this time?"

He felt a stab of disappointment. All business, again. "A half-ounce, I guess. How much is that again?"

"One-forty."

He retrieved the cash from his wallet while she measured out his half-ounce. He struggled in vain to think of something to say. Anything at all. With a half-ounce, he wouldn't have a valid excuse to return for two weeks. But he couldn't ask for less than a half-ounce, either. That would be too obvious.

She took the money, and handed over the bag. As she gathered up all the supplies, she said, oh-so-casually, "Hang out awhile. I have a little something different I've been saving for you."

"Sure," he said quickly.

He watched her carry everything upstairs. He finally noticed that she had been playing music on her stereo, at very low volume.

He hoped that was a good sign.

He got up, and went to inspect the LP cover beside the stereo. Nico, *Chelsea Girl*. The androgynous German voice sang, "I had a lover / I don't think I'll risk another these days."

He hoped that wasn't a bad sign.

He was so nervous he was sweating. Atop an old rolling bar cart near the stereo, he found, among other things, a basket full of those tiny airplane-sized bottles of liquor. It was obvious her guests were meant to help themselves to whatever they found there.

He heard the floor still creaking in her bedroom just overhead. He helped himself to four mini-bottles of vodka and chugged them as fast as possible.

When she returned, she carried her bong and another, different little box. She set the bong on the table and brought the box over to him. She opened the lid and held it under his nose.

He smelled grapefruit. "Wow."

"Yummy, isn't it?" She closed the lid and handed him the box. "Pack the bowl. I'll get food."

She had already filled the bong with water upstairs, so he got down to work. When she returned from the kitchen, she was carrying a tray with some exotic-looking stuff on it: black bread, she explained, and a sort of Jewish cookie called mandelbrodt.

"It's like biscotti. My grandmother used to make it for me in Russia, but I never learned how."

"You're Jewish?"

"Well, that depends on who you ask. My father is Jewish, but I'm *Ivanov po materi* – 'Ivanov by mother,' as they say. As ethnic Russian as they come. So according to Israel, I'm not a Jew."

He had finished packing the bowl, so she gestured to it, inviting him.

"Ladies first," he offered.

"I am not a lady," she quipped. But she lit the bowl, and sucked back for a few seconds. He watched as the white smoke passed through the water, into the chamber. She lifted the slider, and inhaled. Held it a few seconds and exhaled, obscuring her face in curls of white smoke.

When the smoke dissipated, he said, "How often do you do this?"

"Not very," she said. Passing the bong to him, she added, "It's been a couple of years."

"Really?"

"I don't enjoy smoking it alone. And I have to feel comfortable with whoever I'm with, or else it makes me paranoid."

She felt comfortable with him. She hadn't felt this comfortable with anyone in a couple of years. At least, not comfortable enough to smoke a bowl with them. Which maybe wasn't saying much.

Nevertheless, to conceal his pleasure at her disclosure, he lit the bowl. The aroma and flavor of grapefruit filled his senses. By the time he exhaled, a floating sensation had already hit him right behind the eyes.

"Oh. *Wow.*" He took another rip. "What is this?"

She smiled. "It's my little secret."

The floating sensation spread down his body. No couch-lock. Colors were vibrant. The gender-ambivalent German singer? He knew her life story already; she didn't have to tell him. He already knew the notes of her wistful song by heart, and if Haze handed him a guitar right now, he could start playing it right away.

> And if I seem to be afraid
> To live the life that I have made in song
> It's just that I've been losing so long

After a minute, he reached for the bong again. She put her hand on his.

"Take it easy with this."

The closest he had ever come to anything like this had been when he was thirteen, when he tried shrooms with Mike. But this wasn't a scary trip, like that had been. This was a pleasant, albeit mind-blowing, little jaunt.

They ate the black bread with salami and butter on it – real butter, from the Russian market; not that space-age crap that Julia's father served at Dunphy's.

Haze got up, reached into the cabinet below her television, and popped a tape into the VCR player. She turned her head back and said, "Are you ready for me to ruin your childhood?"

"Yes." He had no idea what she was talking about, but it didn't matter. He was ready for it.

For a long time – William wasn't sure how long – they sat there eating mandelbrodt and taking bong rips and watching *It's The Great Pumpkin, Charlie Brown!*

Snoopy, atop his flying doghouse. The oscillating background colors; the pitch and dive of the engine. The staccato of the gunner.

William said, "Wait. Go back. I want to see that again."

She smirked, leaned forward and retrieved the VCR remote from the coffee table. They watched the scene again, the colors strobing their faces like flashing neon signs.

"This is definitely not ruining my childhood," he observed.

"You'll never see it the same way again, though, will you?"

About halfway through the second viewing, the sensation of her hand sliding over his reverberated peculiarly through his nervous system. His sense of touch seemed mysteriously wired into his visual cortex, and her fingertips set off colored Fourth of July sparklers.

There was nothing unusual about her hand except, perhaps, for the little occult-like symbols that adorned her slender fingers in lieu of rings. Otherwise, it was a normal, feminine hand, the skin just a shade darker than his own. The fingernails unpainted.

He flipped his own hand over and allowed her fingers to settle between his.

A few minutes later, they lay in her bed, naked. Turned on as he was, he felt no great urgency about the matter. Neither, apparently, did she. *It's The Great Pumpkin, Charlie Brown!* still played downstairs, but barely registered in his consciousness anymore.

They faced each other on their sides, and she allowed him to explore the images on her body. What he had mistaken for more animals peeking over the top of her neckline were actually three cupolas of a Russian Orthodox cathedral, flanked by a pair of eyes. The rest of the cathedral spread itself down her torso, over her breasts.

He had no concept of how much time passed before he pressed into the warm velvet oblivion of being swallowed, squeezed. As he moved inside of her, he had a brief moment of detachment, just long enough to register –

The iridescent aquamarine mermaid tail. The rivulets of copper, swept over her left shoulder.

Two years ago, that very day.

He gasped, rolled away. Flopped onto his back alongside Haze, and stared up at the ceiling.

She propped herself up on her elbow. "Are you okay?"

He sat up. Put his head between his hands, massaged his temples. She sat up, too, and rubbed his back where his caged albatross was.

"I guess you were right," he admitted. "I should have taken it easy."

"I'll get you a cup of water."

She swung herself out of bed, and he caught a glimpse of the Madonna and Child on her back before she shimmied into a short white satin kimono. He heard the water running in the bathroom sink, and a moment later she returned with the cup.

While he slowly sipped, she rubbed his back some more. He felt suddenly, acutely embarrassed at his failure. He blurted, "Sorry."

"No, not sorry," she said. She took his hand, pressed it against her lips.

He kissed her, and after making out with him for a while, she said, "I have a suggestion."

"Okay?"

"Next time, save the vodka for *after* you light up."

He couldn't help laughing. "How could you tell?"

"I'm Russian. You breathe oxygen. I breathe vodka fumes." She took his hand. "I noticed the missing vodka bottles when I went to the kitchen. I was going to make a drink later."

"Oh." He felt keenly embarrassed again. "Sorry."

"Get dressed. I'm taking you somewhere."

It was just before midnight. As Haze had predicted, the streets of the Mission District were just now getting into full swing. As nervous as it made William to be walking there at this time of night, she didn't seem remotely concerned. Come to think of it, everyone gave them a wide berth. Someone hurled the word *bruja* after her, and he turned to see who had said it, but no one was looking at them.

Well. It *was* Halloween.

She led him all the way to Valencia Street, to a dark and shuttered storefront. It looked pretty firmly closed and locked to William, but she took him right to the front door. She startled him by grabbing the chain around her neck, and using it to pull a set of keys from between her breasts. He had thought she was only wearing a necklace. He looked up at the sign above the door: Haze Tattoo and Piercing.

"Um..."

"Don't worry; no tattoos tonight. Only a sketch." She opened the door, flipped on the lights. Closed and locked the door behind them. "I like to leave work at work. And sketching is still work."

Unlike the comparatively sedate colors in her house, the vibrant studio had lots of red and black and white on the walls, and pops of turquoise splattered here and there, and display cases full of jewelry. Flash hung on the walls and there was more flash in binders for the customers who needed a bit of inspiration.

She led him to a room in the back where she consulted with her customers. She had him sit across a table from her there, and took up his left arm.

The receiving arm, she had said.

"Sitting on the rocks, looking out at the water," she said. "Her hair swept over her shoulder, revealing her slender back."

She got out the art supplies, and began to sketch.

NOVEMBER 1993

"NICE EQUIPMENT, FOR A SIX-YEAR-OLD."

At eleven o'clock on Thanksgiving morning, William walked down Santiago in the rain, three blocks closer to the beach. He turned down 47th Avenue to the late-Doelger-style house that was a carbon copy of his own. With the umbrella in his right hand, he tucked the bottle of Chardonnay under his left arm and held the bouquet of chrysanthemums in that hand.

At the Dunphys' front door, he jabbed the doorbell with his elbow.

The footsteps clattered down the stairs inside - light footsteps, hers - and a moment later, the door flung open.

She stood on her tiptoes to kiss him, then took the flowers and the wine. "My mom will be a total sucker for these," she said while he folded up his umbrella.

She stepped back into what had once been a tunnel entrance, now enclosed to form a foyer of sorts, and shut the door behind him. He stood blinking at her in the relatively dim light. She wore one of her floral baby doll dresses with black tights and a bowler hat. Smiling, she kissed him again and handed back the wine bottle.

87

"Don't worry," she said as she took his hand and led him upstairs to the living room. "My mom is your first obstacle. Dad's in the kitchen."

Julia had invited him over more than once for sex after school, but William had never taken her up on it. It was not only her house - it was his boss's. So she had always contented herself with sex in his bedroom, and he had never seen the inside of her house.

It turned out that the floorplan of her house was identical to his own, right down to the ground-level addition where the garage had once been. But where the faded lava-orange shag carpeting lingered in his living room, the Dunphys had pulled theirs up and refinished the parquet floors beneath. In his house, the dark wood-paneled walls and mustard-yellow polyester curtains swallowed the light. But Karen had painted their walls a nice clean white, pasted an English rose wallpaper border just below the ceiling, and raised the Roman shades to admit the sunlight.

They found Karen in the dining room, setting the table. She came forward to greet William with a hug and exclaim at his offerings. "You didn't have to bring these! You already provided the crabs for dinner."

William smiled and didn't admit that his mother had shoved them into his hands as he walked out the front door.

Still holding the flowers, Julia took his hand again and whispered, "Come with me." She led him past the dining table to the entrance of the kitchen. She released his hand to go rummage through the cabinets for a vase. She took her time, and he lingered in the doorway, watching Paul at the stove. Paul hadn't noticed him yet, and William was tempted to turn and flee before he did.

Paul was a Catholic Republican with an abiding love of profanity and a penchant for launching volleys of it when under pressure. He certainly was not immune to unleashing it upon William, but unlike some of Paul's other cooks, William didn't take it too personally.

The other day, he let it roll off his back when Paul snatched the spoon from his hand and sampled his puttanesca sauce.

"Tastes like balls," Paul said, slinging the spoon he had just put his mouth on right back into the saucepan. "Start over."

So William added less garlic this time and smiled privately to himself, wondering how Paul knew what balls taste like. Those moments were Paul's way of teaching him. William could either get bent out of shape, or he could learn. And then he could savor the almost proud look on Paul's face the next time he tasted William's puttanesca sauce.

William could probably count on one hand the number of meaningful interactions he and his own father had shared over the past year.

All the times over the past three weeks that Julia had straggled home late, or not at all... and then Julia telling her father only yesterday that William was coming over for Thanksgiving. Paul might be peculiarly conservative, but he was neither stupid nor naïve. He would have put two-and-two together by now: his daughter and his employee were sleeping together.

He turned around and spotted William. Paul's lips pinched like a drawstring purse before he turned back toward the saucepan.

"Well," said Paul, in a tone of inevitability. "Come on in."

William obeyed wordlessly. At the kitchen cabinets, Julia finally located a vase. In William's current state of nerves, he was barely able to appreciate the utilitarian efficiency of Paul's kitchen. Clearly this was his domain, not Karen's.

William spotted the crabs already simmering in the pots. Through the window of the illuminated oven, he saw the brussels sprouts roasting. The salad and the loaf of sourdough waited on the counter.

Paul didn't say anything more. Didn't even look at him. He was making a simple garlic and clarified butter sauce for the crab. William watched as the milk solids settled to the bottom of the pan, and Paul began straining the clarified butter from the top.

"Is that for the crab?" he asked.

The drawstrings tightened a bit more around Paul's lips. "It is."

It never got easier, challenging Paul. But William sensed that Paul liked that about him, in spite of himself. It didn't hurt that William had mastered the timing of his challenges and that he never challenged Paul unless he knew damn well what he was talking about. After only a few short months of working together, William had learned how to do it with merely a tone of voice and a facial expression.

Paul turned his body one-quarter to face William. "So this is the first thing you say to me, the first time you come into *my* kitchen, in *my* house."

William smiled slightly. "I said something?"

"So tell me, since you're obviously the expert here – what do the people want, if not to taste the crab? This lets them taste the fucking crab."

"It does."

Julia had found a vase and came to the sink to fill it. Still taking her time, clearly eavesdropping.

"Don't tell me," Paul said to William, pouring the clarified butter into ramekins. "You've got another one of your hallowed Sicilian grand-mother's recipes."

William tried not to wince at Paul's characterization of his Nonna as *hallowed*. "I do."

"Of course you do." Paul stepped aside, gestured to the counter and the stove. "It's all yours."

William gaped. "What?"

Paul crossed his arms over his chest. "It's your big opportunity. Don't blow it in front of your girlfriend."

Out of the corner of his eye, William spied Julia casually arranging the flowers in the vase, as if she weren't hanging on every word. He said, "Really?"

Paul opened the cabinet doors and drawers one at a time, revealing cookware, knives, and kitchen utensils. He gestured to the hanging baskets: onions, garlic, scallions, and lemons.

William cleared his throat. Gathered his thoughts, trying to recall his grandmother's recipe by heart. Realizing that by this point, he didn't really need a recipe – he had the basic skeleton, and could wing the rest through intuition.

Paul still stood there, arms crossed, watching for William's next move. Julia was still there, too. She smiled at him for courage, but said, "Don't look at me. My dad fired me from his kitchen."

"I tell you what," interjected Paul, "it's Backwards Day. You play chef, I play prep cook."

"Now that is something I have to see to believe," said a voice behind

William. He turned to find Julia's sister in the doorway, balancing stacks of pinstriped pastry boxes.

William sprang forward to relieve some of Alison's burden. Together they set the stacks of pastry boxes on the table in the corner of the kitchen. To his dismay, Alison assumed a seat on the built-in banquette with a clear view of the action and started plating the pies she had brought with her.

At least Julia's mother wasn't there to watch him sink or swim. But he intended to swim.

He pointed to Paul. "Chopped parsley and a cup of butter." From the kitchen table, Alison cackled at his flawless mimicry of Paul, but he ignored her and pointed to Julia. "You. Open the wine."

"Aye aye, captain."

For his part, William peeled, trimmed, and minced the garlic and scallions. When Paul finished with the parsley and the butter, William ordered him to juice lemons, and then he boiled down a quarter cup of wine in the saucepan.

While he boiled and Paul juiced, Julia carried the vase of flowers into the dining room. A moment later, as he added the butter, salt, and garlic to the pan, he noticed that Julia now hovered in the doorway with her mother.

That's what he liked about cooking – once he got started, it didn't spare any psychic energy for his nerves.

When the butter melted, he waved Paul over with the parsley and the lemon juice. Paul threw them in the pan, and William followed it with a couple of pinches of cayenne pepper. He tasted. Added more cayenne.

Paul tasted, then shot William a look that was a combination of surprise and annoyance, as he often did when William proved himself right. But he only said, "That's a lot of dipping sauce for five crabs."

William shook his head. "You pour it over the crab."

Paul looked skeptical, but said nothing. He pointed to the ramekin of chopped scallions, still on the counter.

"Garnish," William explained.

Silenced, Paul pressed his lips together. Julia and her mother exchanged knowing glances, and Alison smirked.

Paul strained the crabs from the pot and William rinsed them briefly under cold water. The women whisked the other dishes to the dining table while William and Paul brought the crabs and the sauce.

Julia sat beside William, and Paul served the wine while William demonstrated how to pour the garlic parsley sauce over the crab. Beneath the cover of the dining table, William tapped his foot nervously while everyone cracked their crab and tasted.

Paul said nothing, of course, but he ate every bite and washed it down with the buttery Chardonnay.

"You can admit it now, Dad," Alison said to Paul as she served him a slice of pie.

"Admit what?"

"William knocked it out of the park."

Karen laughed out loud, and beneath the cover of the table, Julia's hand squeezed William's.

Later, as they walked the three blocks together in the rain back to his house, William slid his arm around her waist and sheltered her under his umbrella. Julia balanced two boxes of Alison's pies, one on top of the other. Her canary-yellow raincoat struck a cheerful contrast to his sober black umbrella.

The first things to accost them as he opened the front door were the blare of Thanksgiving football on the TV, and the overpowering wall of tobacco smoke.

"Un-fucking-believable!" Mike's voice bellowed from the living room.

"Can you believe this fucking game?" came another masculine voice.

William cast Julia a sheepish look, and she grinned good-naturedly. That was the thing about her – if his family's rough edges offended her, she never let on.

They ascended the staircase to the living room and found Mike, Uncle Frank, and William's father slouched on the sagging avocado-green furniture, their eyes riveted to the TV screen, scores of empty beer bottles and smoking ashtrays scattered on the coffee table in front of them. William cleared his throat, but they still didn't notice. He glanced at the TV and asked who was playing.

"Dallas and Miami," said Uncle Frank.

William frowned again at the screen, at the ice and snow on the football field. "This is in Miami?"

"Texas Stadium. But still." Uncle Frank looked up and finally spotted Julia. "Oh, hey, honey. Nice to see you."

Mike and William's father noticed her then, grunted their greetings, and turned back to the game.

William shrugged and steered Julia toward the kitchen, where his mother and sister darted around like balls in a pinball machine. His mother gave Julia a breathless greeting and a hasty peck on the cheek.

"Can I help?" Julia offered while his mother accepted the pastry boxes.

Kelly shoved a tray of antipasti at Julia. "Take these to the dining table."

While William helped Julia with the antipasti, the house erupted in such a deafening uproar that he nearly dropped the platter. The men in the living room leaped to their feet, bellowing obscenities with such fervor that William thought there must have been a fight, except that their eyes were fixated to the TV screen.

"What happened?" said William.

"Live ball!" spluttered Uncle Frank.

"The idiot touched the ball," William's father explained. "The Cowboys were going to win, but they just handed Miami the game."

"Good," Mike declared. "Fuck the Cowboys."

William again looked sheepishly at Julia. But she smiled and gamely said, "I didn't know you swung that way, Mike."

The men in the living room turned to her with a stunned look, then broke into snickers. Uncle Frank gave Mike a noogie and said to William, "She'll fit in just fine around here."

With the game over, everyone gathered around the table to help themselves to prosciutto and salami, tomatoes and mixed olives, marinated peppers and artichoke hearts, burrata and provolone and crostini. An hour later, William's mother brought out a lasagna, and an hour after that, the traditional turkey, stuffing, and vegetables.

"Your family Thanksgivings are epic events," Julia observed as

William poured her a third glass of prosecco and his mother served Alison's pumpkin pie.

"We're Italian," Uncle Frank pointed out. "We take our holiday dinners very seriously."

William's mother handed Julia her slice of pie, and Julia told them about the more modest crab feast at her house.

"You should have seen the sauce Will made for the crab, though," she added. "All I'll say is, the only pie my dad ate today was humble pie."

Warmed by the prosecco and the smile Julia turned on him, William reached for her hand. He no longer cared if everyone could see his feelings on open display. It didn't even irk him when Mike made a gagging noise and said, "Jesus, get a room."

There was something almost primordial about the feeling it gave him to sit there like that, holding her hand in companionable silence while eating with the other hand. A feeling akin to pride of ownership, almost. It definitely wasn't evolved.

But the thing was, her family liked him. His family liked her. Their families had been connected for generations, through both shared community and shared trade. On top of all that, she was the most beautiful thing in the room. And she was *his*.

Predictably, by ten o'clock, his father, brother, and Uncle Frank were well on their way to being thoroughly sloshed. Pretty soon they'd start up on the crude humor, and Mike would no longer bother hiding the way his wolfish leer raked over Julia's body every time she crossed his path.

At least they were all happy drunks.

William announced, "I'm going to walk Julia home."

Slurring their farewells, his family staggered to hug and kiss Julia, and William followed her downstairs to the enclosed tunnel entrance. But instead of leading her out the front door, he pulled her into the in-law unit.

William wasn't delusional – he knew his family no longer bought his bullshit about walking Julia home, if they ever did.

He flipped on the light in the in-law unit and locked the door behind them. She turned her face up to his. He wanted so badly to undress her, to unwrap her like a present to himself, that his ears buzzed.

He reached behind her, found the top of her zipper. Peeled open her dress. Ran his fingertips down the groove of her spine.

She brushed her hands over her shoulders. Let the dress fall to the floor.

A while later, in his bed, he draped her halfway across his body, the back of her head against his chest. He was content and satiated and tired, and yet he couldn't fall asleep. He lay there, a hand grasping one of her breasts, and stuck his nose in her hair, breathing her heady perfume of sex and shampoo.

This was going to be one of the happiest memories of his life. If he lived to be one hundred, this day would be just as fresh in his mind as it was now. He had already had a lot of days like that with her, and this was another one.

She started to roll away, but he squeezed her to stop her. Her eyes flickered open and lifted to his.

He twisted some of her hair through his fingers. "I'm going to apply to UCSB."

She rolled over, propped herself up against his chest to look at his face. "The deadline already passed."

"I'll apply next year, then. If all else fails, I'll work in a kitchen. There are plenty of restaurants in Santa Barbara."

"But you've got a full ride to USF."

He shook his head. "It's not set in stone."

"Oh come on, Will. I really must insist that you toot your own horn occasionally. You have a 4.0 GPA and you got a 1510 on your SAT. You're well on your way to being a National Merit Finalist."

He was forced to admit that she was probably right – it did seem inevitable. There was no point in playing coy about it. And he felt like he owed it to Nonna to go to college. If it weren't for her, he never would have had the opportunity in the first place. He'd probably still be stuck in Special Ed, or some school for the emotionally disturbed.

He got up, went to his closet. Retrieved a bankers box and brought it over to the bed. Lifted the lid, and pulled out his old Nikon camera.

"My grandmother gave me this when I was six."

She accepted it from him. Inspected it. "Wow. Nice equipment, for a six-year-old."

"I didn't talk for a whole year."

She looked up sharply. "What?"

"I had to repeat a grade because of it. For a year, I wouldn't talk to anyone except my grandmother."

"Huh," Julia murmured thoughtfully. "Just like Maya Angelou."

"Yeah, except in my case, no one ever figured out why. They called it selective mutism. My grandmother gave me this camera as a way to express myself. Since I wouldn't do it in words, I could do it in pictures."

He gestured down into the bankers box. From inside, she pulled out a whole stack of photos and began flipping through them.

"I don't really have a very good storage system for all these," he explained. "So I just put my pictures in here, after I develop them."

"You develop them yourself?"

"I use my bathroom as a darkroom."

She burst out laughing. "That's so completely dorky, it's awesome." His cheeks grew warm, and she added, "You know I mean that as a compliment, don't you?"

He smiled, and she dug down further through the box and found photo after photo of varying sizes, some in black and white, others in color. She pulled them out one by one. The Cliff House. The Sutro Baths. The Camera Obscura. Land's End. Hang gliders launching from Fort Funston.

"These are beautiful, Will," she murmured. She pulled more from the box: a homeless man in Golden Gate Park with a shopping cart full of overstuffed plastic garbage bags. A hoary Vietnamese fisherman with deep arroyos carved in his face. The underside of the Golden Gate Bridge as he sailed beneath it.

"Why don't you frame some of these?" she asked.

"My mom did frame one or two. They're upstairs."

"I know you said you don't want to do photography for a living. But maybe you could still major in it in college. I mean, since you don't know what else to study."

He shook his head. "USF doesn't have a photography major. I've been thinking of majoring in Hospitality Management."

She lifted an eyebrow. "Hospitality Management?"

He accepted some of the photos she held out to him. Began reorganizing them into neat stacks. "I could manage a restaurant, or open my own someday."

She began pulling out more photos. Looking at them, one by one. "Well, I think you've missed your calling. You should reconsider."

"If you want any of these, you can have them."

"Really?"

"Sure. They're just sitting in there, anyway."

"Well, I like the ocean ones," she said, going back through the whales, the waves, the boats, and setting some aside.

She reached the bottom of the box, and seized upon a photograph she hadn't noticed before. A photo of a bunch of plants in his backyard, for his science project.

She gaped at him. "You're already working on that? It's not due until March."

"What can I say? I'm overzealous."

"You're a shameless geek, is what you are. Who are you trying to impress, Dr. Benson? She's a lesbian, you know. In the meantime, you're making the rest of us look bad." She picked up the photo and looked at it again. "What are you doing your project on?"

"Hydroponics. I'm exploiting Mike for his considerable experience."

"Mike?" she said, and then she got it. "Wait, those aren't pot plants, are they?"

It was his turn to laugh at her. "Don't you know what a pot plant looks like?"

"Oh no, not you too. 'Julia, you're so naïve.'" She let go of the photo, and took his hand. "That day on the beach – you know, around the bonfire – you told me that you used to smoke weed, but you had been trying to stay away from it for a while."

He nodded. "I started smoking it around the time my grandmother died. It helped take my mind off things, but it got to the point where it was the only thing I wanted to do. The only thing that snapped me out of my funk was the fact that school was about to start again. I felt like…" He picked at some lint on his comforter. "I don't know how to explain it. I guess I felt like I couldn't dishonor my grandmother that way."

She shifted her weight. Tucked her legs beneath her. "Dishonor your grandmother?"

He tried to explain. Despite his rejection of Confirmation, William knew he had made his grandmother proud in the last months of her life – he'd be the first in his immediate family to go to college, at no expense to either himself or his parents.

Then again, maybe going to college hadn't been the inevitable thing, after all. Maybe meeting Julia at Holy Cross had been the inevitable thing.

Julia touched his cheekbone, bringing him back to the moment. She kissed his lips, and her hair tumbled over his face. He felt the stirrings of his libido again.

Clearly she noticed it, too, because her eyes flitted down briefly to his lap, and one corner of her mouth tilted up. Sitting up, she gathered everything back into the banker's box and set it on the floor. Then she pushed him down on the bed again and shifted to straddle his hips, peering down at him with sultry eyes.

He ran one hand up and down the silky skin of her thigh, while reaching with the other to toy with a lock of her hair. His heart was so full to bursting that it actually hurt sometimes. "*God*, Julie... you are so beautiful, you know that?"

"So you keep telling me," she murmured, smiling tenderly. "Right back at you, by they way. How did I ever bag such a hunka hunka burnin' love?"

He assumed his best Elvis impression, complete with lip curl. "Well, bebbeh, I guess it's because *I can't help falling in love with you.*"

"Oh my God, *not* sexy!" she half-groaned, half-cackled, playfully swatting at his chest while he carried right on signing the lyric. He allowed it for a few seconds, enjoying the way her perky breasts bounced with the effort; but then he seized her wrists, grinning as she pretended to keep struggling. He reveled in the flush that painted her freckled porcelain skin – a heady cocktail of laughter, exertion, and arousal. He drank in the way her eyes bunched up at the corners with her full-throated laughter. And of course, he basked in the glow of her smile that never failed to flood his chest with warmth.

She turned him on so fucking much, and she was *everything*.

He nudged her shoulder, urging her closer, and she tumbled forward, taking his mouth in an urgent kiss. With a muffled groan, he finally released her wrists so he could run his fingertips up her back, lightly tangling them in her hair. The way she whimpered and wriggled on top of him drove him insane.

He reached down between their bodies, guiding himself to her; and with his other hand, he gripped her hip, already shaking with anticipation. Breaking their kiss, he lifted a brow in question. Her hooded eyes locked on his, and she answered by sinking down onto him, eliciting a hiss of pleasure from them both.

"Jesus, I'm already so close," he gritted out in amazement.

She sat upright, reaching with slender arms to lift her hair up off of her shoulders and breasts, giving him access to all of her. He took it eagerly, raking his eyes and palms down her beautiful body as she started moving on him. She was all soft, creamy skin and sweet curves, with a slender waist flaring out to feminine hips, and an eminently-grabbable ass. Sexier than anything he had pictured in his wildest fantasies.

"Julie..." he whispered, his voice tinged with awe. "You're perfect. So fucking perfect. I'm barely hanging on by a thread here."

She moved faster on him and sucked in a breath through clenched teeth, releasing it in professions of love, of how good he made her feel. Of how he, and this, were all she wanted, all she could think about.

He gripped her breasts, kneading them – perfect little handfuls. "If I went to Santa Barbara – if we moved in together – we could have this every single night."

She slowed but didn't stop entirely, grinding on him instead in tight, maddening circles. She was gazing down at him, her forehead creased as if deeply conflicted. But she murmured, "Don't worry, Will; it's ten months between now and when we start college. That's a lot of time to figure it all out."

After a moment's hesitation, he decided now was definitely not the time to belabor the point. So instead he did a sort of curl-up and took one of her flawless pink nipples between his lips. Whimpering, she arched into him, threading her fingers through the hair on the back of his head and holding him to her.

Yes. There was only one thing in life he was really sure about, and that was Julia. So as he pleasured her with his fingers and dialed up their pace to frantic, he knew he would apply to UCSB. He wouldn't get in, but he would move down there with her anyway.

Julia knew exactly what she wanted to do with her life, and he didn't. And as she came apart on him and he spilled into her with a groan of relief, he knew he would follow her and be happy until he figured it out.

JULY 1992

"AND SUDDENLY I SAW THE HEAVENS UNFASTENED AND OPEN."

*N*ine days closer to William's seventeenth birthday. Nine days closer to when he would embark with Frank on a three-week albacore tuna-fishing trip. One hundred and fifty miles offshore, all the way to the warm water edge. That far out, the stars would float above them in full relief, undimmed by the city lights. Meteors would streak through the Milky Way's arms, so vivid that it seemed they might crash into Uncle Frank's outriggers. And during the day, they might even see blue whales.

Or an albatross.

In the sanctuary of his bedroom, William had begun writing poems again. And on Sunday, after the usual family dinner, he and Mike had indulged in a mini jam session. For the first time in nearly two years, lyrics flew freely from his pen and melodies from his guitar, while Mike supported on bass. They riffed for hours without breaks, knowing it was only a matter of time until their mother yelled at them to pull the plug;

their father was trying to sleep. And they both knew that *trying to sleep* was code for *passed out drunk on the sofa.*

But the poems… those were still private. Those were just for William. And maybe, one day, he would share them with his grandmother. After all, she was the one who had freed the *poète maudit* from its cage.

Watching Mike pack up his bass guitar, William suddenly blurted, "Can you draw me an albatross?"

Mike's hand froze with the guitar case halfway shut, his head swiveling to gape at William. "Can I what?"

As much of an idiot as Mike was in most respects, there was no denying his artistic talent. He had never received nor needed any formal training. It was like he sprang from the womb, a fully-formed Leonardo da Vinci.

In the artistic department, anyway. Definitely not in the genius department.

"Draw an albatross. For me."

"What the fuck, man?" Mike emitted one of his cretinous laughs. "Where did *that* come from?"

To hide his burning cheeks, William went to stow his guitar case in the corner of his bedroom. "It came from the fact that I want you to draw an albatross for me. Standing with its wings spread, as if readying for flight. Can you do it or not?"

"Okay, clearly you're going all Bruce Wayne on me here. Just promise to use my powers for good, not evil."

William smirked, and didn't tell Mike he would use it as a cover for his first book of poems. The one he would present to Nonna when he graduated from high school.

Now, today, it was Monday, and Nonna had asked William to bring home five salmon filets for supper. She knew Frank would bring in his catch that day, and that William would help him offload it. And since his parents worked later than he did, and his sister Kelly was away at some soccer camp, Nonna tasked him with bringing home the goods.

Now he strode home from the bus stop, the butcher paper-wrapped filets tucked under his arm like a football. The fog was so dense, it swallowed not just the sights, but even the sounds of the neighborhood.

He wasn't sure what to credit for the extra spring in his step. Maybe it was just his inner *poète maudit*, finally liberated from its cage. It was a cage Jimmy had constructed for him, but he had finally realized that he was the only one keeping himself there.

Maybe it was the lingering buzz from jamming with Mike last night.

Or maybe it was the surprise of finding Julia Dunphy on the bus, just two rows in front of him, in the thrall of Pablo Neruda. Her lips silently formed the poet's words as her eyes traced them over the page:

> something started in my soul,
> fever or forgotten wings,
> and I made my own way,
> deciphering
> that fire
> and wrote the first faint line,
> faint without substance, pure
> nonsense,
> pure wisdom,
> of someone who knows nothing,
> and suddenly I saw
> the heavens
> unfastened
> and open.

He still hadn't worked up the nerve to speak to her. Besides, he hated it when anyone interrupted *him*, mid-Neruda.

His house finally came into view, emerging suddenly out of the fog. But even as he retrieved his key from his pocket, the hairs on the back of his neck prickled.

Something was wrong.

He knew it, even before he heard the smoke alarm. Even before he crossed the distance to the front door in a handful of long strides, and the acrid stench of something burning assailed his nostrils.

"Nonna?" he shouted over the relentless shriek of the alarm. He touched the doorknob – it was cool – then unlocked the front door as quickly as his shaking hands would allow.

The alarm's wail intensified, as did the acrid smell. A haze of thin smoke billowed from the open door. Even over the alarm, a faint, almost spectral groan reached his ears from somewhere upstairs.

"Nonna!" Dropping his backpack in the foyer, dropping even the package of salmon, he sprinted upstairs, two at a time. The burning smell intensified, as did the moaning. His long legs propelled him through the living room and into the kitchen in three strides.

Supine on the kitchen floor, limbs sprawled. Eyes wide, mouth slack, a grotesque death mask. Drool streaming from one corner of her mouth, pooling on the linoleum.

"Nonna!"

His shriek pinballed around inside of his head, the voice unrecognizable even to himself. As he fell to his knees, her eyes slowly slid over and locked and with his. An unnatural groan ripped from her throat, and to his horror, he realized she was fully alert and aware.

"Nonna! What's the matter?" He snatched one of her hands and squeezed, willing her to squeeze back. But she didn't. "Nonna, please, say something!" But she only stared. Somehow, he instinctively knew she was trying to stay brave for him. Trying to reassure him with her eyes.

Tears gushed down his cheeks. "Nonna... tell me what to do!"

She groaned louder, her eyes sliding in the direction of the stove. That's when the burning smell returned to the forefront, and he understood. Springing to his feet, he flipped the knob on the stove, extinguishing the burner. The pan above it contained the charred, smoking remnants of whatever she had been cooking. It was unrecognizable now. Quickly deciding it wouldn't catch fire, he didn't waste any more time on it – he returned to squat at his grandmother's side.

"It's okay, Nonna; I turned off the burner. I'm going to call 911."

She only stared at him, unable to even nod. Springing to his feet again, he snatched the receiver from the wall-mounted phone and spun the three digits on the agonizingly-slow rotary dial.

"Come on, come on, come on..."

With the receiver still pressed to his ear, he returned to Nonna's side, the coiled phone cord stretching to accommodate the short distance.

"911, please state your–"

"My nonna – I don't know – she's on the floor and I–"

"Sir, please slow down. Your *what?*"

Nonna's eyes were still locked on his, and it was like she was channeling messages straight into his brain: "Deep breaths, niputeddu miu. I'm okay. You've got this, my smart, capable boy."

"Sir?" came the operator's sharp voice. "I can't hear you. If that's a fire alarm, you should evacuate immediately."

He burst to his feet again and ripped the smoke alarm from the ceiling, silencing it. "Nonna – my grandmother – something's wrong," he stammered into the phone. "She's collapsed on the kitchen floor. She can't move or talk. Please hurry."

William kept his eyes locked with Nonna's as the 911 operator dispatched help and talked him through a series of questions that he spluttered answers to.

Awake.

Breathing.

Alert.

Aware.

Oh God, she was *aware* of everything that was happening to her!

"Don't worry, Nonna; you'll be okay. The ambulance is coming. I'm here."

"I'm already okay," her eyes seemed to answer him. "You'll be okay, too."

"No," he choked out.

"Yes you will, and don't you forget it."

"They'll fix this." He heard the sirens wailing now. "Nonna, I'm just going to roll up these dish towels and put them under your head–"

"Sir," came the urgent voice on the other end of the line, "do not move her; she may have a spinal cord injury."

Choking on an anguished sob, William fixed his eyes on Nonna's again. "I'm just going to flag down the ambulance and let them in. It'll only take a minute, okay? I'll be right back."

"Go on," Nonna said with her eyes.

The next few minutes were a blur that William barely registered – first responders rushing upstairs, William trailing closely. As Nonna vanished into the center of a circle of paramedics, he snatched the rosary hanging on the kitchen wall. Hopefully loud enough for Nonna to hear over the commotion, he prayed.

I believe in God,
the Father almighty...

The ring of paramedics opened briefly, and he saw it – Nonna was moving!

No, wait, she wasn't moving, she was–

Blessed art thou among women,
and blessed is the fruit of–

Snatches of words he didn't understand, like *myoclonus* and *tachy* and *hemorrhagic.*

–thy womb.
Holy Mary, Mother of God–

A few he did understand, like *seizing* and *airway* and *cardiac arrest.*

pray for us sinners,
Now and at the hour of our–

I'm sorry, son. She's gone.

An inhuman wail ripped the curtain dividing reality from nightmare – a wail he didn't recognize as his own until he collapsed to his knees.

"Are you Catholic?"

The gruff voice beside him belonged to one of the paramedics. A middle-aged man with a dark mustache.

"Let's pray together for her, son."

I commend you, my dear sister,
to Almighty God,
and entrust you to your Creator...

Only then did William remember – he had forgotten to tell her he loved her.

"THAT ONE'S FAR FROM HOME."

Numbness.

After the wailing, praying, and crying, that's what rushed in to fill the void they had carved out – pure numbness.

His birthday came and went. So did Nonna's funeral. Immediately after, William plunged headlong into a three-week trip with Frank, actually hoping to sweat and freeze and suffer – but all to no avail. Now, back on land, he remained firmly entrenched in the numbness.

On that horrible day one month ago, someone must have alerted Andy. He arrived at the same time as William's distraught parents, followed quickly by a stunned Mike; then administered last rites before the coroner carried Nonna's body from the house. He stayed to comfort an inconsolable Kelly, who hadn't been able to get home quickly enough to say her goodbyes.

Andy had spoken at length to William, but his words sounded like a squawking trumpet – like the adults in a Charlie Brown TV special. A bunch of meaningless nonsense. Canned. Trapped.

Numb.

After William returned from his three-week fishing trip, Andy visited him again at home. This time, William heard more of the words.

Stages of grief.

Not your fault.

With the Lord.

At peace.

"Pray with me, Will."

At those words, Andy snap-zoomed into focus. And that's all it took to open the floodgates to the next stage of grief.

Rage.

William sprang to his feet, tipping the dining chair backward, his fists balling at his sides. Beside him, Andy flinched, eyes wide. William felt the crevasses forming in his forehead, and his teeth nearly shattered under the clench of his jaw.

"I prayed," William seethed. "I prayed while she died surrounded by a bunch of strange men. I told her everything would be okay; but that was a lie. And not only were my last words to her a lie, I never once told her I loved her."

Andy's wary gaze softened, his shoulders lowering a bit. "She knew that, Will. She always did. Even if you'd had time to tell her, you didn't need to."

"But I *did* have time!" William spat out. "She was aware of everything, even though she couldn't move or speak. She was on the kitchen floor with the smoke alarm blaring in her ear, wondering how much longer before the house burned down around her. She was aware enough to tell me – to show me with her eyes that I needed to turn off the burner. I had plenty of time to say I love you, but I forgot. I *forgot!*"

"Will–"

"She was the only person in this whole family who made it okay for me to not be some – some *caricature* of manhood, like Jimmy or Mike. She was the only one who didn't look at me like I was a huge disappointment to her. She never gave me shit, just because I wanted to write poems instead of play sports or fix up old cars or, I don't know, beat people up and play beer pong. Do you know what my own father told me when he read one of my poems? 'That's good, Will, but don't spend too much time on that shit – it'll give you a limp wrist.'"

Granted, his father had said it in a superficially teasing way; but it was one of those teasing ways that suggested he half-believed it. And that was par for the course with the rest of his family.

"Well, now you're old enough to know how ignorant that is," Andy pointed out.

"Yeah, but you know what else? Nonna was the only person in this entire goddamn family who tried to get my parents to do the right thing and kick Jimmy out of the house. Oh, and that was *after* she tried to get them to take Jimmy to rehab, but they wouldn't do that either. My own parents let him turn the in-law unit into a fucking meth house and terrorize me night and day because they were either too busy or too hammered to notice."

"Will..." Andy was visibly grasping for words; William could tell. His face contorted with the effort, his lips forming syllables his voice never gave substance to. Finally, he huffed out a sigh. "You need to tell your parents all of this, every single bit of it. Tell them how it made you feel – how it *still* makes you feel."

"What difference would it make? They know they screwed up, but there's nothing they can do about it now. If I pick at that wound, they'll just work and drink themselves even stupider. And now, Kelly doesn't even have Nonna to compensate for their absence."

"Or maybe it would be a wake-up call for your parents."

William scoffed. "Fat chance."

"At the very least, maybe it would give them an opportunity to offer you a long-overdue apology."

"Even if they did, so what? Jimmy's still in prison, Nonna's still dead, and I'm still stuck with a family who's convinced I got switched at birth."

"No," Andy insisted, slowly rising to his own feet. "Don't you remember what we talked about? Your power is in your response, Will. Use yours to honor your grandmother. Use it to defy Jimmy and anyone else who tries to drag you down. Would your nonna want you to turn your back on all of your talents and opportunities, just because she's gone?"

Suddenly wracked with sobs, William collapsed back into a chair – one he hadn't yet upended. He thought he had gotten all of the crying out of his system a month ago, but apparently not. Andy pulled another chair up beside him and draped an arm around his shoulders, murmuring words of encouragement and comfort.

That's when an unexpected image intruded into William's consciousness: Mike's albatross drawing. The one William had commissioned from him.

Mike had produced it not long after Nonna died, his eyes serious for once, as if he had guessed what it meant to William. It was astonishing and beautiful, with its wings outstretched and its head turned in profile. Its beak open, as if scoffing at all the world's snares and cages.

Sitting there at the dining table with Andy, the image was so clear before him. And that's when he remembered

"That one's far from home," Uncle Frank had said. It was during their three-week albacore tuna fishing trip. They were just off the Farallones. He was standing on the deck, shielding his eyes from the sun as he looked up.

William followed his gaze. "What kind is that?" It wasn't the first albatross William had ever seen, but it was the first one like this – white body, dark wings. The iconic albatross look. Not like the dark-all-over black-footed albatross more common to these waters.

"Laysan albatross," Frank grunted. "Usually they nest in Hawaii, but when breeding season is over, you'll occasionally see one around here. Still, it's pretty rare."

They resumed working, but every so often, when William paused for a drink of water or a bathroom break, he spotted it, still circling overhead. Still following them, as if waiting to snag a meal from their by-catch. But it never did. It just circled, watching over them. Late in the afternoon, when they were wrapping up operations, William glanced up to find it gone.

But William was still there, stumbling with clumsy feet over the deck of his uncle's boat.

"Will."

Andy's voice snatched William back into the present moment. He had no sense of how much time had passed, but William had cried himself dry again. Andy was still there, but he seemed to be waging his own internal battle.

Finally, Andy lifted his gaze to William's. "I'm going to say this once, and this is all I can say about it. But maybe you've heard the expression before: 'Hurt people hurt people.'"

He peered intently at William, as if waiting for the words to sink in. It was clearly important to him, so William rallied his last shred of mental energy to try and understand.

Hurt people hurt people.

But was Andy talking about Jimmy? Or his parents?

"It's not an excuse," Andy added quietly, wearing an oddly defeated look that William didn't understand. "Just context."

A long time ago, Nonna had told him about a bird that her own mother kept as a pet – some kind of dove or pigeon she found on the sidewalk with a lame wing. When Nonna asked her mother why she kept him in a cage instead of releasing him back into the wild, her mother answered, "For his own safety. If I set him free, something will catch and eat him. He was bred for food, or maybe to be released during weddings. But he doesn't know how to survive out there, which is how he wound up with a crippled wing."

Hurt people hurt people.

That evening, after Andy went home, William shut himself in his bedroom again. Reaching into the drawer of his bedside table, he retrieved his address book, thumbing through it until he landed on the *T* section.

Temkina, Serafima.

He dialed her number, and the ringback tone sounded in his ear.

Click.

"Hello?"

"Haze? It's–"

"William."

Surprised, he said, "How did you know?"

"Caller ID."

"Oh. Right."

A beat. "Are you okay?"

William gave a rueful huff, but said nothing.

"I'm sorry," she rushed out, breathless. "Of course you're not okay. Mike told me what happened. I'm so sorry."

"I'm fine."

From her silence on the other end of the line, he assumed she could tell that was a lie. After several beats, she ventured, "Will... did I ever tell you I found my mother dead when I was eleven?"

"No." It came out flat, so he quickly added, "I'm sorry."

"I'm not telling you so you'll console me. I'm telling you because even though my experience may not be exactly the same, I do know a little something about it. And I know from experience where it can take you when you try to forget at all costs."

After a moment to allow her words to sink in, William said dully, "Thanks." But the truth was, he wasn't calling to talk about forgetting, or not forgetting.

He was calling to talk about safety.

Clearing his throat, he plowed ahead. "Haze... how old do I have to be to get a tattoo?"

"A tattoo?" she echoed skeptically. "Eighteen, of course. With brothers like yours, I would have thought you'd know."

"I do, but... how old do I have to be to get a tattoo from *you?*"

A few beats ensued, in which William heard nothing but his pulse swishing through his ears.

Finally, she asked, "What kind of tattoo are we talking about?"

"An albatross. I already have the design, but don't tell Mike. He drew it, and he's trying to establish himself as a tattoo artist; but I don't want him coming anywhere near my back with a needle."

She gave a knowing chuckle. "So is that where you want it, then? On your back?"

William hummed in confirmation. "And Haze? There's just one more detail I'd like you to add, if possible."

"What's that?"

He sucked in a deep breath, welding the final bar in place.

Numb.

"Can you put my albatross in a cage?"

NOVEMBER 1995, PART I

*W*illiam parked his motorcycle illegally in the alley behind Dunphy's, against the back wall of the building. After stowing his valuables in the break room locker, he exchanged his motorcycle jacket and helmet for a white chef's coat and skull cap. He had finished prepping the grill and was readying his mise en place when Paul approached him.

"William," he barked. "My office."

William delayed only long enough to scrape the parsley he had been chiffonading into a prep bowl, then dropped the bench scraper on the counter and followed Paul.

He knew better by now than to ask questions. Besides, William could tell just from the tightness around Paul's lips.

She had told him.

When? And how did it unfold?

Of course – her birthday. Her mother had called to wish her a happy birthday. She had told her mother, and then her mother told Paul. Or, she came into town for her birthday – after all, it was Sunday this year –

113

and she had told them both together, at the same time, sitting over her birthday cake at their dining room table.

"Why isn't William here?" they would have asked. And it all would have come out.

Maybe she had even come to the restaurant. Maybe she had even *worked* there. He looked around himself. It was as if her hypothetical presence – maybe even in the very spot he stood now, in her father's office – changed the air in the room. Perfumed it.

Paul closed the door behind them and gestured to the empty chair in front of his desk. "Have a seat."

William complied, of course, and waited for the ax to fall.

But Paul took his own seat, and folded his hands on top of the desk. The same green-gray eyes as hers. The same long, thin, freckled face.

"I know you and Julia broke up." He had never been a man to beat about the bush. "I really hope we can keep working together, without any awkwardness. I know I've never told you this, but you're the best line cook I've got. One of the best I've ever had, in fact. I think you have a real future in cooking, and I hope it's in my restaurant; I really do. But if not, I want you to know that you'll always have a great reference from me, wherever you go."

To William's horror, a sudden, involuntary chokehold gripped his throat. He bit his tongue - a little trick he had picked up over the years. "Thank you."

"In fact, you've more than proven yourself on grill lately. And I want you to take over that position, now that Hector moved on."

"Wow," said William, gobsmacked. "Thank you."

Of course, if Paul promoted him to grill at age twenty, he shouldn't read too much into it for himself. Hector had taken over from Mark, who had opened some up-and-coming Asian-fusion joint in Hayes Valley. And now Hector had moved up to sous-chef at a swanky Vegas hotel.

All the best staff were jumping ship. Stuck on Fisherman's Wharf with a rapidly-graying patronage, these days Dunphy's was only a springboard for promising cooks like Hector. And now, apparently, for William.

Yet that wasn't even the greatest appeal of his new promotion. The greatest appeal was knowing that maybe Julia would hear about it. Maybe she would even visit Dunphy's one day, and then she would see him there, at the grill, or maybe even working rounds cook. And then she'd have to know that he was going places, despite her previous dismal assessment of his drive and ambition. And then one day, when she heard he was opening his own restaurant, she would be sorry she had dumped him all those years ago.

But if he moved on from Dunphy's – when and where would he ever see her again?

He went straight to the griddle and attacked it with everything he had. He would do his damnedest for her dad. Either way, stay or leave, she would hear nothing but good things about him.

It didn't sink in until he went home – she had never responded to his overtures at reconciliation. She had just ignored them, like they weren't his very lifeblood, painstakingly extracted over their past two years together.

She was never coming to Dunphy's, at least not while he was there. She was never going to just show up on his doorstep, like she did in his dreams.

He would never hear from her again.

Her thrift store style; her bright smile that he had once dismissed as showing too many teeth. Her capricious conversion to Islam, until praying five times a day proved too burdensome.

The way she squatted behind him on Ocean Beach in her pink bikini and teased him about the caged albatross on his back.

The way the wind whipped her hair on his uncle's boat when he kissed her.

The way the Halloween soundtrack, the other revelers, the entire *world* faded into the background as she snap-zoomed forward in the mermaid costume. The rapture when he asked her to come home with him, and she did.

"I'm never taking it off," she teased him when he gave her the ring. "You're never getting rid of me now."

All of that. All for absolutely nothing. How was he ever supposed to get that out of him?

There wasn't enough weed in the world.

He burst out of his bedroom and ran up the stairs. His mother had already been in to pluck the Jameson from his snoring father's grip and cover him with a blanket. William knew from experience that by now, she was already sound asleep in bed, and he was in the clear.

He found the key to the liquor cabinet and swiped another one of his father's bottles. Brought it back downstairs to his room. Opened the cap, and poured a generous helping.

"Next time, save the vodka for after *you light up."*

Or, as Mike would say, "Grass then beer, you're in the clear."

He set the whiskey on the bedside table, untouched.

He had enough weed to sustain him for the next two weeks. He had no real excuse to call or visit Haze again. And it was eleven o'clock at night; he couldn't go over there now.

Half an hour later, he knocked on her front door. Only then did it occur to him – she might not be home. Or even alone.

Just as he was about to give up and leave, the chain on the door slid, and the locks turned. She had been sleeping; he could tell by her eyes. She wore the same short white satin kimono as yesterday, with nothing underneath; he could tell by her nipples poking through the fabric.

She stepped back inside the foyer. Opened the door to him. After she closed and locked it again, she came to stand in front of him. Looked up at him, waiting.

He stepped closer. Slid his hands inside the opening at the front of her kimono. She untied its sash, and allowed him to peel it off of her shoulders. Allowed it to pool at her feet.

Upstairs in her bed, he shifted himself down. Just below her navel was a spider, with a line of Cyrillic script at its feet:

надейся только на себя

Tracing the script with his fingertip, he found a ridge, streaking horizontally above the triangle of dark hair between her legs. He lingered, exploring its rough, puckered texture.

He propped himself up a bit on his elbow to get a clearer look at her sphinx-like face. "Appendix?"

"C-section," she replied matter-of-factly. She put her hand in his hair, massaging his scalp.

His eyebrows lifted in surprise. He held her gaze for a moment, waiting, but she didn't seem inclined to elaborate.

He ran his fingertips over the scar. Planted a string of kisses along its length. Shifted further down, and she opened herself to him with some mild Russian epithet of contentment.

An hour later, they lay in her bed, shotgunning hits from a joint. The same strain she usually sold him; more indica than yesterday's sativa.

"I wasn't sure if you'd be here or not," he said.

"I'm pretty much a homebody these days. After a day at the studio, I just want to read a book and go to bed."

He traced the onion domes atop her Russian Orthodox cathedral. "What are you reading?"

"Pushkin," she replied. "And Tyutchev."

She offered him the joint and reached for a book on her bedside table. Its cover bore writing in both Cyrillic and English and had long since faded to the color of dust.

"I came to the U.S. when I was nine, so I can still read Russian. But sometimes I need a little help." The pages crackled with age as she turned them to the spot she had marked. She looked up at him with a little smile, and added, "You should like this."

He rested his head in the crook of his arm and puffed on the joint while she read to him:

> *Live in your inner self alone*
> *within your soul a world has grown,*
> *the magic of veiled thoughts that might*
> *be blinded by the outer light,*
> *drowned in the noise of day, unheard...*
> *take in their song and speak no word.*

"What is that?" he asked after allowing it a moment to sink in.

"*Silentium,* by Fyodor Tyutchev. The translation is by Nabokov, but it doesn't matter – a translation can never do the original justice."

William nodded, thinking of *L'Albatros* by Baudelaire. It didn't seem right to share that with Haze, though. Julia was the only person in the world who had ever guessed what his tattoo was about.

So he passed the joint back to her and reached out to touch her gray-streaked hair. "Where in Russia did you grow up?"

"Novosibirsk." When he drew a blank, she added, "It's in Siberia."

"Siberia," he echoed.

"People take one look at me and assume I grew up in a gulag," she said, gesturing to all of her tattoos.

In fact, she explained, she grew up in Akademgorodok, a college town within Novosibirsk. For a while, it was one of the best gigs in the Soviet Union, so far in the middle of nowhere that people could get away with the unheard-of. Exhibitions of banned Soviet artists. Risqué poetry readings. Nude seminars on a manmade riverside beach. And the freedom to practice frowned-upon disciplines like genetics – her father's field.

"We actually lived in a *house*, wonder of wonders."

"Then why did your parents decide to leave?"

"Because by the time I was old enough to remember anything, all of that was gone. Brezhnev stagnation, in the seventies. My parents heard there was a big Russian community here, and my dad got snapped up by UCSF." She reached for the roach clip on her bedside table and used it to grasp the joint's dwindling nub. "And also, my dad thought my mom could get better help here."

He propped himself up on his elbow. "Your mom?"

He watched her take a final puff from the roach, and accepted the clip when she handed it to him. She said, "My mom had some sort of mental illness. She committed suicide two years after we moved here."

"Oh." The roach clip remained frozen in suspended animation.

He remembered her telling him, three years ago, that she was the one who found her mother dead. He knew from personal experience the trauma of something like that; but he couldn't begin to imagine the abject horror of finding someone he loved dead from suicide – much less a parent. Having to live with that image, and the questions of *why* and *what if*, for the rest of his life.

His own trauma suddenly paled by comparison.

Unsure what else to say, he added, "I'm so sorry." Then he cringed inwardly at the almost comical inadequacy of it.

She put her hand on his. "Save the roach. We can put it with some others and smoke it another time."

After she deposited the joint's remains on her bedside table, he reached for her and pulled her head down onto his chest. Her fingertips traced circles there.

They fell asleep tangled together like that, and when he next awoke, the sun was already up. So was he. He glanced at the bedside clock and felt a stab of panic – 7:36. His exam started in less than an hour.

She lay curled on her side, facing away from him. The sheet covered her only from her hips down. His eyes traced the curve of her spine, the Madonna and Child on her back. A six-winged seraph below that, matching the gold pendant she wore around her neck. Four lines of indecipherable Cyrillic script below that:

> Духовной жаждою томим,
> В пустыне мрачной я влачился, —
> И шестикрылый серафим
> На перепутье мне явился.

Painfully hard, he scooted over and wrapped his arms around her, spooning her. Planted kisses on her ear. Massaged her breasts until she stirred and murmured in greeting.

She turned her head back, smiling. Their mouths met, exploring, tasting. Deepening. Then, finding selflessness impossible, he slid inside of her.

She drew a sharp breath and held his stare with her own keen one. He seized her chin, unable to pace himself, unable to change positions, unable to do anything except submit to his own lust.

She drew her knees up, pushed his thighs with her feet and threw him back off of her. Spun around and, in one swift movement, pinned him onto his back with the weight of her body.

"You will not finish before me," she declared.

Her breasts dangled just above his lips, swinging like fruit on a branch as she rocked her hips, and each time that he craned his neck to sample, he felt himself tumbling over a precipice. But she wouldn't allow it. She reached between their bodies to stanch what had seemed inevitable moments before, as if twisting the shutoff valve on a hose. She reduced him nearly to a whimper, again and again. Losing patience, he made swift, tight circles with his fingers around her most sensitive spot, and she threw her head back with a groan of appreciation. At the end of an interval both too long and too short, she shouted unspeakable things in two languages and finally, blissfully permitted him to tumble headlong over that precipice with her. She crumpled into a spent heap on top of him, and he nuzzled her hair with his fingertips – he didn't know how long – until they caught their breath.

"Jesus," he panted finally. "*Wow.*"

She lifted her head, and said, "Good morning."

He gave a ragged sort of laugh, and she smiled in return. She reached behind his head, pulled him to her in a kiss, but he didn't close his eyes. The clock behind her read 8:02.

"You need to go?" she guessed.

Deeply conflicted and feeling guilty because of it, he kissed her again. "No. Do *you* need to go?"

"Not until eleven. I know where we can get breakfast."

Aware that he lay in a pool of sweat, he said, "I could use a shower."

He helped her strip the sheets off of her bed, then she took his hand and led him to the shower. Which turned out to be nearly futile, because at the end of it he wound up on her bed again, between her legs, pleasuring her on top of the towels they had spread over her mattress.

While she recovered from that, he lay alongside her in silence, stroking the skin between her navel and pubic bone with his fingertips. Tracing the line of Cyrillic writing that concealed her scar.

"Rely only on yourself," she translated for him.

He said nothing, just looked up at her and continued to caress her skin. She peered back at him for a while in that stoic way of hers. She said, "Remember when I was so unfriendly that day? When you came to my house to buy more weed? This is why. I tattooed it on myself, in case the scar wasn't enough of a reminder."

He still said nothing, waiting to see if she cared to elaborate. But she didn't.

"That makes me sad," he offered. "I'm glad you changed your mind."

"Me too," she replied, but she watched him rather warily, he thought. After a moment, she startled him by swinging abruptly out of bed, saying, "How about that breakfast?"

They got dressed and walked down Van Ness to a restaurant called Los Jarritos, where they were the only white people in the building. William ordered nopales con juevos and chilaquiles for them in Spanish.

"I guess I should learn to speak Spanish, since I live here now," Haze remarked while they waited for their food. "How did you learn to speak it so well? The processing plant?"

He shook his head. "You know that restaurant right across from the processing plant? Dunphy's? I'm a line cook there now."

"Really? When did that happen?"

The waitress delivered their coffee, and he took a huge chug. "A couple of years ago." He gulped down the rest of the coffee and lifted his mug, signaling the waitress, who ignored him. So he reluctantly turned back to Haze. He watched her watching him, making the connection.

She said, "I have an appointment at twelve, but then I'm going to start getting ready for the Festival of Altars."

"The what?"

"It's Día de los Muertos, you know."

"Oh. That's like Mexican Halloween, right? Where they dress up as skeletons?"

"*Calacas*," she clarified. "They're inviting their departed loved ones to celebrate with them. Building altars, with food and other things their loved ones enjoyed. And there's a procession through the Mission District, with music and Aztec dancers."

The waitress delivered their food, and while they dug into it, William weighed his options. He could call in sick to work, but he had promised himself he would never give Paul a single reason to complain. Julia would only hear good things about him.

Besides. What if – remote though the odds may be – Paul mentioned something about her? Or her mother did? Just to hear her *name*, for Christ's sake...

Haze derailed his train of thought by offering him a bite of her nopales con juevos. "Where do you have to be, after this?"

He chewed, glanced at his watch. 9:47. The exam had started at 8:30. "I have rehearsal at two. And I'm supposed to work at five."

Her eyebrows lifted. "Rehearsal?"

"Yeah; I'm filling in on lead guitar for Mike's new band. Just until they find someone permanent."

"Really? Why aren't *you* the permanent guitarist?"

"The band is Mike's dream, not mine."

"Fair enough, but it still sounds fun. What kind of music is it?"

"Irish pub rock. We haven't even had our first show yet. It's next Friday."

"Where?"

He could see where this line of inquiry was heading. He offered her a bite of his chilaquiles. "It's just at MacGowan's Pub, in the Sunset."

After chewing and swallowing, she said, "I'd love to see that."

"Of course," he said a little too quickly, a bit annoyed that she had just gone ahead and invited herself. For one thing, he worried he would fall flat on his face during his first show, and he didn't want her to witness it. But also, he wasn't sure how he was going to explain her presence to Mike. He didn't look forward to Mike's relentless ribbing. And he wasn't sure he was ready to come out as her boyfriend yet.

On their way back to her house, she tugged his sleeve and said, "I need to stop in here a minute."

He peered through the open door of the gift shop to the interior. A jumble of items, including accoutrements for Dia de los Muertos. He followed her as she gathered marigolds, votives, and colorful, lacy-looking paper.

"*Papel picado*," she explained. "For decoration."

At the counter she tried to explain to the clerk, in English and broken Spanish, that she was here to pick up something called a *calavera*, but the clerk didn't seem to understand. William stepped up and intervened, and in the end, the clerk emerged with a small decorated skull, a name written across the top of it: "Oksana."

Haze held it carefully, displaying it to him. "It's a sugar skull. It's a tradition to decorate these with the name of the loved one you're honoring."

"Your mother," he guessed, and she nodded. The votives and *papel picado* she placed in her bag, and the flowers she handed to William. But the *calavera* she carried in her hands the rest of the way to her house.

He followed her into the kitchen, where she deposited the flowers into water. By then it was eleven o'clock.

"Well, listen," she said. "In case you develop a little cough and need to call in sick to work, I'll be in Garfield Park at six, by the *Primal Sea* mural. You should like that one. I'll be in full *calavera* make-up, but you'll find me by my tattoos."

As he drove home, he wrestled with a sudden moment of clarity. Was he really going to let Julia stop him from living his life? She had made it abundantly clear to him with her silence – he had blown it, for good.

Madness to have assumed that his first love, a high school flame, would last the rest of his life. He was twenty years old, for Christ's sake, and Haze had already proven to him how much he might have missed out on.

He wasn't oblivious to the interest he attracted from women. Besides Cindy and Haze, there was the chick who sat in front of him in Macroeconomics and kept turning her head back to steal a glance. There was the girl at the gas station, checking him out as she filled up her GTI.

Who got married at age twenty? Who had sex with only one woman, his entire life?

Ridiculous.

"WHAT'S THE LONG CON?"

At home he showered again, rinsing the rest of Haze's scent from his beard, and grabbed a quick nap. Made a sandwich, slung his guitar case over his shoulder, and took the bus to the house in West Portal with the soundproofed garage beneath it.

The homeowner kept the garage door permanently shut, so he knocked on the front door of the house. Mike frowned and grumbled about something as he admitted him; something about someone "significantly lowering the average pussy magnetism in the room."

"Mike, what are you bitching about now?" William demanded. But soon enough, Mike opened the door from the interior of the house to the garage. William discovered for himself the assemblage of peculiar instruments on the floor, and the thirty-something man fiddling with them. A mandolin. A bodhrán. A concertina, and a tin whistle. Even a banjo.

Niall, wearing a flat cap and his signature sweater vest, sprang forward from the corner of the room where he assembled his drum set to clap a hand on William's shoulder. "There you are! Let me introduce you to Christopher."

The thirty-something's head popped up from the mandolin he was tuning, and Niall said, "Christopher, our lead guitarist, William. William, our Irish multi-instrumentalist, Christopher."

"I'm Northern Irish, actually," clarified Christopher, coming forward to shake William's hand.

"And I'm the *temporary* lead guitarist, actually," William further clarified, still feeling peevish from his last argument with Niall on the subject. He eyeballed Christopher and understood why Mike had been complaining. Not that William really cared about such things, but Christopher, with his desultory expression, his slight paunch, and his receding hairline, wouldn't add any sex appeal to their lineup. Not even his earrings, heavy black claws that stretched his earlobes and seemed tacked on as an afterthought, would help on that front.

"See, I told you I'd come through," Niall declared, beaming. "A single man who could do it all."

While William unpacked his guitar and plugged it into the amp, Mike wandered over and grumbled, "I don't see why we needed all that extra shit."

"You said it was Irish pub rock, right? Part punk, part folk? Well, where did you think the folk was going to come from?"

"Yeah, but *folk*, not a fucking polka band!"

"Just give the dude a shot. It can't hurt anything, for one rehearsal."

Mike took himself off, now grumbling some bullshit about Christopher being a "fuckin' Orangey;" and William finished tuning his guitar.

He strummed a few chords lazily. He watched Christopher strike the bodhrán with its double-tipped beater, then nimbly pump out a few verses on the concertina. Watched Mike depart the garage in search of the bathroom.

A song emerged from the chords William strummed – a song he knew by heart. Mike had long ago taught him to read music well enough to learn his favorite Pink Floyd and Led Zeppelin songs; but he had never bothered writing down the music to the melodies he created. He stored all of that in his head.

Niall's voice at his shoulder startled him from his reverie. "Does that melody have lyrics to go with it?"

William had mailed the lyrics to her in the shoe box. He shook his head no.

"It's a shame. Do you think you can come up with some?"

William said nothing. Changed to a tune they had previously worked on together.

"Listen," Niall persisted, "Mike can bitch all he wants about Christopher and his 'significantly lowering the average pussy magnetism in the room.' But Mike significantly lowers the average *IQ* in the room. No offense, friend; I know he's your brother, but it's the truth."

"No offense taken."

"But you know what would significantly *raise* the average IQ in the room?"

"You need to learn to take no for an answer, dude."

Niall clapped a hand on his shoulder. "You have no faith in me! I was going to say some thoughtful tunes with some well-crafted lyrics. As sort of a counter-balance to all of Mike's manic energy. To give the audience a bit of a rest, you see."

"I don't think rest is the vision Mike has for the band, or the audience."

Niall grinned and squeezed William's shoulder, as if humoring him. "That's because Mike is not a strategic thinker. He doesn't understand the long con."

"Okay, I'll bite. What's the long con?"

Niall squatted down beside William. Stretched his arm out with a faraway look, as if surveying a vast expanse in the distance. "We're playing in a pub. And guys don't come to a pub to hear the music. They come to the pub to meet girls. But how many girls are coming to hear Mike's version of the band?"

"I don't think Mike cares about that. Mike's end game is to resurrect old-school punk."

"Yeah, but all that stuff he worships? The Tool and Die, The Farm, The Deaf Club? All that was dead and gone before he hit puberty. Nobody wants punk anymore. At least, not unless it's cleaned up and dressed all pretty for MTV, like that Green Day shite."

"I kind of like Green Day. They're not horrible."

"Exactly! That's exactly my point, my friend. So why did Mike sign on for pub rock if he really wanted punk?"

"I don't know, Niall. Shouldn't you be having this conversation with Mike?"

Niall gave him a deer in the headlights look, then unfurled one of his contagious laughs. "You're right. But I think you're the man in the best position to get through to him."

William never thought he'd see the day when Mike, of all people, had the most artistic integrity in the group. At least Mike didn't want to compromise his vision for mercenary commercial reasons. But then again, there was a balance to be had somewhere between pure artistic integrity, and flopping.

"You're framing it to him all wrong," William offered.

"How's that?"

"The girls. We don't sell ourselves to girls so we can attract the guys. We sell ourselves to girls, for ourselves."

Niall's jaw dropped, and he slapped William's shoulder again. "I can't believe what a plonker I am."

Mike returned to the garage then. Niall leaped up and declared, "Right! Let's get started, shall we?"

What happened over the next few minutes was a revelation. Christopher's additions elevated the set list from a collection of punk songs whose lyrics coincidentally celebrated the working class, women, drinking, and Irish nationalism – to *Irish pub rock*. William's eyes traveled from one bandmate to the next. Christopher, suddenly wide-awake and freed from the constraints of his surplus flesh. Mike, slack-jawed at the overthrow of all of his dismal expectations. Niall, beaming triumphantly.

William felt his spirits soaring. He had no idea if their set would be the "pussy magnet" Mike hoped for. But for the first time, it was fun as hell.

After the first song, Niall started to give some feedback, but Mike cut him short by dropping his bass guitar and going to wrap Christopher in a hug, slapping him on the back. Christopher's initial shock and Niall's amusement at the spectacle triggered William's own laughter, burbling up quite involuntarily from somewhere deep in his gut.

When the rehearsal ended, William approached Niall as he dismantled his drum set.

"You asked me earlier if my melody had any lyrics to go with it."

"Yeah?"

"I lied. It does."

The lyrics were so ambiguous and metaphorical that he knew no one would ever figure out who they were about, anyway. He played it for him, and Mike and Christopher eavesdropped while they finished putting away their instruments.

"Can you play acoustic guitar?" Niall inquired when he finished.

"Of course."

"I think that's the way to go on a serenade like that."

William nodded and helped him load his drums into the van. When he returned to the garage, he found Mike wrapping up cords. It was mid-afternoon, and foggy, and William's energy was tanking precipitously. He watched Mike light a cigarette and take a drag. He said, "Hey, can I bum one of those?"

Mike turned to look at him, startled. "You're smoking now?"

William shook his head. "I'm just really tired. I didn't get enough sleep last night."

"Right on," Mike ribbed, which didn't bode well for what William was about to tell him. Mike held out the pack of Camels, and William selected one. While Mike flicked the Zippo, he said, "Come get a drink with us. We're going to MacGowan's."

William took a couple of puffs from the cigarette and shook his head. "I can't. I told Haze I was coming over."

Mike shrugged. "So come over after you score some."

William couldn't help giving a short laugh at Mike's choice of words. He turned to look at him, but said nothing.

Mike's eyes widened, and he appeared to nearly lose all muscle tone. "You're fucking kidding me."

William turned away again. Took another drag from the cigarette.

"Oh – no way. Just – no way." Mike gave one of his jackhammer laughs. Clapped his hand on William's shoulder, and shook him. "How did you manage it?"

William blew smoke. "Manage what?"

"Oh, shut up!"

William couldn't help giving a bit of a snicker.

"Wow. I stand in awe of you, little brother. I never would have seen it coming, but you have managed the nearly impossible - you have surpassed both me and Jimmy. Of course, you did have the very best teachers."

"Give it a rest, Mike. I only told you because she's coming to our show next Friday. So keep your mouth shut when you see her, okay?"

Mike lifted his hands. "For my brother's girlfriend? Perfect gentleman."

"Thank you; but she's not exactly my girlfriend."

"Best friends with benefits?" suggested Mike, quoting a line William recognized from a song on the radio. Some pissed-off chick named Atlantis, or something.

"I think she's a bit wounded," William explained, thinking of the C-section scar.

"You're right, you know. She closed down shop and left San Francisco in…" He turned his face up to the ceiling, squinting through one eye. "I think it was in '92. Yeah, it had to be '92, because it was right after she gave you that tat. I heard it was for a man, but I didn't believe it at the time because I thought she was a dyke."

"Why, because she wouldn't sleep with *you*?"

Mike dealt him a good-natured punch to the shoulder. It hurt, but of course William didn't let on. "She was gone for… I don't know. I guess she only came back a few months ago. And the next time I saw her, she had all those new tats."

William considered a moment, then made up his mind. "Hey, will you take me home?"

"Sure, man."

"Wait for me a second. I just have to make a phone call."

He left the garage and found his way to the telephone mounted on the wall in the kitchen. Lifted the receiver, and dialed the number he had memorized for Dunphy's. Asked for Paul, and called in sick.

"YOU CAN CALL ME SIMOCHKA."

At six o'clock, he found the *Primal Sea* mural in Garfield Park and looked for her tattoos. He found her, in the same torso skeleton tank top she had worn on Halloween, her gray-streaked hair crowned with a tiara of marigolds, her face painted with expert intricacy in *calavera* makeup. She hadn't spotted him yet, so he hung back, watching her. She had placed a box on the ground, and atop that she draped a red blanket. Part of the blanket also draped the ground in front of the box. On top of the makeshift altar, she placed an ornate picture frame with a black and white photo of a young woman. Blond hair, light-colored eyes, broad face. Almost Mongolian features. Haze surrounded the photo with marigolds, exotic sweets, and containers of mysterious libations labeled in Cyrillic script. Votives, which she attempted to light.

Women and girls nearby tried to talk to her in animated voices, but she couldn't understand them.

"They want to know who did your makeup for you," he said, by way of announcing himself.

She didn't even look up. She recognized him by his voice alone, and smiled. "Tell them I did it myself."

"Lo hizo ella misma," he told them.

They looked startled to find him speaking Spanish to them. A volley of exclamations followed, one tumbling over the other so he couldn't understand them. He decided to take advantage of the mass confusion.

"They want to know if that's your mother," he lied.

"Si," Haze replied to the women and girls. "Mi madre. Oksana."

Of course they looked confused by her response, and William put a hand over his mouth to stifle his laughter. But one of the ladies graciously replied, "Era bellisima, su madre."

"Tan hermosa," agreed another.

"Si. Hermosa como la hija," agreed William, turning to smile at Haze.

Another volley of exclamations followed, from which he discerned that they approved of his flattery of his *novia*. The next thing he understood was one of the women asking, "¿Era china?"

"Claro que no," replied another, "Mira su pelo rubio."

"Rusa," William clarified.

"Ah, si, claro, rusa."

Haze was having a hard time lighting the votives in the wind. He crouched down beside her and cupped his hand around the rim of one while she lit it. She still smiled.

"I see you caught a cold during your rehearsal," she said.

He watched her face the whole time. He wanted to kiss her, but he didn't dare mess up her perfectly executed face paint. Her eyes were black smudges, ringed with fuschia blossoms and purple jewels. A teal-colored bindi-like jewel on her forehead, surrounded by a lotus blossom. The vines spreading with tiny blossoms and jewels over her cheeks. The white and teal of her face, and the pink of her lips all blending, contouring together seamlessly. The sharp black nasal cavities and the gash from ear to ear and across her mouth. The vertical black stitches atop her pink lips.

He never would have seen it coming, such breathtaking artistry; but then he wondered why not?

"Help me set up my *ofrenda* to my mother," she invited him.

He helped her string up the *papel picado* like bunting over the altar. Helped arrange the sugar skulls, including the one with her mother's name on it.

They drank with her mother – *kvas*, she explained, a sweet non-alcoholic beer; and *mors*, a fermented berry drink. They ate the *pastila* – various small, square confections made of sour apples, honey, and egg whites.

They toured the other *ofrendas*, including a popular one to a dead singer named Selena, and stopped at a "tree of life," where they could write notes to departed loved ones on slips of white paper. Haze grabbed one and scrawled something in Russian, presumably to her mother, since one of the first words he picked out was "мама." He couldn't help noticing the closing greeting, as well:

Люблю,
сима

He pointed to the last word. "Is that your name in Russian?"

"Yes – the short form. Sima. In Russia, friends and family never call each other by their full names." She clipped her note to a wire branch of the tree and said, "Do you have anyone to write to? It doesn't have to be to someone who's dead. It can be to someone who's not with you tonight."

For half a second he considered writing something to Julia, but for obvious reasons he quickly dismissed that thought. His next idea still felt way too raw and vulnerable to reveal to Haze. But something about Haze in her face paint and this place encouraged him to throw all caution to the wind. Before he could change his mind, he seized a piece of paper and a pen, and wrote:

Dear Nonna,
I'm sorry. I'll do better.
Love,
Will

He did not look at Haze, and thankfully she didn't say anything. He felt the choking sensation. He bit his tongue – hard – until he tasted blood. He clipped the note to the tree branch and watched his slip of paper fluttering alongside hers.

She took his hand, wove her fingers through his and led him silently to the procession. They watched the drummers and took in the homemade floats, constructed atop pickup trucks and bicycles. Mictecacihuatl, queen of the Aztec underworld, pulled on a wagon altar. The thirteen standards processed by – snake, rat, wolf, and more. They watched the Aztec dancers, their ankles festooned with bands of beads that clacked like castanets, their colorful, sometimes sparse costumes glittering, their headdresses soaring with spikes of tall, colored feathers. And everywhere, the *calacas* and *calaveras*, like Haze in her face paint and skeleton tank top, which she now covered partially with a black leather jacket.

The atmosphere was festive, yet respectful; the air perfumed with incense and the occasional whiff of cannabis.

At the end of the procession, they returned to Garfield Park, where William helped disassemble Haze's *ofrenda* and load the components into the wagon she had brought with her.

"Are you hungry?" she asked.

"Starving," he admitted.

They were on Mission Street now, walking north toward her house. She pointed across the street to a storefront with a mural of the Virgin of Guadalupe. A lighthouse on a yellow awning below that proclaimed it as "Taqueria El Farolito."

"Let's get a burrito and take it back to my place," she suggested.

In her kitchen, she invited him to dig in to his burrito while she washed off her face paint, an offer he happily took her up on. He also helped himself to an airplane mini-bottle or four of tequila to wash it down.

She joined him at the table, fresh-faced without a speck of makeup. She usually wore a little something – some black eyeliner, perhaps, or a smear of brick-red lipstick. After sex or sleeping, her makeup smudged, and then she freshened up as soon as she got out of bed.

Now, as she took her seat across the table from him and unwrapped her burrito, she smiled at him a bit self-consciously.

Impulsively, he seized her hand. "What days do you work?"

"Every day except Sunday."

"I don't work Sunday, either. Do you want to do something?"

She gave a wry smile, withdrew her hand, and snagged one of his mini-bottles of tequila. Unscrewed it, and took a swig.

"My dad doesn't speak to me anymore, but when he did, he kept asking me why I don't just date a nice Jewish boy. I tried to explain to him – the nice Jewish boys he has in mind would never date a girl like me, anyway."

"Why not?"

"Well, I mean…" She held up her arms, wrapped in animal tattoos, and flicked the ring in her nose. She hesitated a moment, then pointed to the cupolas above her neckline and the eyes that flanked them. "These are supposed to be prison tattoos, you know."

He felt his stomach lurch. "You were in prison?"

She laughed. "Not exactly. I was in Brighton Beach." When he still drew a blank, she explained, "Little Odessa? The American headquarters of the Russian Mafia? It's in Brooklyn."

"Really? And you got those there?"

She nodded. "After our mother died, my brother and I went to live there with my father's relatives."

"You have a brother." He had always assumed she was an only child – an orphan, for all intents and purposes.

"I have two, actually," she clarified, sipping her tequila. "Kirill – he's an Orthodox priest. And Vasya – the one who went with me to Brooklyn. He still lives there. He and I got into a lot of trouble, playing around like real *vor*."

"*Vor*?"

"You know, like – made men."

"Did you actually know anyone in the Russian mafia?"

"You couldn't run the streets unsupervised like we did without bumping into one or two. They made a big impression. We took all that *vor* crap very seriously. We gave each other our first tattoos." She patted her knees, where he had earlier spied what resembled compass roses. "Stars. They mean, 'I kneel to no one.' He was sixteen, but I was only twelve." She took another bite from the burrito. Chewed thoughtfully. "I told you about my other brother, Kirill – the priest. He lives in Anchorage."

Anchorage. "Alaska?"

She nodded. "There's a large Russian Orthodox community up there, left over from its days as a Russian colony. Kirill knew of a good rehab facility up there – you know, after all that crap with Jimmy – and he convinced me that the change of scenery would help sobriety stick."

William plucked a black bean from his burrito and popped it in his mouth. He reached for her hand again. Examined the ring tattoos on her fingers – a circle with a dot inside of it. A skull inside of a square, and a circled A. An Orthodox cross inside of a diamond.

She abruptly withdrew her hand and got up to retrieve more salsa from the kitchen counter. When she returned, she said, "Vasya was nose-diving and taking me along with him. My relatives sent me back to San Francisco, but by then I was fourteen and I had already started dealing. And using."

Once again, he reached across the table and took up her hand. Touched the animal tattoos, running his fingertips up the length of her arm.

She looked down at them, and smiled. "The Siberian ice maiden."

"What?"

"A mummy they found in Altai Republic, where my mother was born. They found the ice maiden in 1993. She was buried alone, surrounded by all her things for the afterlife, including a container of cannabis."

William couldn't help laughing out loud at this last detail. "How perfect."

"But the most amazing thing was her tattoos. Like this one, here on my shoulder." She pointed to the bucking deer-griffin hybrid, with the flowering antlers. "There were other mummies, too, and I totally ripped off all their designs. This may sound crazy, but when I saw the pictures in National Geographic, it was like my mother was there, looking at them with me. Like I was seeing them through her eyes, or something. I knew that's what my arms had been waiting for all these years."

"I don't think that's crazy," William murmured.

"My son – Asher – he was born in February of this year. His father, Matt... my ex-husband..."

She paused here and peered up at William, as if to gauge his reaction. Whatever she saw in his eyes must have satisfied her, because she continued.

"Matt is an Alaska Native. A lot of Alaska Natives are Russian Orthodox. I met him at my brother's church, at a Narcotics Anonymous meeting. And that's where we got married – at Kirill's church. But Matt is an addict, like me, and he relapsed, and then he cheated on me. And I had no way to support Asher by myself. So after he was born,

I left him with Matt's mother, and came back here to try and get a business up and running."

"I'm so sorry," was all that William could think to say.

"I had just come back to San Francisco in April when I saw that National Geographic article." She looked down at her tattoos, at William's hand caressing them. The grooves between her eyebrows deepened. "You know, some cultures use tattoos as medicine."

"I know." He again considered telling her about his albatross tattoo. He just couldn't. Sacrilege.

"Medicine, and armor," she clarified.

"What do you mean?"

She shrugged. "Pretty much the only guys who fetishize this are white American guys, like you."

"Is that why you think I'm with you? Because I fetishize you?"

"Don't you?"

"Well... yeah."

She burst out laughing. He had never seen her laugh so freely before, and he couldn't help smiling at the way it revealed lines in her face and around her eyes that he had never noticed. He added, "But not because of your tattoos. Not for any reason, actually – I was just teasing."

"I'm not quite sure how to take that," she said, still snickering.

"I just think you're a beautiful woman, all around. It's a shame if anyone doesn't see that. Their loss."

She gaped in disbelief, then leaned across the table and kissed him. "Yes. I'd love to do something with you Sunday."

Upstairs, in her bed, she said, "This is all I could think about, all day."

"Me too," he lied.

As she kissed her way down his torso, he gave a little shudder of anticipation and said, "Sima." It was out of the blue. He had no idea where it came from.

She looked up at him, and said, "Simochka."

"Hm?"

"You can call me Simochka."

After she dropped off to sleep, he lay awake a few minutes longer, despite his physical exhaustion. His mind racing, still buzzed from all the alcohol and weed and confusion.

He understood now. Sex with Haze was good because of her experience and skill. But Julia's entire *being*, physical and otherwise, lit him on fire. Every single nerve ending in his body scintillated, even when he merely thought of her. It was that total quenching, that ultimate spiritual and physical consummation, that he craved.

But it didn't matter. He would never have that again, certainly not with Julia. Meanwhile, here was Haze. Sexy, smart, talented in so many ways. Kind, generous – but no pushover. And into *him*.

He could work with that. That could grow. He could have that ultimate consummation again.

DECEMBER 1993

"I FOLLOWED YOU AROUND FIRST."

The week after Thanksgiving, for the first time ever, William accepted Julia's invitation for sex in her bedroom after school. Nobody was home, she assured him, not even her sister. Nevertheless, when he arrived, he made her check every room of the house, and he himself plotted all possible escape routes.

"Should I check under my parents' bed?" she teased as she led him by the hand and pushed open her bedroom door. "What about the attic?"

But he didn't answer because there he was – his first foray into the mysterious habitat of a girl (his sister didn't count). Julia closed the door behind them and twisted the lock. She gave him an almost shy smile, and said, "Welcome to my lair."

What jumped out at him immediately was the tropical aquarium that, though shallow in depth, spanned the width of nearly the entire opposite wall. Like a giant lava lamp, it burbled and swirled with an ever-shifting palette of aquamarine, gold, scarlet, and neon purple. In addition to the half-dozen or so species that he didn't know, he recognized a seahorse, a sea star, and various corals.

One spectacular fish drew him closer to the tank – a striped mandarin, she explained. At first he didn't even think it was real, painted as it was in the neon version of almost every color of the rainbow.

He slid his arm around her waist and watched it for a while, along with the other aquarium inhabitants. It was hypnotic. He wondered what would become of all of these creatures, once she moved to Santa Barbara and couldn't care for them anymore. She'd have to find new homes for them all.

Eventually he looked around some more, and his eyes settled on the colorfully-framed photos on the wall.

"Oh," he said.

She took his hand and led him to the nearest one – the Castro Theatre, illuminated at night. She had matted it inside of a rectangular frame, covered in turquoise fabric and bedazzled with sparkling beads in various colors. Next to that, the Guatemalan textile market in the Mission, its square frame covered in fabric with a gold and white chevron pattern. Further along the wall, the crab boats at sunset. The sea lions on the Farallon Islands. All of the photos he had given her at Dunphy's on his birthday.

Then the photos of the blue whale that they had seen on his uncle's boat, where he had kissed her for the first time. He had given them to her in October, for her birthday.

"Did you frame these yourself?" he asked. The eclectic hodgepodge of frames reflected her quirky personality to a tee.

She nodded. "I made the frames especially for them."

He had expected to find New Kids On The Block or Johnny Depp paraphernalia on her walls. And okay, so he did find a *Benny & Joon* movie poster opposite her bed. But the fact that she had dedicated one whole wall to his photos touched him more deeply than he could have imagined.

He slid his arms around her waist again. Turned her face up to his, and spent a while kissing her. She reached for the belt around the waist of his khaki school uniform pants and lazily unbuckled it.

When his pants crumpled to the floor, she looked up at him again with a sly smile. But she must have seen something in his face, because she said, "What?"

He smiled back, shook his head. "I don't know. I just... I followed you around helplessly for so long, and for some reason you took a liking to me."

As she reached into the front of his boxers, she pinned him with a sultry look. "Hey, Captain Oblivious - don't you know? I followed you around first."

Later, as he ambled home down Taraval, his brain awash in post-coital chemicals, he passed the window display of a jewelry store with signage only in Chinese. A silver mermaid pendant on a necklace display stopped him in his tracks.

The Halloween party at her cousin's house. The music, the fellow revelers, the entire world had faded into the background. Purple clam shells clinging to her breasts. Copper hair swept across one shoulder, rippling in waves down the front of her body. Iridescent aquamarine mermaid tail, hugging her spectacular, perky little rump as she sat in his lap. He had been utterly powerless to conceal from her the effect that she was having on him.

Not long after, she had relieved him of his virginity.

It was almost five o'clock; the jewelry store was about to close. He pushed open the door; bells on the door jangled, announcing his presence. The Chinese woman cleaning the glass display cases peered up at him in some surprise. He wondered if he was the only white person who had ever come into this store. He wondered if she could even speak English. He pointed to the window display and asked to see the mermaid necklace. She lifted it from its display and handed it to him.

It was a bright silver pendant, only about half an inch long, on a thin silver chain. The mermaid was shaped like an S, with her tail tucked under her body and her hair rippling over one shoulder, just like Julia's.

He asked how much. Twenty-five dollars. He held his wallet open to show her – he had only a twenty dollar bill. She said some things, mostly unintelligible, from which he discerned that she would sell it to him for twenty dollars, including tax.

While she placed the necklace into a black box and rang him up, he peered inside a display case in front of the register. The case's interior glinted with rubies, emeralds, gemstones he didn't even know the names of – and of course, diamonds. He squatted to look closer. Among the necklaces, earrings, and bracelets was a small selection of rings.

William recalled the last time he and Nonna cooked together, when she taught him how to sweat eggplant to keep it from turning greasy. Nonna had said, "Will, if you ever fall in love with a woman, don't degrade her by living in sin."

It was one of her old-school Sicilian platitudes that she occasionally scattered among the pearls. He humored it, then tucked it out of mind. Yet now his memory exhumed it, for some reason. Probably because until he met Julia, Nonna had been the only one in his life who had ever reassured him he wasn't some wing nut, something *less than*, just because he liked poetry, songwriting, and cooking. But then Julia had taken it a step further – she had helped him see that his more artistic inclinations were actually good things. Something desirable – preferable, even. Something worth embracing.

Yes. There was only one thing in life he was really sure about.

Interrupting his train of thought, the clerk pointed to the display case and said, "You want to see?"

He nodded. She unlocked the display case and brought out the ring display with all the different rings to choose from, including the diamond ones. Despite everything, he still felt slightly ridiculous doing this at all, let alone in front of a total stranger who barely spoke English. His palms were moist. He swallowed the lump of embarrassment welling in his throat and pointed to the ring with the largest stone.

"How much?"

Twenty-three fifty. He knew she didn't mean twenty-three dollars and fifty cents.

He pointed to the next smallest one. Sixteen-fifty.

To hell with what his Catholic grandmother would say – this was the nineties. He would go right on living in sin.

She asked, "How much?"

He realized she was trying to ask how much he wanted to spend.

How much *did* he have in mind? He couldn't fathom being able to afford more than five hundred. In response, they went back and forth in mutual misunderstanding for a minute, until the lady shouted back into some covert compartment of the store.

A previously-hidden teenage girl emerged. Oversized glasses, long stringy black hair, braces on her teeth. Her eyes locked on his, and with a jolt, they recognized each other.

"William!"

"Michelle." From AP Biology. "You work here?"

"Of course! This is my parents' shop. And this is my mom." Then she shot William a quizzical look. "What are *you* doing here?"

"Uh..." His face burned, and he glanced around himself. How quickly could he escape?

Before he could come up with some cover story, the clerk assailed Michelle with a barrage of Chinese. Michelle's jaw dropped, and she turned again to William.

"Oh my God!" she gushed. "You're getting an engagement ring for Julia?"

"I... uh..."

She clapped her hands. "Oh my God, that is so beautiful! She's going to be so excited!" She turned back to her mom and unleashed another barrage of rapid Chinese, after which her mom turned to William with a big smile and said, "Ahhhhhh!"

Once again, her mom exchanged a few words with Michelle, after which Michelle said to him bluntly, "Oh, you don't want a five hundred dollar engagement ring."

Taken aback, William said, "Um..."

Michelle seized the smallest diamond ring in the lineup and held it up to him – five hundred dollars. She snatched the ring next to it – also a quarter-carat, identical in every way as far as he could tell. Same setting, same eighteen-karat white gold.

Nine-fifty.

She held them, side-by-side, just underneath his nose, inviting him to spot the difference. His face still radiating hot embarrassment, he leaned over the rings.

"No," Michelle said, snatching them from the shadows created by his head. "In the light."

He looked again, this time taking care not to shade the rings with his head. And then he saw it – the nine-fifty ring blew the five hundred ring out of the water. It was noticeably clearer. More brilliant.

"I – I don't think I can come up with nine-fifty."

"You can put it on layaway," offered Michelle.

He hesitated for just a moment. Then he waved it away. "That's okay. Not now."

"Aw, really?" Michelle sucked her teeth in dismay. "Well, if you change your mind, you know where to find us!"

Obviously annoyed, Michelle's mom whisked the ring display away. William snatched the box with the mermaid necklace, mumbled his thanks, and high-tailed it out of the jewelry store as fast as possible.

At least he had a nice Christmas present for Julia.

"I'D LIKE TO PUT IT ON LAYAWAY."

After the semester ended, William did something unprecedented and requested an entire week of winter break off of work. Julia followed suit, and they had the whole week to spend together. He put her on the back of his motorcycle and showed her all the hidden spots around the Bay Area that he had discovered on his own, spots that no one else seemed to have discovered for lack of adventurousness or persistence. She was game for anything that he was game for.

One morning, Julia propped herself up in his bed and looked at him. "Every time I come here, that guitar case is sitting in the same spot against the wall, looking all shut up and forlorn."

"Oh, no you don't."

"Oh, yes I do. Can you play it?"

"No."

"Liar."

He laughed a bit. "Mike taught himself to play when we were kids, and then he taught me. We used to think we were going to have a band one day, Mike and me. Actually, come to think of it, I think that was mostly Mike's dream."

"Well, I can't picture you as a rock star. But I can picture you playing it for me."

He shook his head. "I want to get you back in my bed again someday."

She sat upright, completely naked. It was one of many things he adored about her – her complete comfort with her own nakedness. She had never shown a moment's shame or timidity on that score.

"Oh, see, you have it all wrong," she said. "You won't get me back in this bed again if you *don't* play for me."

"You are a vicious tyrant." But he grinned and got out of bed to retrieve the guitar. He spent a few minutes tuning it, then began strumming.

He had a secret passion for cheesy folk music and singer-songwriters from the sixties and early seventies. He was tempted to play *As We Go Along*, by The Monkees. He just couldn't. He'd choke.

A Pink Floyd tune emerged from his fingertips.

"You forget, your brother told me all your secrets," interrupted Julia. "I know you can sing."

He put his hand on the strings. "Oh no, I only agreed to play."

"You have nothing in writing."

He shook his head. "Please don't make me."

She grabbed his hand. "I have a confession to make. I'm getting back in your bed again, no matter what you sound like."

He grinned and began strumming the guitar again. Played the intro to *Wish You Were Here*. Paused just before he was about to start singing, reddened and laughed nervously. Started over again, and sang.

He was nervous to be sure, and his voice cracked a bit in the beginning. He avoided her eyes throughout, looked down at the guitar or across at the wall. But after a while, his voice gained strength, he played competently, and when he finished, he lifted his eyes to hers with a little smile. She rewarded his efforts with her own bright smile and applause.

"Now I know the real reason you're such a Pink Floyd fan," she said. "You sound just like what's-his-name, minus the British accent."

"Don't insult him."

She sucked her teeth and admonished him with a little shove on the shoulder. "Your modesty and hero worship are cute. But why such a sad song?"

It genuinely startled him that she interpreted it that way – as merely a *sad song*. "It's a beautiful song. Rips my heart out more than almost anything else I've ever heard."

"Exactly. I demand cheering up after that."

He put the guitar back in its case. "I'll have to find some other way to cheer you up, then."

"Oh, promises, promises," she said as he came to lie next to her.

He draped himself halfway over her and held her face in his hands, inches away from his own. She beamed up at him in anticipation of his next move.

"How do you do this?" he said.

"Do what?"

"Make me wonder why I would ever want to be sad in the first place. Make me feel more like my own self than I have in years."

She gave a short laugh. "In years? You're eighteen and a half, old man." She brushed the hair back off of his forehead, contemplative a moment. "Just be yourself. You don't need me or anyone else to give you permission."

His mind drifted toward his bedside table, where he hid the mermaid necklace in its box. He had planned to give it to her for Christmas, but he yearned to do something for her right now. Something to return just a little bit of the contentment she had given him. Something besides another orgasm.

He poked her in the shoulder. "Let's go get breakfast. There's somewhere I want to take you after that."

"Where?"

"It's a surprise."

They got dressed, and while she braided her hair in the bathroom, he reached into the bedside table and slipped the necklace box into an interior pocket of his coat. They went to eat at the 46th Avenue diner, and afterward, he drove her to a hilly residential area of the Inner Sunset and parked his motorcycle.

"This is obviously not where I was planning to take you," he said. "But it's not far away from here, if you want to walk."

"How far?"

"Just over there," he said, pointing up Turtle Hill. "I think you'll like it."

He led her to a large hill with a long set of stairs ascending it. He took her hand, and together they climbed the stairs to the top of the hill. He helped her gingerly down a narrow path and across treacherous, uneven ground scattered with tree roots and rocks.

Finally, he tapped her on the shoulder and pointed.

"Look."

She caught her breath in a gasp. It was a clear winter morning, and the city spread out before them, with downtown to their right, Golden Gate Park and the bridge in front of them, and the Pacific Ocean to their left. He led her to a bench to sit beside him. There was nobody else there, no one else crazy enough to brave that spot at that time. It was cold and windy, but it was beautiful.

He pulled her close beside him and put his arm around her shoulders to keep her warm. "I didn't just bring you up here to show you the view and freeze your ass off. I wanted to give you a Christmas present. But I'm warning you, please don't get too excited."

"You can't give it to me now," she protested. "I don't have your present here with me."

"That doesn't matter."

He reached into the inside pocket of his coat and pulled out the necklace box. He opened it, and held up the silver chain with the pendant swinging from it.

"This is lame, I know, but it's just a promise," he said, fastening the chain around her neck. "I promise I'll never stop loving you, no matter what."

She lifted the pendant to take a closer look, and smiled. "A mermaid. Now why on earth would that make you think of me?"

He squeezed her around the shoulders. "I'll never forget that night as long as I live. I was so in love with you, and when I saw you, I really thought I could have died a happy man, right then and there."

She looked up at him again, her eyes wide, her mouth hanging open slightly. She searched his face and, apparently finding it sincere, she laced her fingers through his. After kissing him, she whispered, "You make me so happy."

"Good," he murmured, touching the pendant. "Wear it as long as you still feel that way."

She wrapped her arms around him, and they sat there for a long time, not saying anything, surveying the world spread before them. To him, at that moment, it seemed like a vast, open expanse with limitless possibilities.

"Will," she ventured after a few quiet minutes. "What did you mean earlier? When you said I make you feel more like yourself than you have in years?"

William gave a sheepish laugh and tightened his grip around her shoulders. "You remember when I told you about my brother Jimmy? And how my Nonna was the only one in my family who really supported me?"

Julia turned her gray-green eyes up to his, searching with such earnest concern that his face melted into a tender smile. He paused just long enough to kiss the tip of her nose before continuing.

"After Nonna died, I just kind of gave up on writing poems and songs for a while. And by a while, I mean until I met you."

"Oh," she breathed, her face a riot of different emotions – elation, compassion, sadness.

"I shouldn't have given up, though. She wouldn't have wanted that," William admitted.

"You were grieving."

William hummed. "I let myself wallow in it, though. I just... I guess I felt alienated. But now I know it was mostly self-imposed."

"It sounds like depression," Julia said matter-of-factly.

William considered a moment, then slowly nodded. "I guess so."

One corner of her mouth tipped up. "But you're not anymore?"

"Depressed?" His features softened again into what he knew was a derpy-looking smile. "Definitely not. You reminded me I had the key with me the whole time."

She tilted her head quizzically. "What key?"

"The one to the cage."

Understanding dawned over her face as she rubbed his back, right over his albatross tattoo. His pulse suddenly galloping, he dove his head to capture her mouth in a kiss. She gently tugged at his bottom lip with her teeth, and he answered by licking at the seam of her lips until they parted for his tongue.

After several minutes of heated making out, during which their coats somehow migrated off their bodies and onto the ground, Julia whispered, "You still owe me a cheering-up, from earlier." Cupping his rigid length over his jeans, she added, "Promises, promises, remember?"

A rumble escaped from somewhere deep in his chest, and William whipped his head around – they were still alone. Then, like a starved man, he devoured her mouth again while she unzipped his fly, snaking her hand inside. He tipped his head back with a hiss of pleasure as she stroked him over his boxers.

"I thought you said I owed *you*," he gritted out. She giggled, but her only reply was to shimmy her hand down inside his boxers.

Approaching voices had them both groaning in frustration, then snickering as William scrambled to contain himself back inside of his jeans. "Come on," Julia suggested, "let's get an early lunch at the Cliff House. Hand jobs make me hungry."

Thirty minutes later, while they awaited their food beside the floor-to-ceiling windows overlooking the ocean and the waves, she excused herself to the restroom. She was gone a long time, so when she finally returned, he said, "I was about to send out a search party."

"Sorry," she said with a sheepish smile and no further explanation.

After lunch, they went to explore the Musée Mécanique below the Cliff House, and the Camera Obscura above. They kicked around the ruins of the Sutro Baths and watched the sun set from Ocean Beach.

Once the horizon swallowed the orange disc, they drove to Block-buster, where she selected *Groundhog Day*. She had been bugging him to watch it with her for ages.

"It's very Buddhist," she tried, and he laughed because he had threatened just the day before to chuck it all, move to India, and become a monk.

"You're a hedonist. You wouldn't last two days," she teased him at the time. And of course, she was right.

Today he felt inclined to oblige her every whim, so he handed over his Blockbuster card.

When he unlocked the front door to his house, the scent of his mother's cooking greeted them. Turkey tetrazzini, by the smell of it – lately his father's favorite, made with thawed leftover Thanksgiving turkey.

He popped into the in-law unit for a moment to drop off the video. He flipped on the light, and froze in his tracks.

A dozen or so picture frames adorned the opposite wall, each containing one of the photos he had shown her on Thanksgiving Day. The Cliff House. The Sutro Baths. The Camera Obscura.

Julia followed him into the in-law unit and smiled complacently at him. Not only that, but his mother appeared behind her in the doorway.

"What the...?"

Julia laughed, and the story came out. She had spent all the weeks since Thanksgiving making frames for the photos he gave her, as well as some of the other ones he had shown her that day. The hoary Vietnamese fisherman. The homeless man in Golden Gate Park. The underside of the Golden Gate Bridge.

A week or so earlier, Julia and his mother had conspired to hang the photos in the in-law unit some day when he wasn't home, as his Christmas present.

But after he gave her the mermaid necklace, she decided the surprise couldn't wait any longer. When he thought she had fallen into the toilet at the Cliff House, she had really been placing a call to his mother, begging her to hang the photos before he got home that night.

He caught himself looking at Julia in the same incredulous way she had looked at him that morning. He glanced from her to his mother, who smiled in the doorway to the in-law unit, with her arms crossed across her chest.

"Well, don't just stand there," his mother prompted.

Julia took his hand and led him to the opposite wall. She had covered the frames in her own room with vibrant patterns and bedazzled them with beads and crystals of every color. But for William's space, she had chosen a more masculine palette – colors of the ocean. Azure and navy blue, like the water at different times of the day. Ecru, like the sand. Ivory, like the caps of the waves. The odd pop of yellow, orange, or crimson, like the sunset. An occasional ticking stripe or geometric pattern.

Land's End. Hang gliders launching from Fort Funston. All the photos they had looked at Thanksgiving Day – they were all there.

He found her monitoring him carefully for his reaction.

"I hope you don't mind," she said. "You seemed so proud of them. I thought they deserved a place of honor."

Mortified that he might have given her the wrong impression, he seized her hands. He was all too keenly aware of his mother's continued presence, so he contented himself with saying, "Mind? This might be one of the nicest things anyone has ever done for me."

"All right, all right, that's my cue – I'm out of here," his mother interjected, backing out of the in-law unit and closing the door after herself, but not before adding, "Dinner in twenty."

William squeezed Julia's hands. "You and my mom really coordinated this together?"

She nodded. "I'm relieved you like it. I didn't know if you would."

"Why wouldn't I have liked it?"

"I don't know... I was afraid you'd think it was presumptuous. Or intrusive." She hesitated a moment, then added, "You're a polymath."

"I'm... what?"

"You're brilliant at just about everything you try. You should be proud of your talents. If nothing else, I'm proud of them on your behalf."

He shook his head in disbelief – at what, exactly? He wasn't sure. Her kindness, maybe. His own good fortune. He pulled her closer and kissed her.

"After tonight," he said, "there's no way I'm not coming with you to Santa Barbara."

"Will, I love you more than life itself, but I don't want to talk about this again. I know as well as you do that you're not going to turn down that scholarship."

He frowned. "But I *don't* know that. Shouldn't I get a say in what happens in my own life? Or in our relationship?"

"Will," she began. Considered her words carefully. "Of course you do. But you've never been to Santa Barbara, so maybe you'll just have to trust me when I tell you that you'd be miserable there. You'd fare better in some foreign countries than you would there. It would be a complete and total culture shock."

"You talk like I'm some kind of unwashed, illiterate peasant," he balked. "If you can survive there, so can I."

"I'm sorry," she said hastily. "I swear, I didn't mean it like that. I just meant Santa Barbara is so... *SoCal*. And you're so... *not*. Trust me, I mean that as a compliment."

He huffed out a laugh. "You think I don't know what SoCal is like, just because I've never been there?"

She stood on her tiptoes to kiss him again. "Please – let's just watch our movie and eat our dinner and go to bed. Let's worry about this another day."

His brows crashed together. "Fine, but I'm not letting it go. We need to talk about this again soon, okay?"

"Of course," she whispered, her lips parted against his. His frustration instantly evaporated when confronted with the unmasked love and heat in her gaze. Suddenly, one appetite overruled the other. Within seconds, the door was locked, their clothes littered the floor, and his face was buried between her thighs.

Later, with dinner eaten and *Groundhog Day* enjoyed, he sat before her on his bed, naked in every sense – his feelings, his arousal on unabashed display. Unrushed at first, building over the course of the night into the sort of crescendo where they chased each other onto the floor, into the shower and out again and onto the bed, still dripping. The kind where he woke in the middle of the night and *Hey! What's this? A naked girl in my bed!*

At four o'clock in the morning, in the throes of their second round, he heard his family spill out of the house on the way to the processing plant. By then, the sheets had long since popped off the bed, landing in a defiled heap on the carpet. He gathered her long hair behind her head, wrapping it around his wrist, using it to lift her face from the bare mattress into which she had been censoring herself. Putting his lips to her ear, he whispered, "Go ahead. Scream all you want."

Afterward, they slept until the sun insinuated itself through the gap in the blinds. Neither of them wished to admit they were awake. Neither wished to acknowledge the time that was passing.

Julia's stomach growled, and they both laughed. She lifted her head from his chest and kissed him, still laughing through lips pressed to his.

He loved, loved, loved her. Stinky morning breath and all. He stroked her hair, pushed it back off her face and over her shoulder.

"You need some hot guy to cook you breakfast," he observed.

She lifted the phone receiver beside his bed and said to the dial tone, "Room service? I'd like to order the eggs benedict cooked by a hot guy. Actually, just bring the hot guy and pour the hollandaise over him – thanks. And bloody Marys for me and the old man."

He took the receiver from her hand and replaced it on the cradle. "Cold mush for you. And decaf coffee."

They got dressed and climbed the stairs, discussing their plans for the day. At the kitchen, Julia gave a yelp and stopped short.

"Morning," croaked William's mother at the stove. She hovered over a tea kettle in her robe, her hair disheveled, a cigarette dangling from her lips. She sucked on the cigarette and promptly doubled over in a coughing fit.

"Mom. You're here," William remarked without thinking. His mother's cough sounded like a sea lion's bark. Julia stood frozen in mortification, her jaw hanging open.

William's mother recovered enough to say, "Don't worry, it's not contagious. It's just my asthma." Then she took another drag from the cigarette.

William knew damn well that it wasn't asthma. His father told him the doctor had diagnosed her with emphysema, but she was too stubborn to admit it.

He also knew damn well that Julia wasn't worried about whether or not his mother was contagious. He watched her spin on her heel and flee back through the living room, down the stairs.

He ran after her into the in-law unit. Shut the door behind them and chased her into the bedroom, where she shoved the few belongings she had brought with her into what she called her "jump bag." It was the backpack she brought with her when she spent the night with William, with her toothbrush and a change of clothes.

She was practically panicking. "Oh my God. She heard everything, didn't she?" He watched her mentally revisiting all the filthy things she had screamed at four o'clock in the morning and cringing at each one.

There were only 1250 square feet in the house – nine hundred upstairs, the rest down – and the thin walls afforded no privacy. Hell, there were times when he heard noises coming from his parents' bedroom, and he had to put on his headphones and drop a record onto the turntable.

There was no chance his mother hadn't heard everything.

Hot laughter burbled up from somewhere deep in his gut, but he stifled it. He stepped forward, stroked her arm and said, "Don't worry. I'll smooth everything over."

"Why isn't she at the processing plant?" she demanded, almost hyperventilating.

"You heard her. She's sick."

She zipped the backpack with a vengeance and slung it over her shoulders. "I have to go. I'm so embarrassed."

He grabbed her by the shoulders to steady her. Touched her chin, and forced her to look him in the eye.

"Calm down. Everything's going to be okay. You know she loves you."

She gaped at him a moment, then gave a ragged sort of laugh. Sprang up to peck him on the lips, then dashed away and out the front door.

He wandered back upstairs and found his mother still lingering over the kettle on the stove. She inquired casually after Julia. She had smoked her cigarette down to the butt. She took a final drag and doubled over coughing again. She wobbled and he caught her by the elbows.

"Here," he said, steering her toward the kitchen table with its built-in banquette, where she finished her coughing fit. He looked over at the tea kettle, and said, "Mom, you didn't turn on the flame."

She gave a short, rueful laugh. "I wondered why it was taking so long."

He lit the burner and watched as, to his dismay, she lit yet another cigarette. After a moment's hesitation, he asked, "Should you be doing that?"

"Probably not," she said drily, and took a drag anyway.

He watched her smoke and noticed she was losing weight. "Have you eaten?"

She waved her hand dismissively. "What's the point? I can't taste anything."

His mother had already cut up a lemon and set the teapot on the counter with its infuser of loose-leaf tea. He opened the refrigerator and examined its contents. Reached in and pulled out a carton of eggs and some jelly. From the pantry he retrieved everything else he needed.

He heated oil in a pan. Whisked the eggs and popped bread in the toaster.

He said, "I hope you know I mean no disrespect."

"Mm?"

The oil shimmered. He turned down the heat and poured the eggs into the pan. "Having her spend the night with me."

"Oh." She took a drag. The tea kettle threatened to whistle. "And broadcasting it to the whole house?"

Embarrassed, he poured the hot water over the looseleaf tea in the pot. His mother chuckled a bit, low and husky, which soon deteriorated into a coughing fit. When she recovered, she said, "Will, I was young once, believe it or not." She flicked the cigarette against the ashtray on the kitchen table. "You're being careful?"

He nodded.

"Good. I'm only forty-six. I'm not ready to be a grandma."

He pushed the egg curds around the pan with a wooden spatula. Sprinkled them with salt, pepper, and Tabasco sauce. Scooped them onto a plate, squeezed honey and lemon into her tea, and spread jelly on the toast. She stubbed out her cigarette as he served her at the table.

"Can you taste them?" he asked when she tried the eggs.

"I can." She sipped the tea and made a sound of relief. "Thanks for this, Will."

He smiled and scooted his chair back, but she squeezed his hand to stop him.

"She makes you really happy; I can tell. That's all that matters to me."

Later that morning, walking down Taraval on his way to Julia's house, he stopped by the bank and made a withdrawal. Then he stopped into the jewelry store with the Chinese signage. Michelle's mom, behind the counter, gave a start of recognition. He asked for Michelle, who emerged from her secret compartment in the back with a look of surprise.

"Do you still have the nine hundred and fifty dollar ring?"

"Oh my God, yes!" she exclaimed, and showed it to him again. He opened his wallet and pulled out a hundred dollar bill.

"I'd like to put it on layaway."

NOVEMBER 1995, PART II

"WOULD YOU LIKE A BOX FOR THAT?"

The Saturday after Dia de los Muertos, after kissing Haze goodbye, he set out on his motorcycle from the bright morning sunshine of the Mission, back into the gloom of the Sunset. His route took him by Grand View Park, where he had given Julia the mermaid necklace. And it took him by the jewelry store on Taraval – the one with the signage in Chinese only.

He had yet another Act the Maggot rehearsal later that afternoon, where he would practice her song, and then that evening he would go to work at her father's restaurant.

Abruptly, he swerved into a parking spot in front of the jewelry store on Taraval and glanced at his watch. Ten til ten.

He would just have to make new memories.

He waited on his bike until Michelle's mother unlocked the front door. She gave a start of recognition, and beamed up at him.

"Ahhhhhh!" she said.

For a moment he was surprised that she even recognized him, until he remembered that he was probably the only white guy who ever came into this place. She opened the door wide to admit him, and then shouted back into the interior of the store. Michelle emerged from the rear of the store and stopped dead in her tracks when she spotted William.

"Oh my God! William! Long time no see! What are you doing here?"

In the past two years, she had traded in the Coke bottle glasses with the square black frames that swamped her face for a more stylish pair with thin oval frames. Not only that, she had shed her braces, and had apparently learned to comb her hair.

Without waiting for him to answer her first question, she chirped, "How's Julia?"

His guts wrenched themselves inside-out. "We broke up."

Michelle's face fell. "Oh my God; no way! I can't even imagine that. What happened?" At the look on his face, she clapped a hand over her mouth. "I'm sorry; that was a stupid thing to say."

He waved his hand dismissively. Then, she looked like a deer in the headlights.

"You've come to return the ring, haven't you? It's way past the return window, you know." She pointed to a sign beside the register in Chinese characters. "It says you have thirty days to return any purchases. You'll just have to take my word for it."

"I'm not here to return the ring. I'm here to buy a necklace for my..." Michelle wasn't a bad-looking girl, in her businesslike emerald-green sheath dress and blazer. "For my sister."

"You mean Kelly?" The look on her face was skeptical. "She never seemed like the jewelry-wearing type to me. Unless that's changed?"

He thought fast. "It's for a special occasion. Our mom is making her get all dressed up."

She smiled now and, holding his gaze, peeled off her blazer. The sheath dress underneath was sleeveless, and fitted. She tossed it onto the glass display case, then leaned across the glass toward him, her elbows and forearms planted on the countertop.

"So, what do you have in mind?" Her voice was suddenly different, more sultry, and he realized with a jolt that Michelle – he and Julia's former lab partner in AP Biology – was flirting with him.

He took a step backward. Smiled sheepishly. "Ah – I'm not too sure, to be honest."

"Well," she said, reaching into the glass display case and pulling out a necklace display stand, "we just got these in."

She set the stand on the glass countertop. Each necklace was a silver chain with an occult-like symbol at the end of it. At his look of confusion, she explained, "Zodiac symbols."

Intrigued, William peered at each pendant. They did look like something Haze would like.

"What's Kelly's sign?" asked Michelle.

"I'm not sure," he admitted.

She grinned and leaned across the countertop again. Her neckline puckered at the front, and he quickly averted his eyes from the shadowy glimpse of her bra and cleavage. "When's her birthday?"

When *was* Haze's birthday? Oh yeah – March. She had once told him she was born on the spring equinox.

"Huh," Michelle remarked, pulling one particular necklace from the display stand. "I wouldn't have pegged Kelly for a Pisces."

She held it up to him, the pendant draped across the palm of her hand, and he stepped forward for a closer look. The silver pendant looked a bit like a letter H, as in Haze, with the vertical strokes curved inward, and the horizontal one streaking all the way through the vertical ones.

It was perfect.

Then, to his dismay, Michelle seized his hand and pressed the necklace into his palm. She still flashed that coy grin.

He met her gaze now, the heat rising to his face as it always did when a girl flirted with him. But he didn't step away this time. And he smiled back.

"How much?"

"Ten bucks." When his eyebrows raised at the cheap price, she leaned across the countertop again and added, "And a cup of coffee."

Still smiling, he reached into his back pocket for his wallet and pulled out a twenty. "Keep the change. I'll take a rain check on the coffee."

She stood up slowly, accepted the twenty. Held it by the edges, stretched it out. Peered coyly at him over the top of the bill. His face still aflame, he forced himself to hold her gaze.

"Receipt?" he prompted.

Wordlessly she reached into a drawer hidden behind the glass display case and pulled out a receipt pad. Scribbled on it, tore it out, and handed it to him. Just before his fingertips grasped it, she snatched it back.

"Would you like a box for that?"

"Um – okay."

Still, even as she turned away, her eyes lingered on his. She sauntered back into the storeroom and emerged a moment later with a black necklace box. Took the necklace from him, allowing her fingers to brush his as she did so, and placed it into the box. Smirking the whole way.

At last he accepted the box and the receipt from her. Held them up and nodded by way of acknowledgement. Smiled and turned to go, holding her gaze as long as possible, as she had done before.

It wasn't until he got home and looked at the receipt that he realized she had written her phone number on it.

"SO, WHAT ARE *YOUR* LIFE PLANS?"

The next morning, he drove to the Mission to retrieve Haze. His loud pipes announced his approach, and her front door swung open before he could even kill the ignition.

She wore a pair of fitted black jeans tucked into the tops of Doc Martens, and a black quilted motorcycle jacket with sharply squared-off shoulders. And with her hair pinned up the way it was, she looked like she had stepped right off the set of Blade Runner.

It was a promising beginning.

"So. Where are you taking me?" she shouted over the roar of his engine.

"It's a surprise," he replied. Just as he had with Julia.

With a grin, she slid on a pair of mirrored sunglasses and lowered her helmet over her head. Tossed her things into the saddlebag and swung herself gamely onto the back of his motorcycle. Squeezed him tight around the waist.

Without another word, he blasted away from the curb.

As they tore across the city toward the Inner Sunset, William was aware that they turned heads wherever they went. He convinced himself that it was not just because of his loud pipes, but also because of how great Haze looked on the back of his bike.

Just as Julia had turned heads, with those sensational long legs, and her messy copper braid flying out from beneath her helmet.

At the foot of Turtle Hill, he found a parking spot as close as possible to the one where he had parked with Julia on that cold day nearly two years ago.

"It's not far from here, if you want to walk," he told Haze, pointing up a long set of stairs that climbed the hillside. Just as he had told Julia.

Haze smiled and nodded, so he took her hand and led her up the stairs. Across the treacherous, uneven ground strewn with rocks and tree roots. Pointed, and said, "Look." Haze caught her breath at the sweeping view.

But nothing else after that was right. It wasn't as bright and clear of a day today as it had been then. Fog and clouds obscured too much of the view. It wasn't quite as cold and windy, so when he brought Haze to the bench, there was no need for him to put his arms around her, to keep her warm.

He had brought his camera with him, just as he had back then. So he rose from the bench to snap some photos of the city spread out before them, and of Haze, standing before the vista. But her smile was reserved and close-mouthed, not bright and joyful, as Julia's had been.

He could feel the necklace box, inside the inner pocket of his coat, pressing against his chest. But it was wrong – all wrong.

So he put Haze back on his bike and drove her out of the city, down Highway 1. To Año Nuevo, where he held the camera out in front of them and snapped photos of them, with the elephant seals in the background. Past Monterey, past Carmel, past the cliffs slicing into the blue ocean. All the way to the park that shared its name with *her*. To the eighty-foot waterfall, plunging onto the sandy beach.

He snapped the photos of Haze in front of the view. But she didn't ask to take any of him, as Julia had.

The necklace box stayed in his inner jacket pocket.

"Are you okay?" Haze asked as they ate their picnic lunch.

Only then did he realize how long he had been frowning out at the falls, brooding. With a pang of guilt, he smiled halfheartedly at her. Finished chewing his bite of sandwich, and swallowed hard. "I guess I've got a lot on my mind."

"Like what?"

He shrugged, took a gulp of his soda. Thought quickly. "School."

"Oh," she said, peering closely at him. "I almost forgot you were going to school."

Huffing a rueful laugh, he screwed the lid back on the soda bottle. "Me too."

"Remind me again, what are you majoring in?"

"Hospitality Management," he said dully, stuffing another bite of sandwich into his mouth.

Her eyebrows raised. "Hospitality Management?"

He shrugged. Gulped down his morsel of sandwich, which had suddenly turned dry and crumbly in his mouth. "I figure I can use it in the restaurant industry somehow."

"If you want to be a cook, you could just go to culinary school."

He felt irritable, having to explain this to her. "I got a full-ride scholarship to USF. The priest at our church connected me with it. Otherwise, I wouldn't have been able to afford to go to school, anywhere."

She nodded slowly, her eyes still trained on his. "I get that. It just doesn't seem like you're very interested in what you're studying."

His stomach suddenly churned with nausea. "The truth is, it was my grandmother who connected me with the scholarship, through the priest. And... you know. She died a couple of months after that, so..."

He watched her connecting the dots. "Oh. And you feel like you kind of owe it to her?"

Wincing a bit at her frank characterization, he turned to look out over the vista, at McWay Falls. The same waterfall he and Julia had admired when he proposed to her.

He slipped the ring onto her left hand. "I'm coming with you to Santa Barbara. I'm not going to USF. And I'd like you to marry me."

He held her hand in both of his, and she spent a whole looking at the diamond sparkling on her finger, still in shock. The diamond was modest, but it was clearly a new ring. She looked up at him and brushed back the bit of hair falling over his forehead.

"I'll wear your ring, and I'll marry you someday. But I won't let you give up your scholarship."

"I won't change my mind. I'm going with you."

"No," she said gently. "I told you, I won't forget about you."

"I know you won't, because I'll be there with you."

She touched his face, made him look her in the eye. "I love you. We'll have a good life together. But you need to get your degree."

"I can be a cook."

"I know that's not what you really want."

With a note of desperation, he said, "Why won't you believe me when I tell you I don't know what I want to do with my life, except to love you until the day I die? I'm not going to give up a sure thing for an unsure thing."

She watched her melting under his words as she took his hand in hers. But she said, "You're right, this is a sure thing. We'll see each other once a month, at least. At holidays, during breaks. I'll call you every single week, maybe every day. Write you letters. And, you'll figure out what you want to do and get your degree."

She watched his face, watched him look out on the vista. Touched his forehead to smooth the worried furrows in his brow. Held up her hand for him to see.

"I'm wearing your ring. I'm never taking it off. You'll never get rid of me now."

He smiled halfheartedly.

"Listen to me." She made him wrap his arms around her waist. "I'll never forget this day as long as I live."

"Me neither."

"What?" Haze's voice jerked him back to the unwelcome present.

"What *what*?" he hedged.

"You said, 'Me neither.' You neither, what?"

He would never forget how quickly all their promises to each other had fallen by the wayside – *that's* what.

And now, look at him. How pathetic was he? What the fuck was he doing *here*, of all places, with Haze?

He set aside his sandwich now, half-eaten. "Besides, if I was going to go somewhere of my choosing, it would be to UCSB."

Again, Haze's eyebrows lifted. "You mean Santa Barbara?"

He shrugged, avoided her gaze.

She gave a short, incredulous laugh. "Why there?"

He frowned. "I've been down there once or twice. It's nice."

She said nothing, so he glanced up at her, and he knew – she knew. Quickly, he changed the subject by saying, "So, what are *your* life plans?"

From the look on her face, he knew she had not missed the note of sarcasm. She shifted in her seat on the picnic blanket and set aside her half-eaten sandwich, as he had a moment earlier. "I... I'm not going to lie to you, Will." Her eyes flitted up to meet his. "All of this – my tattoo business, trying to stay clean – is just so I can get my son back. So I can bring him home with me, to San Francisco."

With another pang of guilt, he reached for her hand. "Can't your dad help you?"

She frowned down at their hands clasped together. "I won't take any money from my father." He waited for her to elaborate. Her eyes flitted back up to his face again. "My dad... He's not the nicest person."

"Okay... what about your brothers? Can they help?"

Again, her eyes drifted away from his. "Kirill is a poor priest of a poor Russian Orthodox church in Alaska. And Vasya..." Her face warped with apprehension. "If I had to prove where I get money from – in order to get my son back – it wouldn't look good if I took money from my dad or Vasya."

A sudden thought occurred to him. One that had tiptoed at the back of his consciousness for many years; but now it came fully to the forefront. Carefully, he ventured, "What does your dad do for a living, again?"

She withdrew her hand from his. Plucked a grape off of the cluster of grapes she had brought with her for lunch, and popped it in her mouth. Chewed a moment. "He's a botanist."

He peered sharply at her. Watched her chew. She avoided his gaze studiously.

He didn't contradict her. Didn't bother reminding her that she had once told him that her father was a geneticist.

The bitterness that poisoned his soul on the drive back to the city made it difficult even to be civil to Haze when he dropped her off in front of her house.

"Are you coming in?" she shouted over the roar of his engine when he didn't kill it.

He flipped up his helmet's visor so she could hear him. "I have to catch up on my studies tonight," he replied.

"Oh. Okay." She looked disappointed, but she moved toward him, as if expecting a kiss. Begrudgingly, he lifted the helmet off of his head, and gave her a quick peck on the lips.

"I'll call you later," he said.

She nodded with a sober look, but said nothing. As she backed away from his bike, he fastened his helmet back on and peeled away from the curb. He told himself that he hadn't lied to her. He really did need to catch up on his studies.

But that wasn't really what he planned to do with his evening.

Instead, once he got back to the Sunset, he swerved to park in front of the jewelry store on Taraval. He told himself he was just going to return the necklace.

But it was closed on Sunday.

So he went home and smoked a bowl of Haze's excellent weed. Found the key to his father's liquor cabinet, and swiped another bottle of Jameson. Took a couple of pulls.

He reached into his back pocket and retrieved his wallet. Opened it, and pulled out the receipt Michelle had given him. Unfolded it, and looked at her number.

"WHAT'S YOUR POISON?"

Even if he had been prepared for his Macroeconomics test the next morning, he was too hung over. So he slept until well past noon, until he had to get up and go to his Act the Maggot rehearsal.

When he returned home, a message waited for him on the answering machine. From Haze. With a pang of guilt, he remembered how he had treated her yesterday.

"I'm sorry I didn't call you last night, like I said I would," he offered when he returned her call.

"Will..." she began. "The reason I called is because I wanted to let you know that I have no expectations of what this is."

"Huh?"

"I mean..." She seemed to be grasping for the right words. "I have no delusions about what our relationship is, or isn't."

"Haze –"

"I'm four years older than you. I'm divorced, with a nine-month-old son who will probably come live with me soon. But the point is, I get what this is. I just wanted you to know that."

"Haze, can I just –"

"And I know you're not really free to offer more, either."

He had no response for this. After a long pause, she continued, "I really like you, a lot. I like spending time with you. Let's just let it be that, and don't feel like you have to pretend it's anything more."

Another long pause. "Okay."

"So... with that out of the way – do you want to come over?"

He spent that night, and every night that week, at her house. And he went to every class that week, for a change, though he couldn't quite put his mind to any of them. The impending debut of Act the Maggot that coming Friday weighed too heavily on him.

He had never performed in any way in front of a crowd. Certainly he had never sung in front of anyone before, besides Mike, and Julia, and now his bandmates.

And on top of all of that, Haze had threatened to come to the show. How was he supposed to bare his soul about Julia in front of her? In front of an entire pub full of drunken assholes?

It didn't matter that none of them knew what the song was about – *he* knew. And Haze was perceptive; surely she would figure it out.

Around midnight Friday morning, he sat up in Haze's bed. She lay facing away from him, breathing softly in her sleep. The only light illuminating her filtered through the gauzy curtains of her window.

Her mini-bottles of liquor downstairs called to him.

He slowly swung his legs out of bed, trying not to wake her with his movement. But the creaks in the hardwood floor as he stood up betrayed him. She stretched and turned to look.

"You okay?"

"I'm just going to the bathroom," he lied.

She propped herself up on her elbow. Peered at him. "You've been tossing and turning a lot."

"I'm sorry. I can go sleep on the couch, if you want."

She sat up. "No, I don't want. But I've got something that might help you sleep, if you're willing to give it a try."

He hesitated. "I don't want to be too loopy for class tomorrow."

"You won't be. Can I turn the light on?"

He relented, and with her bedside lamp illuminated, she swung herself out of bed. Still completely naked, she squatted in front of the bedside table, opened a drawer, and pulled out a box that he hadn't seen before. Packed the bowl of her bong with its contents.

"Still nervous about your first show?" she speculated.

"Yes," he admitted.

"You've been practicing all week. You're ready."

"I know."

She brought the bong over to his side of the bed. Sat on the edge of the bed beside him. "I'll give you some of this to take with you tomorrow."

"Where do you get this stuff from?" he ventured, as casually as possible.

She took a rip. After exhaling, she said, "You know I can't talk about that."

He took a rip of his own, and tried again. "Secret family recipe?"

She cast him a sharp look. "What do you *really* want to know, Will?"

"Nothing," he said quickly.

A ridge appeared between her brows. "You want to know if my dad is a Russian mob boss?"

Suddenly ashamed, he looked away and tugged at his knuckles. "I..."

"That's what everyone says, right?" she persisted. Her tone carried a faint edge he had never detected there before. "How else would I have access to goods like these? Why else would everyone in this neighborhood give me such a wide berth?"

He forced his eyes back to hers, fixing her with an earnest gaze. "I'm sorry."

"For what?"

"For dignifying the idle gossip of a couple of mouth-breathers with my attention."

"Mouth-breathers..." One corner of her mouth lifted. "Jimmy and Mike."

He gave a shaky laugh. "Especially Mike. He's worse than a fucking church lady."

She laughed freely, but volunteered nothing further; and besides, her product was working its magic now. She turned off the light, pulled him down under the covers. Made out with him a while, and attempted a hand job. But clearly this particular strain was no aphrodisiac – he remained limp, and dropped right off to sleep.

She was right; he was not too loopy the next morning to go to class. Even so, he was too anxious to focus on the first lecture of the day. So he skipped his remaining classes and drove straight home. Packed the bowl with Haze's chill-out weed and smoked it all.

Then he started in on the Jameson.

As afternoon waned into evening, he judged it best to walk to MacGowan's, rather than trying to drive. He ambled into the pub and headed straight for the bar, and Cindy.

She spotted him and aimed her megawatt smile at him. Leaned across the bar so he could hear her over the din of the jukebox and the chatter. "Hey, Maximus!" She had been calling him some variation on Mad Max since the first time she saw him. "Ready to rock?"

"Not yet," he admitted, his eyes lingering a bit too long on the abundance of exposed cleavage above her neckline. She had to be at least a double-D. "Can I get a shot of something?"

"Sure," she said, but she cast him a quizzical look. "Have you been drinking already?"

He took a step back. "Nah."

Still, she gazed at him suspiciously, but she said, "What's your poison?"

"Surprise me."

She poured him a shot of gin. She knew he didn't like gin. He knocked it back anyway, and asked for another.

"Give it a minute to kick in, Maximilian," Cindy suggested. "The night is still young."

So he stumbled to the stage, where Mike and the other bandmates were setting up. Clambered up onto the stage with his guitar case, and fumbled around as he tried to help them set up the equipment.

At one point, Mike clapped a hand on his back. "Dude, are you sloshed already?" He was grinning, but his eyes were uneasy.

William waved him aside. "No, man. I'm just comfortably numb."

At one point, as they were doing their sound check, he glanced out at the crowd and spotted Haze, sitting by herself at one of the pub tables, watching him. She waved and offered that circumspect smile of hers. He smiled back, lifted his hand, and went back to work.

Despite the substances coursing through his system, his nerves broke through. Even so, he felt far easier than he would have otherwise.

Someone silenced the jukebox, and the eyes of everyone in the pub veered toward the stage. With a cue from Mike, the band exploded into its first song. During the intro, Mike stepped up to the microphone, gave a rousing salute to the audience, pumped his fist and shouted, "*We. Are. Act the Maggot!*"

It could easily have been cheesy as hell, but Mike's enthusiasm was infectious, as always. The crowd roared its approval, and he roared right back at them, truly in his element.

It was Irish pub rock, all right – raucous and rollicking, with Mike's lyrics celebrating drinking, women, the working class, and Irish nationalism. During one quick break in the set, Mike introduced all of the band members, and then they plunged right into the next song. At one point, William looked up long enough to watch the crowd clap along with the rhythm, and for a moment at least, his inhibitions melted away.

But then Mike stepped up to the microphone and, in a lower voice, said, "I'd like to take things down a notch and let my brother Will sing the next song, since he wrote it."

The liquor churned in William's stomach now, but he stepped up to the microphone, avoiding eye contact at all costs. He knew the song inside and out, like he knew his own soul. He would have known it that intimately even if he hadn't practiced it for weeks.

"This song is called *Copper Thread*," he mumbled into the microphone.

The shouts of the audience reached his ears: "What?!" "We can't hear you!"

Ignoring them, he strummed the intro. Tittering drifted up from the audience, but it subsided the moment the melody unfurled from his fingertips.

His voice cracked at the beginning – just as it had when he sang *Wish You Were Here* to Julia. But now, as then, it quickly gained strength, and midway through the song, he felt confident enough to glance up.

He locked eyes with Haze.

She was smiling, in her usual restrained way. He quickly turned his eyes back down to the stage floor, or up to the ceiling.

The bar had grown remarkably quiet, so he glanced up again. Just long enough to see every eye in the room riveted to him. Especially, he couldn't help but notice, the eyes of the women.

When he strummed the final chord and stepped back from the microphone, a heart-stopping second of brief silence ensued, followed by an eruption of applause and cheers. He allowed himself one final glance up, and locked eyes again with Haze. Her face flushed red as she clapped vigorously, and the corners of her eyes crinkled as she smiled wider than ever.

It was all wrong.

Here he stood before his current "friend with benefits," serenading the incandescent torch he still carried for Julia – for her smile, and her hair, and her *nipples*, for fuck's sake. It didn't matter that neither Haze, nor anyone else in the audience, understood the metaphorical lyrics. The glow in her eyes as she looked at him drove it all home – she was all wrong; the whole thing was all wrong. And he was a consummate dickhead.

"REDEEM THAT RAIN CHECK, MAYBE?"

The next morning, after leaving Haze's house, William drove straight to the jewelry store on Taraval.

"Ahhhh!" Michelle's mother said like always, beaming at him when he swung open the front door. Then, immediately, she shouted back into the interior of the store: "Michelle!"

Michelle emerged and, as before, stopped short when she saw him. But then her mouth curled into an involuntary smile, and she sauntered casually to the counter.

"William!" She had tucked a flowy, gold-colored silk blouse into a black pencil skirt. His eyes traced the line of her legs past the skirt's hem, to the sheer back-seam hose and red pumps. She was petite – at least a foot shorter than him, maybe even shorter. "What brings you back here? Another sister?"

"Actually," he said, reaching into the interior pocket of his jacket and pulling out the black necklace box, "I'm here to return the one I bought the other day."

"Oh," she said, her smile widening even further. "It didn't work out?"

He said nothing; he only smiled back as flirtatiously as he knew how, and hoped it didn't look as awkward as it felt. After handing her the necklace box, he retrieved the receipt from his wallet, and her smile faded somewhat.

"I saved your phone number," he said.

Her coy grin returned, and she held his gaze a moment before turning to process his refund. The cash register popped open, and she counted out the bills into his hand.

He doubted the wisdom of what he was about to do, and did it anyway.

"Can I make it up to you?" he ventured, holding up the cash. "Redeem that rain check, maybe?"

DECEMBER 1995, PART I

"TELL HER I CALLED."

*A*fter his final exams, the inevitable happened – he got the letter informing him that he was on academic probation. His scholarship would be suspended while he worked on improving his grades. But of course, he couldn't work on improving his grades if he didn't have a scholarship to pay for classes.

Could he appeal to Father Molloy? Maybe – if Father Molloy hadn't long ago accepted a position as the headmaster of a Catholic prep school in Boston. They had fallen out of touch after Father Molloy wrote his letter of recommendation for the scholarship at USF.

That was it. The worst had happened, or at least the worst after losing Julia – his academic career was over. There was nothing more to fear.

As he scrounged around the drawer in his bedside table for a bottle opener, he stumbled across an old calling card Julia had given him when she moved away to college. He thought he had used them all, but he must have overlooked this one.

At first, everything had gone according to plan. William exhausted

170

the phone cards Julia gave him, and she sent him letters each week. She came up for her birthday and the holidays, since William couldn't get away from work, and they spent as much of that time together as they could.

After the holidays were over, their parents balked at the credit card bills, and they had to call each other less frequently. The demands of their coursework intensified. Her letters became more sporadic. Sometimes she forgot when it was her turn to call him.

On the rare occasions that they did connect, her talk was full of the work she was doing and the people she was meeting down there. Especially Kevin Beale, a fellow Bay Area native and aquarium hobbyist.

William tried to convince himself that it wasn't what he feared. He reminded himself of all the evidence, running down the mental checklist, ticking off all the boxes: Kevin was just her friend, her *only* friend in Santa Barbara – first, the hapless grad student who had taught her marine biology summer camp. Then, the T.A. in her freshman marine ecology course. Then, the coordinator for her summer internship on the Channel Islands.

She went to his apartment all the time to help him with his saltwater aquarium. She had always been very open with William about that; nothing to hide. Kevin was nearly six years older than Julia, short, bespectacled, and hirsute.

No threat at all, William constantly reminded himself. Nothing to worry about.

But he did.

Innocent or not, Julia's friendship with Kevin was a distraction. Especially after Kevin became the coordinator for her summer internship on the Channel Islands.

"Kevin wants me to stay and help with the preparations for the internship on the Channel Islands," Julia had told him back in May. It had already been two months since William had seen her. He had been counting down the days until she came home. They were going to spend two blissful weeks together before her internship began.

He felt the hot anger rising in his chest. But with forced calmness, he said, "You're not coming home."

"I would be an idiot to say no."

His voice shaking with restraint, he said, "Do you know what this means? By the time the middle of September rolls around, it will have been six months since we've seen each other."

"Did you really mean it when you said you didn't care how long you would have to wait? Because this opportunity won't wait."

He had meant that when he said it back in March. She had came home from spring break and broken the news to him about her summer internship, crushing his hopes of spending all summer with her.

"It's three months out of our whole lives," she had said back then. "Please don't ask me not to do it."

Softening in response, he had picked up her hand and touched the ring on her finger. "I would never do that. I don't care how long I have to wait."

But now?

Carefully, he said, "I did mean that. But I thought we would at least see each other from time to time. That's what you said when you told me not to come with you to Santa Barbara." He hesitated, then added, "I miss you."

"It's not like this is any easier for me."

"You'll have something to occupy your mind," he said bitterly.

"Yes, I will. Am I supposed to apologize for that? I know you don't know what you want to do with your life and you don't love working in the restaurant. But please don't take your frustration out on me!"

Her sharp tone stunned him to silence. Was that really what she thought of him? That he didn't know what he wanted to do with his life? Hadn't he told her, over and over again, that he wanted to love her until the day he died? That the rest was just gravy?

He tried to see things from her perspective. She was lonely, struggling to make friends at school.

"What did you expect?" he had once asked her, mid-way through her first semester. "It's SoCal."

"I guess I expected a university full of people who had to get straight A's in order to get in," she had answered. "I didn't expect to suffer social death if I didn't join a sorority."

She was trying to keep her grades up, but she was finding it harder than expected. In fact, nothing about studying marine biology was what she had expected.

Like an idiot, he had suggested that maybe she could shift her focus to being a naturalist, rather than a marine biologist.

"I don't want to be a naturalist. I want to be a marine biologist," she had snapped.

"Okay, I'm sorry. I shouldn't have opened my big mouth."

"I don't want to sit around talking to people all day about animals. I want to get out there, touch them, get my hands dirty. Help save them."

But at the tail end of her sentence, her voice had started breaking. Gently, he said, "Hey. What's the matter?"

"Nothing," she had said, her sniffles belying the denial. "I'm just afraid you're right. This has been my dream since I was twelve years old. I'm not the kind of person to just give up on my dreams without a fight. But no matter how hard I try, I'm just failing."

He knew she was ambitious and focused; it was one of the many things he admired about her. But sometimes he wondered if she was determined to justify her choices to herself – or maybe even to him – even if it came at the expense of him.

Now, after a long pause, Julia said in a guilt-laced tone, "I'm sorry. But I don't like feeling like I have to choose between you and my lifelong dreams."

"I'm not asking you to."

"It sure feels like you are. And I won't do it."

But she *had* chosen, hadn't she?

He should have followed her down there when he had the chance. Maybe if he had been there to support her, she wouldn't have struggled so much. Since he wasn't, she had to make a choice. She could invest time and energy in rescuing a relationship with someone who lived hundreds of miles away – someone she hadn't even seen in six months. Someone who had no direction in life. Or she could invest them in rescuing her academic career and her lifelong dreams.

All because he didn't listen to his gut and move down there with her.

Surely fences could be mended. When it came down to it, they had everything going for them. It had only been three and a half months. He would use this calling card to tell her how everything had turned out. He would find a job in a kitchen and work hard so she could focus on her studies. He would rent a little apartment for them so she could move out of that noisy dorm and study in peace. He would cook her meals and put them in the fridge so she'd have something to eat, even when he was at work. He would keep his fucking mouth shut, and never again question her choice of major – or her fidelity to him.

He would make her an offer – a month, let's say. *Just give me a month with you in Santa Barbara, and if you don't think it's working out, I'll be on my way.*

He tried her dorm first, but there was never any answer. After a couple of days, it finally dawned on him – she must have come home to spend Christmas with her family. He called her parents' house every day, but she never answered. It was always either a family member, or the answering machine. He hung up every time.

So then he waited until the first day of the winter semester at UCSB. That night, he took a few pulls from the bottle of Jameson at his bedside. It dulled the electricity buzzing through his veins, just enough so he could pick up the phone and follow the instructions on the calling card.

"Hello?"

The Valley Girl accent told him it was her roommate. What was her name? Oh yeah – Tiffany. "Can I, um... is Julia there?"

A pause. "Kevin?"

His stomach heaved violently. He almost said no – almost missed an opportunity – but then he caught himself and said yes.

"Oh! I could have sworn she said she was heading over to your place."

His field of vision reeled. His pulse thudded just behind his Adam's apple and swished through his ears. A giant vacuum of panic sucked all the air from his lungs.

"Tell her I called," he wheezed, and slammed down the receiver.

Nothing to worry about, he reminded himself. No threat at all.

Except that Kevin was a Silicon Valley trust fund kid from Atherton. And he really enjoyed working on aquariums with Julia. Imagine all the aquariums he could build for Julia, with all that money.

William sat hunched over on the edge of his bed, feeling the hot anger rising from some pit of darkness within. Julia wasn't the kind of woman to go after a guy just for his money. But why couldn't Kevin just ask Julia about his aquarium in some innocuous public place?

How could he spend all that time around Julia and *not* fall in love with her?

William would have to be in denial to pretend he didn't see the way Kevin hugged Julia just a moment too long. The way Kevin's eyes lingered on her with the same appetite, the same admiration, the same *love* that William's had.

He had seen all of that in September, when he visited Julia after she returned from the Channel Islands. How stupid did she think he was? How much of a pushover? Was he really just supposed to stand there and pretend he didn't notice another man making inroads on the best thing that had ever happened in his life?

The anger itched his fingers now, as it had that day with Kevin. Compelling him to action.

The anger.

SEPTEMBER 1995, PART III

*E*arly on the morning of September 15th, William drove his motorcycle all the way to Santa Barbara and rented a motel room. Julia had told him she would return to her dorm around noon, so at eleven-thirty, he parked his motorcycle across from Anacapa Hall, took off his helmet, and waited.

And waited.

And waited.

At two o'clock, he pulled a sandwich out of his saddlebag and ate it, growing more and more worried. Had something happened to her boat? Had he gotten the day wrong?

Finally, at close to four o'clock, he spotted her approaching from the end of the street. With some guy.

He watched them approach. They certainly were very friendly with each other. At one point, she touched his arm, laughing at something that must have been very funny indeed. He laughed too, and paused a moment to grasp her by the shoulders. They kept walking, oblivious to William and everything else around them, then stopped in front of the dorm. Julia whispered something in his ear, then flashed one of her bright, beaming smiles at him. They wrapped each other in a hug. Pulled away and looked each other in the eyes.

William cranked the ignition with a roar. Spun his motorcycle around in a U-turn and parked it next to the curb, right in front of them. Only then did they notice him. Along with everyone else passing on the sidewalk.

"Will!" Julia's face lit up at the sight of him, but he didn't notice because he was too busy glaring at her companion. Some bearded dude with curly dark hair and glasses. At first, the guy looked him up and down, his eyes lingering on the motorcycle, as if impressed.

William dismounted and came to stand right in front of him, invading his space. Glaring down at him. Whoever he was, he was barely taller than Julia. The anger itched at William's fingers now, compelling them to flex – compelling him into action. He wanted to tear this prick limb from limb. How dare he put his hairy hands on the best thing that had ever happened to him?

A crowd gathered, no doubt anticipating a fight. At the animal territoriality on William's face, beard-dude shrank back a bit. Glanced back and forth between Julia and William.

"Um… I think I'd better go now," he said.

"Yeah. That would be a good idea," William snarled.

With one last wary look at William, Beard turned around and walked as fast as he could in the direction from which he came. Their disappointed spectators began dispersing – until William turned to glower at Julia.

"Where have you been?" he demanded.

She scowled right back. "What are you talking about?"

"You told me you were getting back to your dorm at noon. It's four o'clock. I've been waiting here since 11:30."

"How was I supposed to know that? I thought you were coming tomorrow. That's what you told me when we talked last weekend."

It was true – he *had* told her that, because he was planning to surprise her a day early. How silly of him to imagine he would be a welcome surprise.

"So," he gritted out, ignoring her answer. "Who was that?"

"That was Kevin," she replied, a note of strain in her voice.

William was shaking now. "I knew I should have trusted my instincts. But I didn't want you to think I was a jealous prick."

Glaring, Julia refused to answer.

"So it's dinner with Kevin tonight?" He nodded down at her ring, keenly aware of the eavesdroppers who still hovered. "Why are you even wearing that thing anymore?"

"Will." Her voice trembled with barely-contained fury. "I'm late because I was at the bank, trying to get the ring back from the safe deposit box. I didn't want to damage or lose it during my internship. Oh, and by the way – when we disembarked, we got a visit from Kevin's fiancée, Nicole. Trustee of a little affair out of New York called the DeSmet Family Foundation. It was a grant of theirs that made our research possible this season, so we all figured the least we could do was have dinner with her tonight."

She waited until it sank in. Waited for the evidence to show on his face. Then she turned and ran into the dorm. Too late, he ran after her, and the door locked behind her.

He stood frozen in shock for a moment, then pounded on the door and shouted her name; but no one would let him in. So he ran back to his motorcycle, jumped onto it. Sped to the nearest pay phone he could find, and dialed her dorm room. Let it ring until it wouldn't ring any more. Found another quarter in his wallet, but this time the phone was off the hook. Sped back to the dorm to knock on the front door again, but this time a campus police officer made him leave.

Nauseous, not really seeing the road ahead of him, he drove back to his motel room. He picked up the phone and tried her number again, but the phone was still off the hook.

Unable to eat or sleep, he tried her number several more times that night, but each time got a busy signal. As soon as the sun rose, he drove back to her dorm, and parked out front.

Finally, at ten o'clock, she came out. The baggy dark circles under her eyes betrayed that she hadn't gotten any more sleep than he had. She froze on the front step when she saw him.

"I just want to talk," he pleaded.

She glared at him. "Then you're going to have to do it right here, in a public place."

Aghast, his voice came out in a wheeze. "I would never hurt you."

"I don't know. They say it only keeps on escalating."

His forehead creased. "I would never, *ever* hurt you."

"You looked pretty hell-bent on hurting someone yesterday."

"I could have hurt him, if I had wanted to. But I didn't."

She had no immediate response for that, but after a moment, she came down the walkway toward him. "How am I supposed to face Kevin or anyone at my dorm again, after the way you embarrassed me yesterday?"

"I'm sorry."

"Kevin is one of the best friends I've ever had. He's the only person down here who gets me, who likes me exactly the way I am. All these people down here? I'll never fit in with them. The other people in my internship? They think the only reason I lasted at all is because I'm sleeping with Kevin. Which I'm not, by the way, so don't even start."

"I know that."

"You need to get a life."

Her words landed like one of Jimmy's sucker punches to the gut. "What?"

"You always have some excuse for why you can't do the things you want to do. You can't make a living as a fisherman. You don't have the personality to be a photographer. You're not good enough to be a poet or a songwriter. All just excuses, so you don't have to try and then maybe fail."

His brows knit together. "What does this have to do with anything?"

"I don't know. Maybe if you found something besides another person for your life to revolve around, you wouldn't freak out when you see me with someone who happens to have a Y chromosome."

His pride wanted him to be angry, to tell her how presumptuous she was, assuming that his life revolved around her. But wrenching though it was, he had to acknowledge that there was a grain of truth in what she said. He did feel like he'd been living in a holding pattern since she left –

just living for the next time he would see her. Maybe he *had* been too needy – too clingy.

Still, he wasn't sure whether to let his pride or his humility win, until he saw her coming toward him, wrestling the ring off of her finger.

"No," he said, springing forward, trying to stop her from taking it off.

She wrenched herself away from him. Glared at him, and took it the rest of the way off. Held it out to him.

"Please, let's go someplace private to talk," he repeated, conscious of the people walking past them who either stared or tried not to stare. "We can't talk about this here."

"What's the matter, too proud to say it in front of everyone? You didn't have too high an opinion of my pride yesterday."

"Please," he begged her. "Just come with me. You have to know I would never hurt you."

She said nothing, just held out the ring.

"I'll take it, but only if you come with me and let me talk to you. If you still want me to keep it after I talk to you, I will."

He watched her feelings do battle on her face as he continued to beg her, "Please." Finally, reluctantly, she nodded, and he took the ring. Put it in his pocket. Led her to his motorcycle. She put on her own helmet and refused to let him help her onto the back.

He drove her to the motel. Let them both inside his room and invited her to sit in a chair. Knelt in front of her on the floor, and put his head in her lap.

Without lifting his head, he said, "My life doesn't revolve around you. But you're the most important part of it."

"Stand up," she ordered.

He didn't stand, but he lifted his head and looked into her eyes. "I know you're afraid I'm going to hurt you. But it's not in my nature to hurt people. Think about Kevin yesterday. I could have hurt him when I had the chance, but I didn't. Why in God's name would I ever hurt you when I wouldn't touch him?"

"No, you don't hurt people. You just bully them with your six feet four inches and your big loud macho motorcycle." But even as she said it, he could see her anger circling the drain.

He grasped her hands. "When we shared those two classes together in our freshman and sophomore years, I always loved the spunky way you shut down those assholes. The ones who called you Horsey Face, and Mosquito Bites. 'You really can't take your eyes off me, can you?' 'I hate to break your heart, but don't start picking out curtains yet.' The whole class would laugh, and sometimes the guys would talk a little more smack just to save face, but then they usually moved on to someone else."

"What does this have to do with anything?" she interrupted.

"Because at first, that was the only thing I admired about you. But then there was your smile. I never noticed until you started coming in to Cardone's. You kept turning that smile on me even though I did absolutely nothing to encourage it. In fact, I think I did everything in my power to discourage it. But that smile... You just never gave up on me. And then there you were, turning that smile on some Cat Stevens doppelganger with glasses."

In spite of her best efforts, he could see her anger circling the drain. Squeezing her hands, he begged, "Please don't let this be it. You have to know how wrong that would be. Think of everything we've been through the past two years."

When she still didn't respond, he put his head back in her lap. His mind and heart were a cacophony of panic and heartbreak as tears pricked at the back of his eyes.

He was going to lose her.

But after a minute, she put her fingertips in his hair, caressing his scalp. He looked up, his forehead creased with anguish. The eyes that met his were grave now, with no trace left of anger.

He reached into his back pocket, pulled out the ring. Grabbed her hand, slipped it onto her finger and held it there, as if to keep it from coming off again. He scooted forward and pulled her forehead down to touch his. Laced his fingers through hers.

Her breath was coming quick now, and he felt his body responding to it.

It was an exquisite contrast, the almost transcendent joy of her forgiveness, coming so close on the heels of almost losing her. He waited for her to lift his mouth to hers before he moved up to her, gathered her up. He helped her undress, taking time to kiss every little part of her body that he uncovered. Snatched his clothes off as fast as he could. The endorphins surging through his body made her weigh nothing at all. He lifted her like a feather, wrapped her legs around his waist. Moaned with the sheer joy of being inside of her. The sounds she made, the way she thrust back against him, demanded every ounce of his focus to not come right then and there.

He spun her around, laid her down on the bed. He stayed on top, delaying the inevitable as long as he could until he needed to see her. Flipped her around on top of him. Held her hands, let her push back against them as she moved fast on him, breathing raggedly. Felt the explosion coming and jammed her hips down, his body bucking, practically howling with the intensity of it.

Completely immobilized, he watched her lay alongside him, run her fingers down his torso and back up again. She kissed him on the mouth, more and more insistently. As soon as he could, he pulled her up onto his mouth, let her brace herself against the headboard. Sucked and flickered his tongue over her the way she had always loved. It had never bothered him one bit that he could taste his own release mixed with her arousal. Within less than a minute, she bore down on him with a string of shouted profanities and flooded him with her orgasm.

But the tension in her body told him that she was far from done, so he flipped her around onto her back, draped her legs across his shoulders. Lapped at her, curling his fingers inside of her. Made her come again and again until her body could give nothing more.

By then, he was already hard again, but he let her float for a while in the afterglow. As soon as he dared, he climbed on top of her and let her rest while he tried to satisfy his seemingly insatiable need.

Food became a secondary concern. When low blood sugar made it unavoidable, he ordered a pizza so they wouldn't have to leave. He sat her in his lap, both of them stark naked, and laughed with her at their attempts to feed each other pizza. They lost patience after one slice apiece, and made love right there in the chair.

When the sun went down, and their bodies were tapped out, he held her against his side, kissing her mouth, massaging her hair.

He whispered, "You have every part of me. My heart, my body and my soul. And you always will."

"I love you so much," she murmured. But as he floated off to sleep, he wondered why she said it as if it caused her pain.

"IF YOU WANT ME, I'M HERE."

A week later, William called Julia to begin making plans for her birthday in October. But as he floated the options to her, her replies came back distant and distracted.

"What's the matter?" he prompted gently.

"I'm not going to be able to get away for my birthday," she said. "I have too much work to do if I ever want to recover from this."

Alarmed that she might be sick or hurt, he asked, "From what?"

"I got bad feedback from my internship."

His heart plummeted to his feet for her. "Oh, Julie. I'm so sorry." But when Julia said nothing more, he added, "If you want to get together another weekend, we can."

"Will..."

Something in her tone filled him with dread, and his pulse ratcheted up accordingly. He feared he already knew where this was headed. Whatever she said in the next few moments was going to alter the entire direction of his life.

"Will," she said again. "It was a mistake."

He felt the world spinning. He knew exactly what she meant, but desperately said, "What?"

"I'm sorry."

With increasing panic, he demanded, "Julie, *what* was a mistake?"

"You know what I'm talking about."

"I want to hear you say it." When she still said nothing, he prompted, "Is it Kevin?"

"It's not Kevin." Drawing a deep breath, she added, "I told you already. I need to focus on school if I ever want to recover from this."

"And I told you already, I won't get in your way."

"My uncle once talked to me about you," she said gently. "He told me that if it's meant to be, the details will work themselves out. Well, the details aren't working themselves out. I can't offer you the time and attention you deserve and still do what I need to do. Not without completely losing the person I am apart from you."

God, he was so tired. Tired of trying to understand, of trying to make something work that felt so one-sided at this point. A couple of minutes of silence ensued, and Julia did not try to interrupt it, as if she knew he needed time to absorb the finality of what she had said.

Eventually, he asked, "Are you still wearing the ring?"

"No."

All of the air evacuated his lungs, carrying his voice along with it. Quickly, Julia added, "I'll give it back."

"I don't want it. Do whatever you want with it," he snapped. After another few minutes spent gathering the last shreds of his composure, he added more gently, "I'm not going to stalk you, Julie. If you want me, I'm here. If you want me to come to you, just say the word."

Her voice cracked. "Okay."

Even so, a month later, he mailed a package to her dorm in Santa Barbara – a shoebox, chock full of his poems, songs, and photos. A final Hail Mary pass.

DECEMBER 1995, PART II

he countdown on the timer had started the moment Julia moved to Santa Barbara. She was focused, ambitious, and driven, and he wasn't. She knew what she wanted; he didn't. Things changed; priorities shifted.

But she wasn't fucking Kevin. She never had been. He could prove it to himself, if he wanted to. Julia had once told him the name of Kevin's fiancée, and that she was the trustee for that foundation that did all the underwriting on NPR.

It wasn't like he was hurting anyone. It would put his mind at ease, finally.

So the next morning, William dialed 411 and requested the listing for the DeSmet Family Foundation in New York City.

"Nicole DeSmet's office; Dawn speaking."

"Hi Dawn; this is the wedding photographer," he said. "I'm calling to confirm the date with Nicole."

Silence. "The wedding is off. I already took care of that with you."

His guts heaved with nausea, but he thought fast. "Ah, right, I'm so sorry; I got my paperwork mixed up here. The reason I had Nicole on my call list is actually because I wanted to let her know that I changed my cancellation policy. Depending on the reason for cancellation, I can sometimes refund a client's deposit. Since Nicole cancelled very recently, I'm reaching out as a gesture of good faith."

Dawn practically squeaked. "Wow, that's so honest, and generous!"

So Dawn was young and naïve. That was promising. "Well, if Nicole ever needs a photographer in the future, I want her to remember me."

"I'm sure she will!"

"So, if you can just share with me the reason behind the cancellation, I'll verify whether or not I can offer her a refund."

"Oh. Well..." She giggled a bit. "I don't know if I should say."

William closed his eyes and crossed his fingers that she was as gullible as she was naïve. "I'm sorry, I should have explained. It's just, the specific circumstances behind the cancellation determine whether or not Nicole qualifies."

"Okay; but, um... maybe I should–"

"For example, was it a mutual decision?" He was desperate now for any shred of intel.

"Um... no." After a moment's hesitation, Dawn added, "Kevin broke it off."

"I see." William's heart threatened to hammer its way right through his sternum: *No, no, no,* it said. *Please, please, please...* "I'm sorry to keep pressing, Dawn, but the attorneys are such sticklers. They'll insist on knowing the exact reason why."

Dawn met his ploy with silence.

"I know – it's incredibly annoying," William plowed ahead with a forced chuckle, "not to mention intrusive. Lawyers, right?"

She reciprocated with a breathy laugh, but still said nothing. Just as William was about to try again, she finally spilled, keeping her voice to a near-whisper.

"He fell in love with another woman – a student of his, actually. Dumped Nicole so he could be with her. And Nicole was the one who funded their research, too. Can you believe it?" Dawn scoffed in disgust. "If anyone has earned a refund on her wedding deposits, it's Nicole."

William wasn't sure why they called it heartbreak, because the pain centered more on the intestines. It felt like someone was using a dull implement – a wooden spoon, perhaps – to gouge them out.

He had seen it in the movies, but he had always assumed it was just melodrama – this curling into a fetal position on the floor, gasping for air. Weeping into a wet spot on the carpet, grasping at the fibers for support. He didn't know that kind of thing happened in real life.

Some time later, he didn't know how long, he managed to pull himself back up into his bed. And he stayed there for a month.

A sixteenth of an inch at a time. Digging down through the epidermis and dermis, the layers of fat, the abdominal muscle wall.

He couldn't breathe. He couldn't eat. He lost half the weight he had painstakingly put on since his growth spurt at age fifteen. The only reason he didn't lose *all* of the weight was because of the Jameson he was drinking to help him sleep.

Disentangling the innards, pulling them out, loop by loop.

His mother begged him to talk to her, to tell her what had happened *this* time. But he had forgotten how to talk. His mother said time heals all wounds, so how was it that every day it only hurt more?

The phone rang, tentatively at first, then more insistently. His mother passed on all of the concerned messages from Haze, Mike, and Paul. She told them he had mono.

It would never, ever be okay again.

Finally his mother threatened to have him 5150ed. And since William had seen *One Flew Over The Cuckoo's Nest*, he got out of bed and submitted to a sandwich at the kitchen table.

"Maybe you should try one of those antidepressants," his mother suggested skeptically. His parents had never been big believers in *all that psychobabble,* as they called it. Instead, wherever a good old-fashioned bootstraps mentality fell short, they supplemented with spiritual guidance. But after Andy's predecessor transferred to another parish, they seemed to have lost faith in that, too.

A few minutes later, Mike arrived. He sat across the kitchen table, the shock of William's wraithlike appearance registering plainly on his face. It was clear that Mike's presence was intended to buck him up somehow – to remind him of all the fun he was missing out on with the band. How much the band mates missed him. How much the girls in the audience missed him.

The girls.

After Mike went home that night, William unlocked his father's liquor cabinet and swiped another bottle of Jameson from its rapidly-dwindling supply. Surely his father must have noticed by now. He sat in his bedroom, consuming it, and thought about the girls.

Haze and Michelle definitely helped him forget his problems, but they weren't always at his disposal. Some days he was left high and dry with his thoughts, and his Jameson. What he realized, as he drained the bottle, was that he needed more of those forgetful days, and fewer of the high and dry ones.

Julia had been right all along – underneath the restrained exterior, he was a roiling, boiling, seething hotbed of passions. He liked to feel good. He *deserved* to feel good, for a fucking change.

He couldn't drink on the job, so he did it before going to Dunphy's. Not enough to dull his job performance, since his talent there was part of his game. Just enough to flirt comfortably with the waitresses, and the new hostess, and the female prep cooks.

Eventually, the alcohol started wearing off in mid-shift, so he stashed some of those mini-bottles of liquor in the interior pocket of his coat. The ones he swiped from Haze's house.

He told himself he was tipsy. And staying tipsy was the key. It carried away the last of his inhibitions, so when a waitress passed his station on the way through the kitchen – or a hostess, or a female prep cook – he invited her to accompany him to the walk-in, or to the alley out back. If she actually obliged, that was a good sign. The things that went on in the walk-in and the alley behind Dunphy's were legendary.

He even succeeded with a customer once, a woman in her mid-forties who asked to pay her compliments to the chef after trying the cioppino, so Paul sent him out. She slipped him her number, and he spent a sleepless night at her condo.

On Fridays at MacGowan's, he ordered Jameson, neat, and then another one. It bolstered his courage so he could get up on stage and broadcast his heartbreak publicly. The girls in the audience practically swooned over that stupid fucking song he had written for Julia.

Afterward, he didn't pack up his guitar and go straight to Haze's house like he used to. He hung out with the guys and had another Jameson, neat. And then another.

Cindy gave him a concerned look as she pushed his third drink across the bar. "You okay?"

He grinned and lifted his glass in response. "Cindy, I'm better than okay. I'm on fire." And he went to mingle with the groupies.

The withholding of his attention was actually his most powerful tool, more powerful than the giving of it – at least where most of them were concerned. It was like catnip. Chat her up a bit, get her number, and then not call. If she came back to the bar the next Friday, sometimes all he had to do was walk her out back. Sometimes he was too lazy to go even that far, and he would lead her to the men's room.

Drinking at MacGowan's was getting expensive, so he learned to start at home. Just enough to put on his best show, but not sloppy yet. After the show, he'd order two or three more from Cindy.

When Cindy pushed his Jameson (neat) across the bar one Friday in May, he thought he detected her disapproval tight around her mouth. Bemused, he watched her retrieve a wet rag and flick it furiously over the bar. He wondered why he had never fully appreciated that curvy bombshell physique before. He had already enjoyed success with one middle-aged woman. Why not this one?

He propped his elbows on the bar and leaned forward. "Hey Cindy, I think I finally just figured it out."

"Amaze me."

"You look exactly like Geena Davis."

She wasn't smiling. "And you're auditioning to be Brad Pitt?"

"If you like."

"Not really." She hurled the rag into a bus tub. "Let me guess. You think hey, she's a single mom, pushing forty, three kids. She wears corsets with her tits spilling out and serves booze to horny assholes all night. I'll be a breath of fresh air. She'll be *so grateful.*"

He recoiled, annoyance tightening his chest. What the hell was wrong with her these days? In the beginning, she had practically thrown herself at him.

She leaned across the bar at him so abruptly that he flinched backward. "When you first came in here, I flirted with you because I saw a cute, sweet kid who needed a boost of confidence. Now I see a pathetic, entitled, drunken douchebag."

He scraped his bar stool back so roughly that it tipped over, and he stumbled. He made sure to bring his drink with him. He staggered across the room, gulping it down all at once and then slamming the glass on the stage so hard that it shattered.

His brother was there, clapping a hand on his back. In a low, soothing tone, Mike said, "Hey man, you okay?"

"Fucking incredible." He clambered onto the stage, snatched the now-disconnected microphone and began parodying his own song. Some girls near the stage looked up at him and giggled.

William paused long enough to stretch his arm out. He tried in vain to settle his pointer finger on the amorphous, wavering female specters below the stage.

"Look, Mike! It works no matter how bad I sing it!"

Mike humored him with an awkward grin. He was climbing onstage but, sensing an intervention, William dropped the mic, leaped from the stage, and draped his arms across the shoulders of two of the girls. Including the one with the copper hair and the cute little overbite.

"Ladies, let me buy you a drink from the waiter in the back room. I'm on the outs with the bartender at the moment."

They giggled and followed him into the back room where the tables were. He didn't remember very much after that, except that he couldn't take his eyes off the Julia doppelganger. She told him her name, but he promptly forgot it – it distracted from the illusion. And he was definitely hitting it off with her, too. She leaned across the table, tossed her copper hair. Flashed her cute little toothy smile at him. Let him buy her drink after fruity drink and offered him sips of it from the same spot that her lips had touched.

Increasingly he ignored her friend, especially after she started letting him nuzzle her freckled throat and slide his hand up her bare thigh. At one point, Mike appeared and bent over his ear.

"Beer goggles, dude. Beer goggles."

William shoved him away, so Mike shrugged and pulled up a chair next to the other girl to play wingman. Then the Julia doppelganger reached into her purse and retrieved a colorful little pill of some kind. With her flirty grin, she held it to his lips, offering it to him.

He eyed it warily, willing it to come into focus. "What's that?"

She leaned into his ear and whispered, "X."

Mike spotted it. "Ohhhh, fuck yeah; share the wealth!"

Even under the influence of so much alcohol, William still glanced around to make sure they weren't being watched as the Julia doppelganger passed pills under the table to both Mike and her friend. Then she retrieved one for herself and held it in front of her lips with a seductive grin at William. Inviting him to take his along with her.

Fuck it. "What do I do with it?"

Everyone at the table laughed, and Mike good-naturedly berated him for his naïveté. The Julia doppelganger took his tablet, placed it on his tongue, and ordered him to swallow it whole. He washed it down with his drink.

Not long afterward, she groped him and whispered, "Let's all go back to my place."

Everything after that was a frenzy of motion, a jumble of voices, sporadic glimpses of flesh. He was aware of being very hot, and insatiably thirsty.

In the midst of it all, a vague memory of his brother's command. "Shove over, Will. Switch with me."

A bolt of pleasure, his eyes rolling back, crying out with the shock of it.

His eyes opened, and it was daylight. Disoriented, he waited for the room to come into focus. He became gradually aware of a body entangled with his. Wincing, he opened his eyes a little wider. Lifted his head.

They were lying on the floor, naked, covered by nothing at all. She snored delicately, her head on his shoulder, her leg slung over his.

He mumbled, "Julie?"

She stirred a bit, but didn't open her eyes. "Brittany."

Seized with panic, he glanced around frantically and found Mike on the bed a few feet away. Naked. With the Julia doppelganger.

William scrambled to a sitting position. Scuttled backward, across the carpet, as fast as he could. Brittany jerked fully awake and rolled herself up to a sitting position. Blinked at him, her bleach-blonde hair a tousled mess, wisps of it falling into her makeup-smeared face.

He sprang to his feet, cursing the pounding in his head, and ran to the bathroom. Heard Brittany say, "What's *his* problem?" He snatched a towel, and wrapped it around his waist.

When he came back into the room, he saw the pills, empty bottles, and pipes strewn everywhere. Brittany sauntered naked around the room in search of her clothes, wholly unfazed. William raked his hands through his hair, trying to stop the room from spinning.

"Jesus Christ."

In the bed, Mike and the Julia doppelganger stirred, stretched. Mike's eyes flew open wide as he took in his surroundings, and then he grinned. "Whoa. Hell of a party."

"What the fuck did we do?!" William demanded, snatching his clothes off of the floor.

Mike glanced around the room. "Everything?"

The Julia doppelganger sat up in bed now. Her copper hair was clearly out of a bottle. What he had thought were freckles on her throat were actually moles. And she didn't have a cute little overbite like Julia's – she just needed an orthodontist.

She swung herself off the bed, only to step in a puddle of vomit on the carpet. "Oh, God."

Mike watched her scrambling into her underwear and observed, "I think we'd better bounce."

William nodded and followed him into the living room, carrying his clothes, still wearing only a towel. After pulling on his boxers, Mike clapped his hand on William's shoulder and said, "Thanks, bro. Best night I've had in a long time. Can't say the best night of my life – there was this time Jimmy and I got twacked with these four chicks–"

"Shut the fuck up, Mike."

"Jesus, dude, what's your problem?"

Thoroughly panicked, William scrambled into his clothes and stumbled out of the apartment, down a set of stairs, and into an unfamiliar streetscape, cringing at the bright sunlight.

He had no idea what neighborhood he was in. He didn't recognize any of these buildings. He staggered to the nearest major intersection and looked at the signs. He frowned – he didn't recognize the street names either. He knew most of the major streets in San Francisco. He had traveled down almost all of them during his explorations on his motorcycle.

Also, there were a lot of black people around here. Was he in Excelsior, or Visitacion Valley? Maybe he was in Crocker-Amazon. He stopped someone and asked which way to the nearest Muni station.

The man's wary eyes traveled the length of William – the rumpled clothes, the facial scruff, the wavy hair darkened with grease and standing on end. "There's no Muni in Oakland."

Fuck me.

It was three o'clock in the afternoon before William made it back to MacGowan's. His motorcycle wasn't there. Had someone brought it home for him? He was a bit shaky by now. He could not wait to get home, eat something, and wash it down with some Jameson. Then he would take a shower and brush his teeth before he had to go to work.

When he finally made it home by foot, he heaved a sigh of relief to find the motorcycle parked out front. Then, to his dismay, he spotted Haze sitting on the front step, a duffel bag at her feet, her knees drawn up to her chin. Dread already welled in William's stomach.

It was going to be bad.

He stopped in front of her. She wouldn't say anything, so he prompted, "What's the matter?"

Slowly, she clambered to her feet. Stepped toward him and looked in his face for a moment with those somber eyes. Then, her face screwed up. With his reflexes as numbed as they were, he failed to anticipate her as she wound back and slapped him hard across the face.

"What the fuck?!" he spat out, clutching his smarting cheek.

She reached into her duffel bag and, to his horror, produced the photos he had taken of himself with Haze. The ones of them together at Grand View Park, and McWay Falls, and all the other places he had taken her in a futile attempt to recreate the magic he once felt with Julia. Haze flipped through them casually, one by one, as if he weren't even there.

His mind whirled. He had left those in his bedroom. "How did you...?

"You didn't come over last night after the show, like you said you would."

His eyes flew open wide, and he froze. He had completely forgotten about it.

"I hadn't heard from you," she continued. "I called Mike, but he wasn't answering. I went to MacGowan's, but they were closed, and your bike was still out front. I didn't want to call your house that late at night, but I came over this morning because I was so worried. I was talking with your sister in the kitchen when the rest of your family came home, freaking out because you were missing. And then Mike said he brought your motorcycle home because you had gone home with some ugly-ass skank. That in fact, she was the ugliest-ass skank you had *ever* gone home with. Your sister tried to shut him up, but he didn't get the hint. Nobody knew I was in the kitchen, you see."

She was still flipping through the photos of herself. She flipped again, and landed on the identical ones he had taken of Julia.

William flinched. His first instinct was to snatch them from her, but he knew that would only escalate things. It might even leave those precious mementos in tatters. Instead, he sat down on the front step because his trembling knees would no longer hold his weight.

He patted the step beside him. "Haze. Please sit. There's something I want to say." At the skeptical look on her face, he added, "I promise – no bullshit."

After a moment's hesitation, she complied. She was holding the photo he had taken of Julia at McWay Falls in Big Sur. The one he had taken of her right before proposing. He almost panicked at the idea of any harm coming to it, but he forced himself to remain calm.

"Everything I've done has been me trying to forget," he said quietly. "It's not an excuse, I know. You deserved so much better. I'm sorry I caught you up in all my crap."

Curling her lip in disgust, she shoved the photos at William and left without another word. He spent a few minutes gathering his wits. His family waited inside; he had to let them know he was okay. He went upstairs long enough to mumble his apologies to his agitated parents and his sheepish brother, who no doubt realized the havoc he had wrought. He grabbed a bag of potato chips from the pantry and retreated back downstairs to his bedroom.

Haze had violently jerked open the drawer of his bedside table – tore it off its runner. It dangled precariously. His address book lay open on his bed – his "little black book" stuffed with feminine names. His closet door was open and the box where he hid his memorabilia of Julia appeared to have vomited its contents onto the floor. He checked to make sure everything was still there, and then carefully replaced it all along with the photos of Julia that Haze had returned to him. Then he went out on the back patio and burned the photos of Haze in the fire pit.

Back in his room, he popped open the bag of chips and sat on the edge of his bed to eat them. Took a pull or two off the bottle of Jameson on his bedside table.

Was he just destined to burn his bridges with every woman who cared about him?

He heard a light knock on his bedroom door. "What?" he snapped.

"It's Mom. Can I come in?"

He glanced around himself at the chaos that was his bedroom. She did not need to see any of that. Instead, he emerged from his room and went to sit on the couch in the in-law unit. His mother joined him there.

William hunched over, his elbows and forearms on his thighs, and frowned down at the carpet. His mother peered earnestly at him. They sat that way in silence for a long time.

Finally, he said, "I gave her an engagement ring. We were going to get married."

Somehow, she knew he wasn't talking about Haze. "I know. But Will, most high school sweethearts grow apart."

"You and Dad didn't."

She opened her mouth, grappling unsuccessfully for a response.

"I should have listened to my gut," he persisted. "I should have gone down there with her."

"It's not your fault, Will. She didn't even try to make it work. It's not like your dad and I haven't had rough patches over the years. There were plenty of times I was ready to leave. We just worked through it because it was worth it. Maybe it was because we had you kids. Or maybe we've just been lucky. But the point is, you deserve to be with someone who thinks you're worth the effort."

William shook his head. "You don't know the whole story, Mom. I fucked up. And also, the timing just wasn't right."

"Son, where relationships are concerned, the timing is never right. If someone is worth it, you sacrifice other things, the way you kept trying to for her. You were ready to give up a full-ride scholarship to go down there and be with her. But she didn't love you as much as you loved her. I'm sorry to be so blunt, but there it is."

He sat up straight now. Looked her in the eye. "I didn't love her in the past tense, Mom. I *still* love her."

"I know you do, Will."

"I don't know how to just shut that off."

She put her arm around his shoulders, leaned the side of her head against his. "I'm sorry she hurt you. But all this stuff you've been up to? This is not you, son." Her voice grew suddenly strained, choked with tears. "I know your dad and I screwed up. I know we weren't around like we should have been. Your nonna did the best she could, but it wasn't her job to raise you, and we never should have expected her to. She was too old and out of touch to keep up with a bunch of rowdy teenagers."

"Mom, it's okay–"

"No, it's not okay, and I'm not finished," she said fiercely, as if the floodgates had opened and she couldn't contain the truth anymore. "First we failed Jimmy, and then we enabled him out of guilt. And by enabling him, we failed the rest of you kids, too. I know that now, and Will? I'm *so* sorry. If I could go back in time, I'd fix it. I'd listen to Nonna and do everything differently. But all I can do now is learn, and do better."

Startled by her sudden, frank confession, William pulled back to look her in the eye. "Mom–"

"That's why I'm telling you now that Jimmy's getting paroled soon." When William flinched in shock, she quickly added, "Don't worry, I won't let him set foot in this house, but I'm sure he'll be hanging around the neighborhood. Getting back into trouble with his old crew. You need to get out of here, Will. Away from him, and Mike, and all the temptations they bring with them. You need to start over somewhere fresh, away from all the associations you have with this place."

He considered a moment. "Where?"

His mother rubbed his back. "Have you ever given any thought to joining the military?"

William scoffed. "Do you really see me marching in lock-step with any group of people?"

"You might find the discipline and camaraderie in the military are exactly what fits the bill," she replied. "And you could get money for college."

William shook his head. "With my drug test results? Not even the military is going to want me."

Her eyes broadcast pain. "Is it really that bad?"

"Bad enough."

"You can clean up, Will. Go to rehab."

"Great; then that will be on my medical records for the military to see."

"It can't hurt to just talk to a recruiter. They might be able to work with you somehow. Or talk to your Uncle Frank. He was a Marine, you know."

William's smile was rueful. "And his Vietnam horror stories are supposed to inspire me?"

She frowned. "Frank's very proud of his service. Ask him yourself, if you don't believe me. He'll tell you it made him a man."

He sighed, and stared down at the floor again.

"Promise me you'll just talk to him about it," his mother persisted.

"Yeah, okay," he grumbled. And without any further ceremony, he stood up, went back into his bedroom, and closed the door.

After finishing the bag of chips and taking another few swigs of Jameson, he glanced at the clock on his bedside table. Four o'clock; his shift started at five. If he hustled, he could drain this bottle before he had to leave. He worked at it until he knew that if he didn't leave for work right now, he would be more than fifteen minutes late.

He parked his motorcycle in the alley as usual and staggered into

Dunphy's through the back door. Slung his coat over the hook so clumsily that he knocked over the entire coat rack. Went to stow his valuables in his locker, but couldn't remember the combination, so he just left them in the chair by the lockers. Staggered through the kitchen to his station.

He scraped the grill to clean it but didn't wipe up the detritus, so it smoked. He slammed the pots and pans until Paul looked up from his station to see what all the racket was about. He sliced his finger open and swore loudly. Seized a towel and wrapped it around his bleeding finger.

Paul rushed over, demanded a look at the injury, and flinched as the wall of Jameson fumes assailed his nostrils.

Slowly, calmly, Paul told a prep cook to go find Karen. Karen was to take William to the bathroom, rinse the wound and bandage it. Then, though it wasn't a very deep cut, she was to take him to the ER and get his finger checked out.

"I don't think he's in any condition to drive," Paul observed, looking directly at William, "seeing as how he's in so much *pain.*"

Karen did take him to the bathroom and bandage his finger. From the grim look on her face, he knew – his employment at Dunphy's was over.

How far he had fallen since eight months ago, when he resolved that Julia would hear only good things about him from her parents.

"Please don't tell Julia about this," he pleaded, his words coming out mushy through his numb mouth and tongue.

Karen froze, still holding his halfway-doctored hand in hers. "Why would I tell Julia?"

"So she can congratulate herself again on dumping me for the millionaire," he sloshed out bitterly.

Karen frowned, as if confused. "What millionaire?"

William scoffed. "You don't have to pretend for my sake. I know all about him."

"About *who?*" she demanded, and he had to admit, her look of consternation was convincing as fuck. Or maybe he was just that drunk.

"Kevin," he spat out.

After a long, searching pause, Karen's eyebrows lifted in recognition. "You mean the TA?"

"The Cat Stevens doppelganger." His voice sounded very, very far away. His head was nodding, his neck suddenly unable to support its weight.

He couldn't make out much of what Karen was saying as she resumed bandaging his finger, but his drink-addled brain seized on certain snippets, like *just a friend*.

Could it be?

All these months of numbing himself – this slow suicide he'd been committing – had it all been for nothing? Nothing but a big misunderstanding?

No.

No.

Dawn had told him... but then again, she didn't exactly say...

What *had* she said?

"He fell in love with another woman – a student of his, actually. Dumped Nicole so he could be with her."

He had interpreted it one way, but now he realized there was more than one interpretation. Dawn had said nothing to suggest that Kevin and the woman in question were a couple. In fact, she had never even mentioned Julia reciprocating Kevin's feelings.

For two seconds, his tattered heart grasped desperately at this tiny thread of hope. And then he remembered – it didn't matter if this unlikely new interpretation was accurate. If Julia could see how zealously he had gone about degrading himself – how callously he demeaned others in the process – she would know he was just another drunken burn-out. Just like all the other men in his family.

And she deserved better.

On their way to her car, Karen led him out the back door and through the alley, where he had parked his own motorcycle. After pausing to vomit into the sewer grate, he swung himself onto the bike without warning – without even putting his helmet on first.

"Wait!" cried Karen, springing forward to touch his arm. "I'm taking you to the ER."

"No, you're not," he shot back. She sprang back at the deafening blast of the engine, and he peeled away.

That was the last thing he remembered, until he woke up in yet another unfamiliar bed. Only this one was hard and cold like the ground. No sheets, no mattress. Loud, testosterone-drenched voices ricocheted off of sterile gray walls around him.

He sat up like a shot, and immediately crumpled back onto the bed. Wherever he was, the entire room was spinning.

Actually, come to think of it, he wasn't in a room at all. He was in a cage with bars. Just like the albatross on his back.

Pain screamed in his finger, and he groaned. He opened his eyes just enough to look – a bloody bandage. He remembered that Julia's mother had put it there.

He opened his eyes wider now. Sat up much more slowly this time. Took in his surroundings.

He was in jail.

"WHERE WILL YOU GO FROM HERE?"

After the jailer returned William's belongings and walked him out, William stopped short in his tracks, not quite believing his eyes.

Haze said nothing; she just looked at him. He stopped in front of her a moment, and she blinked and turned away. Without a word between them, he followed her. She led him to an old Volkswagen Beetle that might once have been green, but was now olive, gray, and rust. Was it hers? If so, he had never seen it before.

She got in the driver's side and leaned over to unlock the passenger side door. It squawked open, and he got in and buckled his seat belt. She started the car and tuned the radio to a Russian-language station on the AM band.

They rode along like that halfway to the Mission before William said, "I'll pay you back."

She still said nothing. Looked straight ahead.

After another minute, William asked, "How did you–"

"Mike called."

They rode in silence the rest of the way to the Mission. She parked the car in front of a neighbor's house and met its owner at the front door to return the keys. Then, with a fleeting glance at William, she turned toward her own house.

Was she really going to let him inside? Was she going to let him follow her, then slam the door in his face, just for theater? He certainly deserved it.

She unlocked the front door and held it open for him. With his hands in his jacket pockets, he shuffled into the foyer. Followed her into the living room and took a seat on the sofa when she beckoned him to.

Without a word, she went upstairs. His hands were shaking almost uncontrollably. He hadn't eaten in a while; maybe his blood sugar was crashing. He didn't *feel* hungry. His eyes wandered in the direction of the cart, with its mini-bottles...

The cart was empty. The party was over.

Haze came back downstairs, carrying a stack of sheets and a blanket. William rose from his seat and tried to help her put them on the sofa, but for some reason his hands were shaking so badly that he almost couldn't control them. Come to think of it, he was a bit sweaty and clammy, too. Maybe he was coming down with something.

He looked up and saw her watching him. Followed her gaze to his trembling hands. He clenched them, trying to stop the shaking. His pulse fluttered in his neck.

She finished putting the sheets on the sofa, then slowly said, "You should eat."

He nodded. He followed her into the kitchen, but she ordered him to sit at the table. She emerged from the kitchen a few minutes later with some kind of soup. He wasn't hungry, and his hand was shaking so badly that the soup sloshed right out of the spoon. His stomach quivered with nausea.

Haze watched him struggle for a few minutes, then got up and went back to the kitchen. When she returned, she carried a can of beer.

"Drink this."

His eyes snapped to it right away. The itching at the back of his throat...

She thrust it into his hands. "You need to drink it. You'll feel better."

"I'm fine."

"You're going through withdrawal."

The words crashed through his wall of denial like a sledgehammer. Still, he shook his head. "I'm tired and hungry."

"I'm Russian. I know alcohol withdrawal when I see it." She popped the top. It emitted a sumptuous hiss. "Going cold turkey could kill you."

He looked up into her eyes, and her face promptly swam. He looked away, blinked rapidly and bit his tongue hard. He accepted the can and drained it all in practically one go.

His hands stopped shaking. The flu feeling vanished.

He dissolved. Folded his arms onto the tabletop and crumpled into them, his shoulders shaking.

She sat in the chair opposite him, but made no effort to console him. She calmly watched and waited until he got it out of his system. The grief, the terror of living, the shame, the denial – all pooled within some swollen, diseased organ of his soul that finally burst.

Spent, he sagged into the crook of his arm. Without even lifting his head, he said, "Why did you bring me here?"

She said, "You need to detox."

He lifted his head. He was past shame, past hiding the ruins of his face from her. He swiped his hand over his eyes and said, "I can't. I don't have health insurance."

"Go to General."

He glared at her. "You're joking, right?"

She pressed her lips together, grim. "Then you'll have to taper."

"I don't know how."

"I do."

He looked up at her again in some surprise. She said, "Do you trust me?"

Did he trust her? He had wronged her, after all. Did he dare put himself in her hands? Did he have a choice?

He said, "How?"

"You're going to have to be completely honest with me. If you are, you'll stay out of the hospital. If you're not, then you won't."

"Honest about what?"

She retrieved a pad of paper and a pencil from her desk and brought it back to the table. With the pencil hovering just above the pad, she said, "You have to tell me exactly how much you've been drinking every day."

He propped his elbows on the tabletop and clutched his head in his hands. Hot shame seared his insides, and his eyes stung again. "At least a fifth of Jameson."

She had that grim look again. "Every day." It was a statement, not a question, but he nodded anyway. Slowly, she set the pencil down on the pad. She hadn't bothered to write anything.

"Call your family," she said. "You'll be with me this week."

She gave him one beer every hour – sixteen per day. The next day, ten beers – one every hour and a half.

The next it was eight, and the day after that, six.

During the day, he came with her to her studio. He sat in the office in the back and she snuck beers to him there. He read English translations of Russian literature that he borrowed from the bookcase in her house. He played games on the computer, listened to the radio or dozed fitfully on the loveseat. At night, he came home with her and she served him porridges of rice or buckwheat that she called *kasha*, and chicken broth with little flecks of dill in it. When he couldn't sleep, she made him a tea of lemon balm, chamomile, and honey.

Now, in the cold light of sobriety, he looked in her bathroom mirror and no longer recognized the man he had become. This scruffy stranger staring back at him had aged five years in just a few months. He had no qualms about using people, including his first and most enduring friend, in a misguided attempt to escape his grief and pain. Not only that, he had allowed people who definitely did not have his best interests at heart to enable his worst impulses.

But also, in that same cold light, he could finally remember the man he once wanted to be. The man his grandmother had raised him to be. The man he had once aspired to be for someone he loved. The only question now was whether he could become that man all on his own because it was the right thing to do – because *he* wanted it – without requiring somebody else to do it for. After so many disastrous judgment calls, could he even trust his own gut? He wanted to rely on it to incorporate the best parts of himself with the best parts of the people he admired, and become his own man.

The sober man staring back at him wasn't sure he could, but he desperately wanted to try.

On the fifth day there was a lull at the studio, and Haze joined him in the office. William sat on the loveseat and picked at the burrito she brought him and watched her as she ate. She sat in the office chair, her shaggy dark hair falling in a curtain over her cheeks, concealing her face from him as she leaned forward to take a bite. She looked different somehow, and it dawned on him that she was no longer deliberately streaking her hair with gray. She looked younger this way – her own age.

Her black halter crop top, with its plunging neckline, and her cut-off denim shorts offered minimal obstruction to the canvas that was her body: the mythical Pazyryk creatures stampeding down her arms. The occult-like ring tattoos on her fingers. The heads of the Madonna and Child on her back. The edifice of the cathedral on her breasts. The fish aligned vertically along the length of her shin.

The sexual urge seemed to have abandoned him, but he felt a yearning of some kind. He wanted to love her in the way he had loved Julia. He should have. He sensed that she wanted him to.

He said, "Why are you doing this for me?"

She looked up at him, startled. Still chewing. Taking her time with it, as if using it to consider her response. Finally, after swallowing, she admitted, "Because I've been holding out on you."

William's heart missed a beat. "Holding *what* out on me?"

After a moment's hesitation, she slowly re-wrapped her burrito. Clearly, this was going to take a while. Or maybe it was going to take something out of her.

"Information," she replied at last.

Blinking, all he could manage was a stupid echo. "Information."

She nodded, wiping her mouth on her napkin, then neatly folding it. Finally, she lifted her eyes to his. They brimmed with something like guilt.

"And I wonder if it might have helped if you knew it all along."

He caught himself leaning forward in his chair. Words abandoned him. All he could do was wait.

"Will..." She winced, then shook her head, as if to clear it. "Did Jimmy ever... do things to you?"

It took William a second to grasp what she meant, but when he did, he recoiled in denial.

She watched him like a hawk for several long seconds. And despite his best efforts, as the seconds ticked by, an unwelcome memory floated to the surface. A memory he had tried in vain to sink beneath years of denial, weed, and booze. The memory of his brother Jimmy, kneeling atop his chest. Slowly unzipping his jeans, one tooth at a time.

I bet you'd love to suck a real man's cock, wouldn't you?

Occasionally, while pinned beneath Jimmy, William detected something rigid pressing into his hip. It disgusted him, but at the time, he attributed it to an involuntary reflex on Jimmy's part – the inevitable and entirely unintended result of physical contact. William knew only too well how little it took, and under the most inopportune circumstances, as well. But now, William wondered how unintentional and involuntary it had actually been.

William swallowed past the rising bile in his throat. "Nothing he really followed through on, anyway." The words came out strangled.

Haze slowly nodded. She seemed to be making up her mind about something. "I'm not proud of what I'm about to tell you, but I'm even less proud of keeping it from you."

William couldn't fathom what was causing her such discomfort. She was usually so cool and collected – notwithstanding that one time she had administered him a well-earned slap. All he could do was brace for the bombshell on the horizon.

"I'm sure you're aware, no thanks to your brothers, that meth makes you do incredibly stupid things," she continued quietly. "And one of the incredibly stupid things I used to do was fuck Jimmy."

William's mouth went dry. The earth shifted on its axis. Summer changed to winter and back again in the time it took him to process her admission. "Wh-*what*?!"

"Yeah," Haze responded drily. "Or at least, I tried to."

The truth opened up to him slowly, like a flower unfurling in the clear light of day. And what it revealed was going to rearrange everything he thought he knew.

"And Jimmy tried to fuck me," Haze added, peering keenly at William, as if willing him to understand. "He really tried."

"But he couldn't," William deduced at last.

She looked relieved that he was catching on. "Most of the time, no."

"Because he was gay." He stated it like it was a fact he had known all his life, even though he had only known it a few seconds. Jimmy was gay. Of course he was.

Haze tucked her legs underneath her on the chair. "You deserve to know the truth, Will. Because even though Jimmy's abuse was horrible and inexcusable, and it hurt you beyond anything I can imagine – it ultimately wasn't about you. Not really, anyway. It was about Jimmy's own internal conflict. His own self-loathing. But he didn't get so messed up in the head all on his own. He had plenty of help along the way."

William frowned. "What do you mean?"

Haze shifted uncomfortably in her seat. "Do you know why the priest at Holy Cross got transferred? The one before your friend Andy?"

William blinked, unsure how the two subjects were related. "I... I heard something about inappropriate contact with parishioners."

Haze gave a silent, rueful laugh and shook her head in dismay. And suddenly, understanding crashed over William like a rogue wave.

"Do you mean...?"

"Jimmy told me the story in a rare vulnerable moment, when he was crashing after a binge," Haze began quietly. "He told me your parents brought him to the priest when he was only eleven in the hopes of 'curing' him or whatever, because back then, even psychiatrists said homosexuality was a mental illness. But I guess your parents didn't trust psychiatrists, and I guess they thought they were protecting Jimmy's privacy by bringing him to the priest, instead. And then the priest abused his position of trust to prey on the exact same vulnerable kid whose parents had sent him."

"Oh, God." William's stomach churned with nausea. "So the priest got reassigned because of what he did to Jimmy?"

"Among other boys, yes," she said.

"Fuck." For the first time in his life, William felt something bordering on compassion for his oldest brother. It was a peculiar new sensation, and he wasn't sure he was ready to embrace it. "Are you telling me they didn't even de-frock that piece of shit? They just transferred him right on to his next batch of victims?"

"From everything I heard, yes. I got most of the story from Jimmy, but I thought the meth crash might have made him delirious. It wouldn't have been the first time, or the last, as you know. But Mike confirmed the story after Jimmy went to prison, and he filled in the rest of the details." She pinned him with her hazel eyes before adding, "Apparently, Mike walked in on the priest raping Jimmy in the church's sacristy. Jimmy was only fourteen."

On the verge of dry-heaving, William could only make a garbled sound of horror.

"Mike told your grandmother what he saw," Haze continued quietly. "He said your grandmother and your parents did everything they could to get that priest de-frocked and prosecuted, but the diocese covered it all up."

It took a minute for William to recover his voice. "So that's why my parents stopped going to church. Even Nonna stopped going for a while. She only went back after Andy became the new priest."

Haze scanned his expression; and again, behind her intensity, William detected the echoes of guilt. "I know Jimmy targeted you, but I just didn't want you going the rest of your life believing it was *because* of you. Or that you had done anything at all to deserve it."

Hurt people hurt people, Andy had said. *It's not an excuse. Just context.* Now he knew.

"I'm glad you told me," he admitted finally. "Thank you."

She searched his eyes for another moment. Apparently satisfied with whatever she found there, she slowly unwrapped her burrito again. But William was still too nauseous to eat.

After many long minutes of heavy, pensive silence, Haze ventured to ask, "What are your plans after this?"

He tilted his head. "Plans?"

She peeled some more of the aluminum foil back from the burrito. "Where will you go from here?"

Flummoxed, he shrugged. "Back home, I guess. But not to stay."

She took another bite from the burrito. Chewed thoughtfully. "Kirill – my brother, the priest – he knows a lot of fishermen up there in Alaska. There's a ton of money to be made in a very short time on the crab boats."

"Out of the frying pan into the fire," he scoffed. "Fishermen are the biggest horde of drunks and junkies you'll ever meet."

Haze shook her head. "Kirill knows which boats are the sober boats."

He gave a short laugh. "The sober boats?"

But she wasn't laughing. After a moment's hesitation, she added, "My husband Matt – ex-husband, now – he's on one of them."

She got up and opened a filing cabinet. Retrieved a folder – a portfolio of sketches – and began rummaging through it. Eventually she said, "You can stay the week. But after that, you have to go."

He nodded.

"If you decide to go to Alaska, my brother Kirill can introduce you to the captains and give you a place to stay until you get a job."

Finally, she located what she was looking for and held it up to him. It was the mermaid she had sketched for him on Halloween. She came over and lifted his left arm – the receiving arm, she had told him. "'Set me as a seal upon your heart, as a seal upon your arm.'"

He drew his arm away. "It's too late for that. She'd never have anything to do with me now."

She withdrew to her chair. Sat down hard on it. Neither of them had ever explicitly acknowledged her before, this other woman that loomed like a specter between them.

"I'm sorry," she said.

He pushed aside his burrito. No hope of choking that down. "No, *I'm* sorry, Haze. For lying to you."

Though her shrug was almost nonchalant, she stared down at the mermaid sketch in her lap and chewed her lip. "You never really lied, though. We weren't exclusive."

"But it was lying by omission. I didn't tell you..." He swallowed past the lump of shame in his throat. "You know."

She lifted her piercing gaze to his. Waiting. Tugging anxiously at his knuckles, he finally owned it out loud, even though, of course, she already knew.

"I didn't tell you I had other partners. And, um... I wasn't safe, so I put you at risk. I don't know how you can stand to even look at me right now, much less help me, but..." Summoning his courage, he pulled himself upright and looked her straight in the eye. "I'm sorry for betraying your trust, especially after everything you went through with Matt. You gave me your friendship, and I treated you with disrespect. That was pure shit of me, and you deserve to hear me say it."

She gave a tiny wince and trained her unfocused gaze on some point in the corner. But in an even tone, she said, "I appreciate the apology."

He continued staring until she finally dragged her eyes up to his again. They sat that way for several long seconds, but somehow, it wasn't uncomfortable.

Finally, the corners of her mouth tipped up almost imperceptibly. "So, no mermaid, then?"

He answered her with a muted smile of his own. "I've been thinking of a compass instead."

"A compass?" She pulled a sketch pad and a pencil out of her desk drawer. "Why?"

He shrugged. "I could use a little direction in life, don't you think?"

Her mouth twisted into a wry smile. She glanced at the clock – a minute past two – then opened her mini fridge and handed him his two o'clock beer.

Then she set to work. He sipped and watched her, bent over the sketch pad. She tucked her hair out of the way, but it kept slipping out from behind her ear. Her pencil flicked lightly across the paper, its whisper the only noise in the office.

At last, she held it up for him – a compass rose, modeled after the eight-pointed stars on her knees. Marking the position of north, so tiny that William almost had to squint to see it – a crab.

A while later, reclined in the chair in her workspace, he listened to the buzz of the tattoo machine as she hunched over his right arm.

THE END

Please leave a review on your platform of choice! https://
Linktr.ee/JennaMalabyReviews, or scan the QR code:

If you enjoyed *The Compass* and want to read more from me, know that **nothing helps indie authors more than reviews.** So please, **leave a review** on your platform of choice by going to **https://linktr.ee/Jenna MalabyReviews**, or scan the QR code below:

Want more of Julia and William? Find out where it all began, in *The Catch!* Go to Books2Read.com/TheCatchByJennaMalaby, or scan the QR code below:

Or read The Hold, the stand-alone sequel to The Catch! Go to Books2Read.com/TheHoldByJennaMalaby, or scan the QR code below:

Let's keep in touch! Subscribe to my monthly email newsletter for freebies and first looks. www.JennaMalabyAuthor/subscribe, or scan the QR code below:

Thank you *so* much for reading (and reviewing!) my books!

With love,

Jenna Malaby (formerly Jenna Miles)

ACKNOWLEDGMENTS

I have so many people to thank for their generous time and attention in helping me to sound as if I know what I'm writing about. My gratitude to each of you is boundless:

Larry Collins, President of the San Francisco Community Fishing Association and of the San Francisco Crab Boat Owners Association, for information about the San Francisco fishing industry; fishing boats and their layout; and the life of a commercial fisherman.

Rod Moore, Executive Director, West Coast Seafood Processors Association, and **Susan Chambers**, Deputy Director, West Coast Seafood Processors Association, for information about the fishing and fish processing industries in San Francisco and Alaska and about the life of a commercial fisherman; for connecting me with Caito Fisheries; and for treating me to lunch!

Jeanette Caito of Caito Fisheries, for allowing me to tour Caito Fisheries' processing plant and answering questions about its operations.

Angel Cincotta of Alioto-Lazio Fish Company, for insight into the San Francisco fishing and fish processing industries and their history.

Maureen Hanhan, for insight into what it was like to grow up in the Outer Sunset in the 80s and 90s.

Jon Greene of Scoma's Restaurant, for insight into the cooking profession in a seafood restaurant.

Thank you to all of my newsletter subscribers, especially **Bridie Newton**. Your support keeps me going, literally and metaphorically! I'm infinitely grateful.

Thank you to all of my beta readers and ARC readers. Your insights are invaluable and I appreciate you all so very much!

Thank you to my husband and children for sharing me with this passion of mine, and for being my biggest cheerleaders. I couldn't do this without your unwavering love.

And of course, thank you from the bottom of my heart to all of my readers!

Love and gratitude,

Jenna Malaby (formerly Jenna Miles)

ALSO BY JENNA MALABY*

***Formerly writing as Jenna Miles**

Keep reading for Julia and William's Happily Ever After!

From the author of *The Catch* comes its long-awaited follow-up, *The Hold*. Equally enjoyable as a stand-alone book, *The Hold* tells Julia and William's story of grown-up love and blended families in a way that's poignant, powerful, and joyful.

Since high school, aquarist Julia Beale and whale watching captain William Quinn have been each other's one that got away. Now a gift from the past has brought them one more chance at happily ever after.

Their bond runs deeper than ever, and their chemistry is still off the charts. But none of that matters if they can't navigate disdainful kids, aging parents, erratic siblings, and the San Francisco housing market – all while staying afloat as small business owners. Along the way, stir in an ex-husband on the rebound, and garnish with an ex-girlfriend reappearing in a major way.

It's enough to test the strongest of bonds, so when fate throws Julia and William one more curve ball, can they hold on to the trust they've worked so hard to rebuild?

Set in 2012, *The Hold* is perfect for readers who can relate to life's shades of gray. It celebrates the full humanity of humans with two X chromosomes – even when they're moms staring down the barrel of middle age.

Buy The Hold at https://Books2Read.com/TheHoldByJennaMalaby, or scan the QR code below:

~

See where it all began with Julia and William!

Poignant and powerful, *The Catch* is a retro Gen X second chance romance with an angsty love triangle. Told in nonlinear fashion between 1993, 2006, and 2012, it captures the nostalgia of young love, along with the relatable trials of motherhood and responsibility.

Julia Dunphy's husband just left her for the second time, her thirteen-year-old won't stop swearing in public, and to top it all off, her four-year-old just asked to buy condoms. Needless to say, this isn't how she expected her life to pan out.

As a teen in the nineties, Julia had bold plans to study marine biology far from home. Not even William Quinn, the working class boy-next-door, could derail her dreams. Not with his blue eyes. Not with his quiet brilliance. Not even with his loyal heart.

Still, despite time, distance, and marriage to another man, Julia's most tender memories revolved around William. Then, after eleven years and countless broken dreams, Julia and William got an unexpected second chance when they imagined a whale-watching business together – until that, too, ended in a rupture too big to heal.

Now, amid the wreckage of her marriage, and despite a fresh start in her own aquarium shop, Julia knows a third chance with her first love is wishful thinking. But when she uses her training as a paralegal to save William's whale-watching business, and he shows up to thank her, she dares to wonder - are third chances possible, after all?

Equal parts witty, heartwarming, and heart-wrenching, *The Catch* is perfect for fans of Colleen Hoover and Christina Lauren, and reminiscent of classics like Jane Austen's *Persuasion*. It offers a guaranteed Happy For Now ending, with a Happily Ever After in its sequel.

Buy *The Catch* at

Books2Read.com/TheCatchByJennaMalaby, or scan the QR code below:

About the Author

Jenna Malaby (formerly Jenna Miles) writes contemporary romance and literary fiction that's swoony, funny, and sometimes angsty. An avid author since she first picked up a crayon, Jenna is a Texas native and still says y'all without warning, despite living in California since 2008. Prior to having a midlife crisis, piercing her nose, and quitting to be a writer, she provided nutrition counseling to people living with HIV. When Jenna is not dreaming up the next drama for her fictional characters, she and her husband stay busy improvising voices for their cats and unintentionally embarrassing their three daughters.

Connect with me everywhere at
https://Linktr.ee/JennaMalabyAuthor

Like sneak peeks, free stuff, and recipes?
Subscribe to my free newsletter at
www.JennaMalabyAuthor.com/subscribe

Goodreads: goodreads.com/author/show/14594436.Jenna_Miles

- facebook.com/jennamilesauthor
- instagram.com/jennamalabyauthor
- tiktok.com/@jennamilesauthor
- amazon.com/author/jennamiles
- bookbub.com/authors/jenna-miles-acc97ec4-fcfc-41f6-ac5a-47777bffd60e
- bsky.app/profile/jennamalabyauthor.bsky.social

www.ingramcontent.com/pod-product-compliance
Lightning Source LLC
Chambersburg PA
CBHW070506300726
48975CB00007B/2342